The Babysitter

Phoebe Morgan

ONE PLACE. MANY STORIES

HQ
An imprint of HarperCollins*Publishers* Ltd
1 London Bridge Street
London SE1 9GF

This paperback edition 2020

1

First published in Great Britain by
HQ, an imprint of HarperCollins*Publishers* Ltd 2020

Copyright © Phoebe Morgan 2020

Phoebe Morgan asserts the moral right to be
identified as the author of this work.
A catalogue record for this book is
available from the British Library.

ISBN: 978-0-00-831487-3

MIX
Paper from
responsible sources
FSC
www.fsc.org   FSC™ C007454

This book is produced from independently certified FSC™ paper
to ensure responsible forest management.

For more information visit: www.harpercollins.co.uk/green

This book is set in 10.7/15.5 pt. Sabon

Printed and bound in Great Britain by
CPI Group (UK) Ltd, Croydon, CR0 4YY

For my girlfriends.
Every penny from these books is going towards our shared home where we'll live when we're all eighty and can't tolerate anyone else apart from each other.

Phoebe Morgan is an author and editor. She studied English at Leeds University after growing up in the Suffolk countryside. She edits commercial fiction for a publishing house during the day and writes her own books in the evenings. Phoebe lives in London and you can follow her on Twitter @Phoebe_A_Morgan, or find her website about publishing and writing at phoebemorganauthor.com. She is the author of *The Doll House* and *The Girl Next Door*, and *The Babysitter* is her third book. Her novels have been translated into multiple languages and are available in the US, Canada, France, Croatia, Italy, Estonia, Norway, Portugal and more.

Praise for Phoebe Morgan

'A spine-chilling tale'
The Sun

'Utterly compelling'
Woman

'A compelling page-turner'
Fiona Cummins, author of *Rattle*

'A terrific read!'
Cass Green, author of *In a Cottage in a Wood*

'Utterly absorbing, I couldn't put this thrilling whodunit down'
C. L. Taylor, *Sunday Times* bestselling author of *Sleep*

'Claustrophobic and unsettling!'
Lisa Hall, author of *Between You and Me*

'A real page-turner'
B A Paris, bestselling author of *Behind Closed Doors*

'Unsettling... I read this with a growing sense of dread'
Louise Jensen, author of *The Sister*

'Keeps the reader captivated until the final twist'
**Jane Corry, *Sunday Times* bestselling
author of *My Husband's Wife***

'Crackles with twists and turns'
Amanda Jennings, author of *The Cliff House*

'Impossible to put down!'
Isabel Ashdown, author of *Little Sister*

'So clever... I didn't guess the ending at all!'
Laura Marshall, author of *Friend Request*

What I don't understand is what happened to the baby. That poor little mite. How did she get caught up in all this? It's enough to make your blood run cold. She was already on our nursery list. I hope to God they find her.
— Penny Speller, owner at Mulberry Bush Nursery School, Ipswich

We didn't know anything about it. Not until the police arrived. I've never seen so many police. I think they were digging behind that row of flats, not far from the harbour.
— Margaret Parkinson, 42 Ludgate Road, Ipswich

I think any one of them could have done it. I mean, why did they bugger off to France? Bit convenient, don't you think?
— Graham Smith, Facebook Group [346 replies]

We need to remember, there's a woman dead too. Caroline Harvey's life matters. #RIPCaroline.
— @rainbows55, Twitter

It was the husband. It's ALWAYS the husband.
— Michelle Rhodes, to her book group over wine [nods of agreement: 5]

Look. All I want is for us to be able to get the story. The whole story of what happened that night. Our readers deserve the truth. Don't they?
— Jessica Coutts, News Editor at the *East Anglian Daily Times*

Prologue

France
13th August
Siobhan

The day my husband is arrested on suspicion of murder is the hottest of the year. Sweat is clinging to the underside of my arms; my top, hastily thrown on at the sound of the bell echoing through the house, is unflatteringly tight around my stomach, dark lines of perspiration beginning to appear on the clingy white material. The bell is an old-fashioned one, pulled by a thin piece of rope hanging by the door of the villa, and the noise of it wakes all of us up – me, Callum, our daughter Emma and my sister Maria. My eyes alight on the digital clock – it is 09.03 and we have all slept late. We are on holiday. France is in the grip of a heatwave; already, it is 33 degrees.

We came to France two days ago, to stay at Maria's holiday house in a tiny village on the baking north-west coast: Saint Juillet, overlooked by a rocky peak that shades part of the garden. There is no police station in the village – just a tiny church that seats forty, a fancy restaurant overlooking the hills, a Saturday fish stall, and a boulangerie, the opening hours of which are random and confusing. The police must have risen early this morning, made the drive over from Rouen or Dieppe, navigated the treacherous, steep hill down to the holiday villa. No cars come down here unless they absolutely have to. Unless it's an emergency.

There are two officers, a man and a woman, both French, with heavy accents that my sleep-addled brain is slow to understand. My husband is in a faded T-shirt and boxers, his feet bare, dark hairs covering his legs. At first, I think that something must have happened at home – my mind goes to my mother, elderly now, a frail 86-year-old living stubbornly on in a care home on the outskirts of Norwich, alone apart from the nurses. Her grasp of reality has diminished severely of late; it has been a few weeks since I've made the dutiful trip to see her and guilt squeezes my insides, fast and unpleasant. Callum's cousin has just given birth, and I worry that something has gone wrong, picturing Rosa on blood-stained sheets in a hospital room. But of course, it is neither of those things.

Behind me, I feel Emma's presence, the pad of her socked feet. She's in her pyjamas, blonde hair tied back in a bun. At 16, this morning she is childlike and innocent. A second later, Maria appears, a blue silk kimono wrapped around her tanned limbs. Our eyes meet; her gaze as familiar to me as my own. She is a mirror of me, a more beautiful version. Our mother often gets the two of us confused now.

Callum is saying something, protesting, his pidgin French failing to convey the anger and shock that his hand gestures show perfectly. My heart is beginning to beat faster, a tiny drum in my chest. The police are stern, their faces set and unmoveable. Too late, I realise that Emma shouldn't be here. Quickly, I turn from the door and take my daughter's arm, trying to pull her back towards the stairs.

'What's happening?' she asks, her voice still smudged with sleep, and Callum whips round, trying to reassure her, using the calming voice he always does when she's anxious. He can be so kind to her when he wants to be, but his voice is still tinged with an edge of uncertainty that only I can hear.

'It's nothing, sweetheart, this is some sort of mistake – Siobhan, will you tell them? This is all a mistake, darling. Maria, you speak to them, will you? Please?' He smiles at my sister, but it's strained, the muscles in his cheeks tight and false.

My French is no better than his – my mind flits back to my O Level teacher droning on, a bluebottle buzzing against the window in a hot, dry classroom, the spill of blue ink of my fingers – but we are both able to pick up the word the taller of the police officers is saying. *Meurtre. Meurtre. Vous êtes suspecté du meurtre.* I am frozen, I cannot move.

We suspect you. Murder. Maria, whose command of the language is much better than ours, steps forward and begins to speak in rapid, urgent French. It is too fast for me; I don't understand.

And then they say the name of the victim, clear as a bell, and I feel my vision begin to blur, panic grip my throat. *It's her. Caroline Harvey.*

One of them steps forward, and in that second, our nightmare begins.

Chapter One

France
11th August: Two days before the arrest
Siobhan

There's barely any signal in this house. We're all eating dinner out on the terrace, red-flagged stones underneath our feet. It's our first night in France, where the air is hot and still and the sound of the crickets is constant and deafening. Behind us, the swimming pool glistens, bright blue because of the little robot hoover Maria drops into it every day. It's a clever little thing that zooms through the water, up and down like one of those uber-mothers at the local leisure centre back home. But Ipswich seems a world away today; Suffolk has nothing in common with the stifling heat of the French coast. The uber-mothers can't get to me here.

'Emma, aren't you going to eat the rest of that mozzarella?' Callum asks, and I flick my eyes over to my daughter's plate, surprised to see it virtually untouched. Her appetite usually outstrips mine – oh for the metabolism of a 16-year-old. But she ignores me; she's playing with her iPhone, shifting it around on the table, trying to pick up 4G.

'The signal's crap here, Emma,' Maria says, 'that's why I installed the landline. Before I bought this place, there was nothing, can you believe it?' She laughs, spears a piece of tuna onto her fork. I cooked it myself, followed an English recipe to the letter. A thank you for having us gesture, I suppose. I don't like feeling in debt to her, or to anyone.

'I know you want WiFi, Ems, I'll sort it for next summer,' Maria continues. 'Mmm. This is delicious, S.'

I feel a flicker of pleasure that she, at least, likes the meal. My sister has high standards, which is why, according to our mother, she's still alone at forty-six. Nobody's good enough. I don't broach the subject with Maria any more. I don't think she likes it. She's always made me feel as though I am the boring one, choosing marriage and kids over freedom and fun. Never getting my own way. *I'm the mistress of my own life, Siobhan,* she always tells me. I haven't met anyone she's been dating for years, although I don't doubt there's at least someone keeping her sheets warm.

Emma shifts in her seat, barely acknowledging Maria, a strand of hair falling slightly over her face. My daughter is wearing a loose, emerald green dress, the kind of thing I could never pull off any more. She and Maria usually get on so well, but tonight nobody is in my daughter's good books, it seems.

My husband's gaze falls on me, and I can almost feel him willing me to step in, to snap at her, to cajole her into coming out of whatever latest strop she is in and eat the food on her plate. In this scenario, i.e. an Emma mood, I'm usually the bad cop. But tonight, I'm not going to be. After all, I'm on holiday. And I've already cooked the meal, done my bit.

Instead, I take a long sip of my wine, sourced from the nearest vineyard, bought for us as a welcome gift by Maria. My sister has owned the villa for two years, and is still in the process of perfecting it. She's an interior designer with her own business, forever carting expensive rugs and must-have lamps to and fro across the Channel. As a result, the house is an enviable mish-mash of English antiques mixed with French chic. It was her idea for us all to come out here this summer and make use of it; partly an excuse to show the place off, I'm sure, but hard to say no to all the same. *You need a break*, she said, and for a moment I wondered if she knew more than she'd let on about Callum and I. But it's doubtful. I haven't told anyone about the latest development, not yet. I'm still deciding what to do.

Callum booked the flights for us a few months ago, and the three of us flew out here from Southend whilst Maria drove a carful of antiques sourced from a Suffolk auction house through the Channel Tunnel, arriving just in time to let us in and see the envy flit across our faces. I was anxious on the way to the airport, worried about how the holiday would pan out. This might be the sticking plaster that keeps our family together. Either that or it's the tear that pulls us apart.

In this second, though, I'm glad that we're here. The wine is delicious, and for a moment, I let myself believe that this is all mine – this sprawling, escapist luxury – but then Emma pushes back her chair and the moment breaks.

'I'm not hungry,' she says, and I watch the hem of her silky dress fall to her ankles as she stands up and leaves the table, disappearing behind the sliding glass doors of the villa.

After a few seconds, music starts – she's turned on the Sonos system in the downstairs basement, blasting angry, loud music that sets my teeth on edge. The house is two storeys, with the basement in reality forming two bedrooms and another bathroom. Emma and Maria are sleeping down there, while Callum and I are on the ground floor, level with the swimming pool. There's an en suite leading off from our room, a power shower and fluffy white towels. Expensive soap and hand moisturiser that smells of geranium.

Callum sighs, the sound familiar. Maria blows out her breath, the worry evident on her face. She's had the same facial expressions since we were teenagers, all those years ago now. More years than I'd like to count, to be honest. I turned forty-four in the spring. Still, I'll always be her younger sibling. That's something, I suppose.

I take an olive from the little black pot on the table, feel the oil slick on my fingertips.

'Change of scenery hasn't helped with the mood swings, then,' Callum says wryly, raising his wine glass to his lips, and I shrug my shoulders, swallow the olive. He smiles at me, his teeth white and his eyes crinkling. That handsome look that I know so well.

'We've been here less than twenty-four hours. Let's give her a chance.' My voice sounds calm, measured.

It isn't how I feel inside. But then, I've got good at keeping my feelings to myself lately. I've had to, after all. Secrets are becoming my forte.

*

We finish the meal, and then with still no reappearance from Emma, move onto the comfy chairs on the veranda and open another bottle of wine – red this time, five euros in the local supermarket on our way over here. Callum's mood has perked up; he is becoming more jovial, his arm around my waist, his voice loud in my ear. I try to relax into his touch, but it's hard.

'I was thinking I'd take you to see Rouen in the morning. I can unload the car of all the junk I brought over so that we can all fit,' Maria is saying, a cardigan wrapped around her shoulders now as the temperature cools. I roll my eyes; 'junk' – the contents of her car are probably worth thousands judging by the rest of the house. Not for Maria the delights of IKEA – the pieces she brings over are each carefully selected, the best she can afford.

We took a taxi from Caen Airport, but Maria in her own car is by far the best driver, able to navigate the narrow French roads with much more ease than either of us. Although she lives in England, just down the road from us in Woodbridge, she comes out to the villa all the time, and every summer she spends a few weeks here alone. By car, the journey is less than six hours. The locals in the village recognise her, at least. 'They always ask me why I haven't got a man,' she told us earlier tonight, laughing, tossing her hair back over her shoulder. 'They ask me when I'm going to bring *un petit chou* to visit them all.'

'They obviously don't you know you that well then,' Callum had said, grinning at her, and she'd laughed again, the sound echoing over the hot red tiles, but the tone of it didn't quite ring true. I wonder if she could be more lonely that we think. I've tried to discuss it with Callum, once or twice, but he's never very interested. I think she was seeing someone more seriously for a while, a man from her work, but she was always very cagey about it and I never got very far in my questioning.

'Rouen in the morning would be lovely,' I say now, waiting for Callum to agree. Since we've been out here, there has been something off about his mood, but I can't work out if I'm just imagining it. There is a nervous energy, a pulse of unease that began on the flight earlier today. He has never been an anxious flyer, but this time he was on edge for the whole hour, his eyes darting around the plane, his fingers tapping on his phone until an air hostess told him to stop. I smiled at her after that, and ordered a glass of wine. Emma stared out of the window the entire time; I could hear the tinny beat of the music coming through her headphones. Callum bought her expensive ones – he's never been able to say no to her. Well, he's never been able to say no to anyone except me. That's why people love him. The ultimate yes-man.

'Callum,' I say, 'wouldn't that be great? Maria's offering to take us to Rouen. I've always wanted to go, actually. See the cathedral, the churches.'

He glances at her quickly, but it's too dark for me to see the expression on his face.

'Yeah,' he says at last, predictably, 'I'd love that. I'm sure Ems would too. Thanks, Maria.'

She inclines her head, then stands. 'More wine, S?'

She's always called me S, ever since we were small, as though saying my full name is a little too much for her. My glass is almost empty; I hadn't realised.

'Yes please,' I say, and she moves away, back into the light of the house, her shadow tall and willowy in the darkness. Her hair is a dark brown waterfall, whilst my own is beginning to be tinged with the odd grey. I wonder if it's time for me to start dyeing it, if Maria would admit to doing hers. I know she does, I've seen the packets in her bathroom cabinet.

'Isn't it great to get away from it all?' Callum says to me

when she's gone, throwing his head back against the cushioned headrest, staring up at the stars. It's dark now, the only light the glow from the house and the shimmer of a couple of anti-mosquito candles. His body language has become more relaxed as the evening has gone on; either that or it's the alcohol working its magic.

'Mmm,' I say non-committally, smiling at him as he points out Orion's Belt, the saucepan, the North Star.

He pulls me closer, lightly kissing me on the forehead, and lets out a sigh of contentment. 'I feel free here,' he says suddenly, 'really free'. The kiss feels like a stamp; I'm his property, after all. *To have and to hold.*

His phone, jammed against my hip, buzzes with a message. 'God, this must be the only spot in the whole place with a reception!' he says, and I turn away as he looks at it, fix my gaze on the bright lights in the distance, wondering how long we're going to carry on pretending. One more night? One more week? One more year? I don't know how much more I can take.

Chapter Two

I miss you, I type out, then watch as the letters slowly erase themselves under the firm grip of my thumb. *How are you?* I write instead, which is better, but not perfect, and then I hit send before I can think about it any more.

I promised myself I wouldn't be like this. Promised I'd keep away. For my own sake. I *know* what he is now, I know what he made me do. The awfulness of it. But it's a Sunday morning, and I've got that particularly horrible, deep in the gut sort of loneliness beginning to form, snaking its way up my stomach and into my throat. The glasses of wine last night didn't help either; I'm going to stop drinking, properly this time; I'm going to stop being dependent on both booze and Callum Dillon at the exact same moment. God, I'm pathetic. Why are bad habits so hard to break?

My phone buzzes and I leap for it, but it's just Jenny, asking if I want to come round to hers for a meal with her and her husband tonight. My fingers tighten around the phone. No, Jenny, I don't want to come for a meal in your posh house and watch as you and Rick coo over your brand new baby. I don't want to stare at your fridge full of wedding invitations, your sweet little high chair, or your giant Smeg fridge. I don't need any confirmation of how full your life is compared to mine.

I take a deep breath, then type out a reply to her and bury my phone underneath the pillow next to me in a vain attempt to stop myself from checking it for messages from him.

It's only a week until they all go on holiday to France. He's moaned about it, told me how difficult it is for him to get time off. He's so busy, *so* busy and important. The two of us went on a rare night away a month ago, stayed in a little B&B in Norfolk, the best he could manage, but of course I lapped it up. He left his suitcase here afterwards, didn't want his wife to find it. He hasn't even come back to get it – he'd rather buy another one than face seeing me again, it seems. It's all there is of him here – no toothbrush, no razor, no crumpled boxer shorts. It's almost as if he's never been here at all. As though our entire relationship has been solely confined to inside my head.

I can't stop thinking about them going away together, picturing it all. He told me ages ago, before everything happened, that his sister-in-law had a place in France they were going to visit, although he wouldn't say much more than that. *Where in France?* I asked him, but he laughed, kissed me on the nose, told me it didn't matter. *Callum, don't worry, I'm not going to turn up on the doorstep,* I said, and he tugged gently on my hair, teasing me. *I wouldn't put it past you.* I tried to find pictures of it after that, googled his sister-in-law's name. Maria Wilcox. She's very pretty, just like Siobhan. Even prettier, in fact, like Siobhan with an Instagram filter. Good genes, the Wilcox clan. I couldn't find a photo of the villa, though. I don't know what it's called.

I don't want to think about them going on holiday together; I can't bear it. Even after what he did to me, the thought of him playing happy families makes me feel sick. I put an end to things, told him it was over. And it *is* over. It has to be, this time. After everything that's happened this year, I need to make the decision to put myself first. It's what my mum would've said to me, if she was here. Eighteen months is long enough to conduct an extra-marital affair, especially one with a man like Callum Dillon. Jenny told me once that she thinks he's a misogynist, and I looked up the definition that night: *a person who dislikes, despises or is strongly prejudiced against women.* Three months ago, I'd have said the exact opposite was true. Callum likes women too much. And women like him. He's charming, at first – he reels you in with a smile, an in-joke. When we first met, I felt as though I'd been selected, as if a torchlight had picked me out of the darkness. Now I wish I'd stayed in the shadows.

My phone beeps again, the sound barely muffled under the cushion, and my fingers scrabble to unlock the screen. *Go on, Caro, please! I'd love to see you. It'll be fun!* Jenny, again. I stare at the exclamation points: so unnecessarily enthusiastic. I hesitate, try to think clearly, to push away the fug of loneliness that is threatening to crowd out my thoughts.

I am still in my pyjamas, sitting upright in my bed, the curtains resolutely closed against the sunlight even though it has gone 11 a.m.. The room feels stale. An empty wine glass stands on the dresser; it will leave an ugly stain. My legs are prickly, unshaven and white. I think of Siobhan Dillon's legs, long and tanned, stretched out on a sun lounger by a sparkling blue pool, the sun a burning hot sphere in the sky above her.

Callum's hand making its way up her thigh. *No.* I force myself to push the images away, to stop obsessing. Obsession's never good for anyone; the therapist told me that after Mum died. But I don't think obsession is something you develop, or get rid of. You're born with it – you either have it or you don't. It might shift focus sometimes, but it never truly goes away.

The day yawns out ahead of me like a blank canvas, and I feel a fluttering sense of panic at the thought of staying here, stuck in this room, waiting to hear from him, even though I have told myself that it is over. What good will that do?

OK. I'll be there, I write to Jenny, and within seconds the reply pings back, a smiley, overexcited emoji that makes me grit my teeth, just slightly. But perhaps I am wrong. Being too harsh. Maybe going to see Jenny will take me out of myself a little; the baby, Eve, will presumably be tucked up in bed, and maybe her husband isn't quite as annoyingly smug as I remember. Perhaps I can have a good time. *Eve.* The christening invite is still floating around the flat somewhere; at the time, I couldn't bring myself to go. It was too painful. But I'm better now. Much better. Or at least, I'm trying to be.

Feeling newly resolved, I force myself to pull back the duvet and ease myself out of bed, my feet touching the cold floorboards. I try to avoid my reflection, because I know what I'll see – my long hair feels greasy and unkempt, my face will be slightly puffy from the wine-induced crying I did last night. I think of the day Callum and I met, how different I am now. I wouldn't want him to see me like this. Not when he's got Siobhan Dillon for a wife.

*

Jenny lives on the other side of Ipswich, right by the south side of the docks. It's a ten-minute walk from my flat on Woodmill Road and I decide the cooling evening air might help me decompress; besides, it's still light. July and August have been kind to us this year, hot and sticky; Suffolk has baked under the summer heat. Normally I'd like it, but in my current mood it feels like a punishment. I think briefly of Callum and Siobhan, limbs entangled on a huge white bed, the doors flung open to stave off the humidity. I think of them emerging from a plane into crisp French air, pulling expensive sunglasses down over their faces, smiling at each other as the first wave of warmth hits them. I bet Siobhan speaks perfect French, on top of everything else.

The docks are lovely at this time of year; the water curves around the harbourside and the sails of the boats chink in the breeze. Ipswich often gets a bad rap, I've always thought, but I like it here – it has everything I need. And it's better than Stowmarket, where I grew up, but still close enough to visit Mum's grave if I want to. I haven't for a while. I think she'd be ashamed of me, of what I've become.

As I walk, the restaurants sparkle in the light, but peering at the glowing windows makes me feel worse. I see a couple, smiling at each other over deep, full glasses of wine on the table in front of them, and my stomach clenches. That could be me and Callum. That *was* me and Callum. A woman comes out of the Pizza Express on the corner, pushing a pram, followed by a tall man holding the hand of a child. The perfect nuclear family – everything I wanted. Everything that is totally out of my reach.

Forcing myself to keep walking, I round the corner and

approach Jenny's house. It's set back from the road, in a nice-looking row of buildings that face the water. I remember when she and Rick bought it, just over a year ago; they posted a picture on Instagram of their faces pressed together, keys dangling in her diamond-ringed hand.

I'll never post a picture like that. I've got nobody to post one with.

Jenny's got little window boxes neatly laden with summer flowers, the leaves wilting a bit in the heat. As I approach the front door, I reach out and push my finger into the soil in the box nearest to me; it is dry beneath my skin. Perhaps I'll remind her to water them. She shouldn't take things for granted that way.

'Caro!'

I've barely knocked when the door is swinging open, and Jenny is engulfing me, her arms tight around my torso, her perfume sweet in my face. She kisses me on the cheek, then takes hold of both of my shoulders, stands back as though appraising me. What does she think when she looks at me, I wonder; does she find me wanting? Not enough?

'Come in, come in,' she says, letting go of me and gesturing inside the house. She's wearing a long cream cardigan and turned up jeans, effortlessly mumsy. I've known Jenny since university, but the woman in front of me is almost unrecognisable from the girl I used to share halls with in Leeds, the girl who'd go out in a tiny dress with a WKD in each hand and too-high heels on her feet. No, that Jenny has well and truly vanished.

'Wine? Tea? Gin? What can I get you? Eve's sleeping, thank God.'

Eve.

'Wine please,' I say, forcing myself not to check my phone for the fiftieth time since this morning. Callum hasn't replied to my *how are you?* even though the cruel blue ticks on WhatsApp make it obvious that he's read it. I follow Jenny into the house, my eyes taking in the shiny silver-framed pictures on the walls, the photos of baby Eve in various outfits – swaddled in blankets Eve, wrapped up for snow day Eve, Halloween Eve, her tiny face poking out of a pumpkin costume. My heart seems to close in on itself, like a tightening fist.

'Caroline, hey.' My heart sinks as I hear Rick's voice, and then he's in front of me, smiling widely and bending to kiss me on both cheeks. The French way. France. Callum's holiday. *No.*

I push the thoughts away and accept the large glass of wine Jenny is holding out to me, my fingers gripping it tightly. It's not that I don't like Rick, exactly, it's more that together with Jenny, the pair of them represent everything I haven't got. Everything I am a million miles away from having, because of how stupid I was.

'I'm so glad Eve nodded off before you came!' says Jenny, her back to me, bustling around with the fridge. 'Really, it's a miracle. It's been so hard to get her down recently, hasn't it, Rick darling? The terrible twos, starting early. Just our luck!' She laughs, the sound high and tinkling, and I feel the words stab into me like tiny poisoned arrows. *You don't know how lucky you are.*

'Have a seat, Caro,' Rick says, and I sit down on one of their high, fashionable stools. They had a breakfast bar installed just before Christmas, part of their house renovation. It must have cost them a fortune.

'I've got fresh pasta,' Jenny tells me, and I smile at her.

'Sounds great.'

The wine tastes weirdly sweet, too warm in the August air.

'So how are you, Caro?' Rick asks, smiling at me. His teeth are very white; perfectly so. 'What's been going on? How's the illustration game?'

I smile back, forcing myself to try to stay in the moment, not to think about Callum.

'It's great,' I say, 'really great, actually. Lots of work coming in. I'm doing a children's book right now.'

'Ah, well, send it our way when it's done! We want to get Eve reading as early as possible, don't we, Jen?' He glances over at her, rubbing his hands together as though the idea of starting a child reading early is his own version of reinventing the wheel.

'We certainly do!' she says, coming to sit down next to me at the table, a glass of wine in her hand, smaller than mine. Sensible Jenny. Her rings glisten under the lights. I remember the day she and Rick got engaged; she posted a picture on Facebook of her hand, fingers splayed, diamonds glittering. *Thank God I'd had my nails done*, the caption said. Thank God indeed, I thought sourly.

'And, so, tell us!' Jenny leans closer to me. I almost want to laugh, it's so quick. They've managed to get any interest in my work out of the way in under a minute. Now onto the good stuff. My love life. The bit we've all been waiting for. I take another gulp of wine, feel it slide easily down my throat.

'How's the dating going?'

Jenny's put a little bowl of olives out on the table between us, and I watch as Rick pops one into his mouth – green and fat. His teeth close around it, like those of a wolf.

'Well,' I say, 'I haven't really done too much lately, I—'

'Oh, Caroline!' Jenny gives a mock-sigh, throwing both her skinny little arms up into the air. 'You promised, this year, this was the summer you were really going to give it a go. Didn't you!' She nudges her husband. '*Didn't* she, Rick! You were there. You remember.'

'You did indeed,' he says, grinning at me, reaching for another plump olive.

Underneath the table, I dig my nails into my thigh with my free hand, feel them make an indent into my skin. I hope it makes a bruise.

Chapter Three

France
12th August: One day before the arrest
Siobhan

I wake up early on our first morning in France, my mouth a little dry from the red wine with my sister and Callum on the terrace last night. Emma didn't appear from the basement and so we left her to it in the end, stayed outside drinking under the stars until the early hours. I went to bed first, with the intention of having some time alone to think, plan out my next steps, but by the time Callum came up I must have been already unconscious, knocked out by the wine, because I didn't hear him slide into bed next to me. Didn't hear anything at all, in fact.

Beside me, Callum is asleep, the covers flung off him, his mouth very slightly open. He is so familiar to me now, after fifteen years of marriage, and another year of dating before that. Emma was born in the January of the year we married, *out of wedlock*, as Maria likes to tease. Sometimes I wonder what would have happened if I hadn't got pregnant, if we hadn't rushed into the wedding, but thoughts like that are useless now. What's done is done. Or is it? For a while now, I've been thinking of a way out, but it's easier said than done.

I watch the rise and fall of Callum's breath, the easy way he lies, both arms above his head. There's something childlike about it, childlike and carefree. I sleep curled up, like a foetus on guard against the world. I'm a light sleeper, usually, but Callum sleeps like the dead. Sometimes he will fling out a limb, crush me with it accidentally. Occasionally, he will sleep in the spare room at home, if he's been working late in his studio, and on those nights I spread myself out, starfish style, feel a splash of guilt at how much I enjoy it. I allow myself to imagine what it might be like to live like that all of the time. To be single like my sister.

Quietly, I ease back the covers and leave the room, glancing at my reflection in the tall gold mirror as I do so. My silky white nightie looks old and tired, my hair is full of split ends that dangle onto my shoulders. A mosquito bite stands out on my arm, red and itchy. Although I've only just got up, I already feel tired at the thought of the day. Another day of pretence.

I pick up my phone, standing on the dresser, but it is resolutely silent, the top right-hand corner devoid of any signal. *We are disconnected,* I think, and the thought makes me feel a wave of relief. It is strangely refreshing not having the usual cacophony of noise first thing – the news alerts, the updates from the uber-mothers, the concerned voicemails from the school headteacher about Emma's worsening grades, her fall-outs with the girls in her year. The bad behaviour that nobody can quite explain. Instead, there is silence, a blank screen. I glance at Callum's phone, on charge over on his side of the bed. My fingers itch for a moment, the desire to unlock it and rummage through his electronic life again is strong, but really, what's the point? I know everything there is to know, now.

His passcode is Emma's birthday – sweet, until you realise it's all a sham.

Downstairs, there's a pile of Maria's new wares in the living room, unloaded from the car: a stand-alone lamp with a twisting, ornate base; a pile of rugs in rich, warm colours; a bookcase painted in a soft teal colour. I run my finger over it gently, wishing I had my sister's eye. And her freedom.

In the kitchen, I select one of Maria's blue ceramic mugs that she got from the pop-up market in the village and pour myself a much-needed filter coffee. I wanted to take Emma to see the market, try to use it as a bonding opportunity for the two of us, but my sister says it's not there this week; it seems its opening hours are as random and sporadic as the little bakery.

Taking a long sip of coffee, I select the sharpest knife from the rack and begin to slice fruit for my daughter: dicing the apples, skinning the kiwis, pitting the cherries. I pile it all into a small blue and white bowl, drizzle fresh yoghurt around the outsides and dot fresh raspberries on top. It looks so pretty that I almost want to take a photo. I would, if I were one of those people. Emma says there are lots of them – food bloggers, Instagram influencers who only need to post a picture of their breakfast to get hundreds of thousands of likes. My daughter's own social media channels are private, closed, especially to me. Believe me, I've looked.

Of course, Emma isn't interested in my efforts. When I tap on her bedroom door before gently pushing it open, she pulls the white sheet over her head, but not before I catch a quick glimpse of her: the pale face already scowling, the low-level teenage anger that seems to radiate from her every limb these days. I stand still for a second or two in her doorway, watching her, but she doesn't move. Silently, soundlessly, Callum appears behind me. His hands go to my waist.

'Let her sleep,' he says softly, and semi-reluctantly I back away, close the door. I feel the familiar tug of guilt that I always feel around my daughter, the worry that Callum *does* know better, that he and Emma share something that I, for some reason, do not. Does my husband know what's right for our daughter? Am I failing so badly as a mother that it's pushing their bond even closer?

My feet are bare on the tiles and I'm still clutching the bowl of beautiful fruit. Callum has a hold of me, and, not knowing what else to do, I smile at him as he bends down and kisses the tip of my nose. He used to kiss me on the mouth, always and without fail, but lately he has started to choose my nose instead, or my forehead, occasionally my hand. *When did it begin,* I often think to myself, *did it begin around the same time as everything else?* I look down at my hands, avoiding his gaze; my fingers are stained red from the raspberries. Little flecks that look like blood.

'I'm going to take a shower,' he says. 'Is Maria up?'

'I don't think so,' I say – the door to my sister's room is resolutely shut. I smile to myself; Maria never did handle hangovers very well. When we were teenagers, she'd always drink more than me, encourage me to join in. I can still remember the sharp scent of vodka as she pushed it towards me in our bedroom, and the funny taste of it from the china cup. Mum never knew, I don't think. Maria made sure of it. She washed the cups in the sink and put them back on the shelves in the morning, soap suds covering up the smell of spirits.

I watch now as Callum retreats away from me, back to our

en suite. I go upstairs, open the huge sliding doors that lead out onto the terrace. It's already hot; the sun is white in the sky. I know we were thinking of driving to Rouen today – Callum does like a plan, an itinerary – but I can feel the pull of the swimming pool already, am visualising myself stretched out on a sun lounger by the water, my husband and daughter twenty miles away wandering the streets of France.

It's not that I don't love my daughter. I do. More than anything. But bit by bit, I am losing her, and for all intents and purposes, my husband is already lost. Sometimes that hurts so much that I simply cannot bear it. Instead, I detach: I disengage from them both, retreat into the corner of my mind that still thinks of myself as an individual, rather than part of a three. It doesn't always work.

Emma has become more and more withdrawn over the last eighteen months, her slide into adolescence much harder on me than I'd ever imagined it might be. I have wished so many times that her hormones would manifest themselves differently; that I could bandage up a wound, administer doses of medicine like I did when she was a little girl clamouring for Calpol. But of course I cannot.

A friend of mine once told me drunkenly that her own teenagers are exactly the same – hissing with an inexplicable rage one moment, all smiles the next, a seemingly impossible merry-go-round of emotions that reverberate around the family. We were sipping white wine in the kitchen of our house in Ipswich, the only two left after a gathering one Christmas. We used to be a lot more sociable, Callum and I. My friend – let's call her Kate – had valiantly drunk the best part of two bottles by the time she began talking about her children (she has one of each – a son and a daughter, not far off Emma's age now) and it was clear she'd wanted to open up to someone for a while.

'Sometimes I just wish they'd disappear,' she had said, gazing gloomily into her glass of Pinot, and I'd felt myself nodding, even though I didn't really agree. I wouldn't swap Emma for the world, in spite of all her moodiness.

'God, I'm sorry,' Kate said, almost immediately after she'd finished speaking, clapping one hand to her mouth, the gesture a little bit sloppy due to the wine. 'That was a terrible thing to say. Please Siobhan, forget I said it.' I watched as a look of panic came over her face. 'You will, won't you? You will just forget it? God, me and my big mouth.' She hiccupped. 'I've had way too much wine.'

It must be said that at this point I was not sober either, but I wasn't as far gone as my friend, whose eyes were beginning to take on the blurry sheen of someone who might be about to cry.

'Don't worry about it, Kate, it's forgotten,' I said to her, the words coming slowly. I was wearing a long white cardigan, and I wrapped it around myself, feeling chilly despite the warmth from the fire in the living room and the twinkle of our Christmas tree lights. We'd gone all out that year in an attempt to cheer Emma up, 'bring her out of herself' as the school headteacher had helpfully suggested. My body felt strange beneath the cardigan, as though it belonged to someone else.

Anyway, it's hard to think back to when Emma began to change. To when my bubbly little girl turned into something different. All parents say that, don't they, that the morphing of child to adolescent is a truly bizarre experience, something you're never prepared for despite how many times you've warned yourself it will happen.

She began to turn in on herself, spending more and more time alone in her bedroom. Whereas before she had been happy spending time with me after school, sitting atop the Aga with her legs dangling down, watching me in the kitchen, now she vanished, a blur of school uniform and long hair disappearing up the stairs. I used to stand at the bottom step, trying desperately to think of the magic words that would bring her back, make us close again, but somehow they never came.

'It's just hormones,' Callum had said at first, shrugging, and for a second or two I hated him. Hated him for dismissing her like that. He and Emma have always got on very well – truth be told, there are times when I look at them both and feel jealous, though that's not something I'd ever really want to admit to anyone else. But despite their closeness, Callum has never really tackled the problem, at least not head on. He buried his head in the sand and it's stayed there ever since. When he did try to talk to her about it, he became too brusque, almost aggressive. I suppose a stroppy daughter didn't really fit into his persona – his TV exec personality, his almost local celebrity status. In spite of how much he loved her, she was becoming a blot on his copybook. But it wasn't as though I was much better. I worried about her, but I was frustrated, too. I wanted her to snap out of it, to grow up a bit. Look, I'm just being honest. I never pretended to be perfect. Despite what people might think.

*

Callum comes outside, his hair wet from the shower, a white towel wrapped around his waist. Our villa is overlooked slightly by the one above us on the hill, but Callum has never been particularly bothered about privacy. When I first met him, he was quite the exhibitionist, forever taking risks and encouraging me to loosen my inhibitions a bit – wanting public displays of affection, snatched encounters outdoors on our dates. I'm not sure he ever really got what he wanted in that respect – not from me, anyway. It was never really my thing.

'Still up for going to Rouen today with Maria?' he asks me. 'We can probably drag Ems along too, don't you think?'

He's grinning at me in that careless way he has, running a hand through the dark spikes of his hair. Whatever odd mood that had gripped him on the plane over here seems to have gone now, faded away in the heat and the wine and the luxuriousness of the swimming pool. Callum is a man who is used to getting what he wants and despite everything, he still has that ability to charm me, to grin like a Cheshire cat and make those old giddy feelings arise in my stomach.

'Mmm,' I say, about to capitulate, and then suddenly I look at him and think better of it. 'You know what, actually, Callum, I was thinking I might stay here for the day, by the pool,' I say. 'Might get a bit of work done, if I can get the internet working.' I pause. 'You don't mind, do you?'

He groans, but it's only a mock-groan, I can tell. He doesn't really mind if I don't come, and I can already see his mind skipping ahead to what this means – a possible father-daughter day for him and Emma. Just Daddy and Ems. No bad cop today.

'We're on holiday, Siobhan,' he says. 'Plus, you said you'd always wanted to visit Rouen.' He pauses. 'You don't need to be working – I work! You need a break. That's why we came here.'

Is it, I ask myself silently, but outwardly I smile, though

I'm bristling inside at his casual dismissal of my need to work. 'I know, I'm sorry. But if I can power through some bits today then it'll free me up for the rest of the time here. I promise.' I'm improvising now.

He relents, as I knew he would, and I settle myself down by the pool, my laptop on my knee, listening as Emma finally rouses herself and the pair of them set about getting ready to go to Rouen. At one point, Emma comes out to the patio, stopping when she sees me on the sun lounger.

'Are you not coming?'

I gesture at my laptop with a rueful sigh.

'Work. I'm sorry, darling. But you'll have fun with Dad.'

'Hmm.' She seems to accept it relatively easily (I could almost be hurt by her lack of protestation) and I watch as she lifts the hem of her white summer dress, sprays her legs with mozzie spray.

'Maria?' Callum is calling for my sister, the sound of his voice bouncing over to where I lie at the pool. It's very hot – I should get a hat. 'Maria? Where are you?'

She emerges from a side door, sunglasses over her eyes and a shopping bag in her hand, blue plastic straining at her wrist.

'Have you been out?' I ask, confused, and she nods.

'Popped to the patisserie, managed to catch it open for once.'

'Oh,' I say, 'we thought you were still in bed.'

She grins at me. 'I handle my hangovers a little better than I used to, sis. Been up and about for hours. Sorry about the stuff in the living room, had to unload the car. Croissant?'

'Emma and Callum are hoping to go to Rouen,' I say. She looks at me by the pool, the two of them ready to go, and seems to assess the situation at a single glance.

'I think I'll stay here with Siobhan, actually,' she tells Callum, the car keys glinting in her hand. 'Here, take these. You're insured on mine, aren't you? You'll manage. Just go slow on the bends. We'll save you a croissant for when you get back.' She's tossed the keys across the patio to him before he can argue; I watch as he catches them deftly. He's always been sure of himself, has my husband, but as he and Emma turn to go, I catch sight of something unreadable on his face. It is there for a second, and then it disappears.

Five minutes later, they are gone. I wait until the sound of Maria's car stuttering up the hill has faded into the distance, then close my laptop, which I never had any intention of using. I don't really have much work to do; my role at a pharmaceutical company has gradually lessened over the years as Callum's star has continued to rise. I took a step back from it when Emma was born, wanting to prioritise my family, prioritise my husband. I've spent sixteen years of my life doing just that, which is why, I suppose, the thought of it all crumbling now is a little too much for me to bear. After the sacrifices I've made, the things I have endured.

I lie back on my sun lounger. Beside me, my sister sets out the croissants on the white plastic table in front of us, then settles herself down. For a few seconds, we are silent, listening to the sound of the crickets, but I can feel her gaze on me, the way I always could when we were younger. She'd always be trying to catch me out, and sometimes I feel as though nothing has changed. 'She's protective of you,' our mother often said, 'she cares about you as if you were her own. Eldest sibling syndrome.' I've never been sure if that's the case, although there's nothing concrete to suggest otherwise.

The pool glistens in front of us, and I reproach myself; we are here because of Maria, aren't we, we are in this beautiful place, in the sunshine, because she has been kind enough to offer it up. Things *have* changed – we are adults now, and I have nothing to worry about. The crickets sound as though they are getting louder. All I want is some time to think – about what I'm going to do, how Callum and I are going to move forward. Whether we are going to move forward at all. But I can't hear my thoughts for the hum of the insects, and Maria's presence next to me is distracting.

'So,' Maria says at last, as if she can read my mind, 'when are you going to tell me what's going on with you, S? I might be able to help.' She pauses. 'You know you can tell me anything, sis. That's what I'm here for. Remember?'

I don't say anything. A trickle of sweat works its way down my neck.

'Siobhan?'

'There's nothing going on,' I say at last, 'really, Maria. Everything's fine.' It has become my party line over the years; the words slide off my tongue like honey.

A silence falls between us, heavy with everything I'm not saying. Briefly, I close my eyes, the hot sun burning an orb of white into my eyelids.

'It's almost forty degrees now,' Maria says eventually, pulling her sun lounger a little bit closer to mine with a slight scraping sound as it shifts across the tiles. She's wearing a white lace smock over her black two-piece swimming costume, looking every inch the glamorous sort of woman that I can't be any more. Her body is unscarred, child-free – the thin silver line from my caesarean stretches across my belly. I haven't really answered her question, her reminder that I can tell her anything. Anything at all. It's what she used to say when we were younger, back when we shared a room – she'd whisper to me in the dark, ask me to tell her my secrets. Truth be told, at that age I didn't have any – most of my thoughts revolved around my homework and what was going on in *Neighbours*.

'Mm,' I mumble, 'it's lovely.' There's another silence for a minute, the only sound the throbbing of the crickets, and the drifting, dull burr of an overhead plane. I follow it with my eyes, and wonder briefly about the passengers on it – are they happy? Are they free?

'Thanks for staying with me,' I say at last to my sister, and she shrugs her shoulders, smiles across at me. Her eyes are covered by her mirrored sunglasses – I stare at my own tiny reflection in her lenses.

'Of course,' she says. 'It's good to have some time alone with you anyway, sis. I feel like we never get to do that any more.'

Beneath me, I can feel my limbs starting to stick to the lounger, the plastic melting into my sticky flesh. Licking my top lip, I taste salt.

'We used to be so close, S,' she says, and now she's angled her body so that it's fully facing mine, a parallel image of my own.

'We still are,' I say, and then, quickly, 'thank you for inviting us out here. You know how much I appreciate it.'

She blinks at me, long dark lashes sweeping smooth skin. She's right, I suppose – we're not as close as we have been in the past; even though she's only in Woodbridge we find ourselves caught up in our lives, me with Emma and the school, her with her interior design business and her mysterious liaisons with men she pretends don't exist but must. There are gaps in our story, times where weeks go by without me seeing her. But still, she makes an effort – she texts Emma, takes her shopping for too-short clothes without batting an eyelid. She's always been a brilliant aunt.

'You do know I mean what I said, don't you? You can tell me anything, S. Whatever's on your mind.'

I am cursing not having my own sunglasses with me; I feel exposed and suddenly vulnerable as she assesses me from behind her protection of dark glass.

'How do you think Emma seems?' I say at last, when the silence between us has become too thick and foggy, and it seems to momentarily do the trick, distract her attention away from me. Focus instead on the girl we both care about. 'She didn't eat much last night,' I carry on, and when Maria doesn't reply, I take this as my cue to continue. 'And she seems so angry all the time, have you noticed? I barely recognise her any more. She's so up and down, as though we've all done something terribly wrong but I don't know what it is.'

'I think Emma's probably worried too,' Maria says at last. 'She's worried about you.' Her voice lowers slightly, changes tone. 'So am I.'

In front of us, the blue water of the pool sparkles. Inside me, it feels as though the pressure is rising, higher and higher. Callum's face flashes in front of my mind, the buzz of his iPhone against my hip, the image of Emma pushing her food around her plate, her eyes glaring at us from across the dining table, the screech of her music blasting upwards to the terrace, the sound keeping her sealed away from us inside.

'Why are *you* worried about me?' I ask Maria, and she gives a little snort, a half laugh, as though my question is ridiculous. 'No, really,' I say, 'I want to know.'

Maria sits up a little, pushes herself to a seated position. Her back is straight against the plastic chair; she always did have good posture. Her stomach stays flat even as she moves herself upright; no roll of fat at all. Neither of us have touched the croissants.

'I don't think you're being fair to yourself, Siobhan.'

My heart is beating fast, and I turn my face away slightly so she can't see my expression. Does she know?

'In what way?' I say, fighting to keep my voice even, not to display the panic bubbling up inside my stomach.

'You and Callum,' she says, 'you're not happy, S. I can sense it. I'm your older sister, I've always been able to tell when there's something the matter.' She shakes her head, blows out her breath. Her lips look glossy, tinted red in the sunlight. 'Is there something wrong between you two?'

'No,' I say dully, 'everything's fine.'

She exhales, gazes up at the sky, impossibly blue and clear. 'I don't know why you ever got married, Siobhan,' she says, 'all it does is bring misery. You should've done the sensible thing, stayed a free agent like me. I can have my cake and eat it, whenever I like.' She stretches forward, grabs a croissant and takes a bite. Golden flakes of pastry glisten on her lips.

'Aren't you jealous?' she says, teasingly, trying to lighten the mood, 'just a little bit?'

Chapter Four

Ipswich
3rd August: One week earlier
Caroline

By the time we've finished our pasta, Jenny's drunk too much. I can tell by the way she's talking and stroking Rick's arm. Her eyes are very bright and her neck is sort of flushed; red mottles peeping out from the collar of her shirt and staining her skin. Perhaps the girl with a WKD in each hand isn't as far away as I'd thought, even if she is wearing a mumsy cardi with a one-year-old in the next room. Speaking of, as it reaches ten o'clock, baby Eve starts crying, little mewls at first that turn into full-blown screams, and Rick excuses himself to go see to her. I hear the creak of the floorboards as he pads upstairs and over to her cot, then the sound of him shushing her. She stops crying really quickly, but he stays upstairs for a few minutes. Jenny and I are quiet. And then she says it.

'So what's going on with Callum, Caroline?'

There's something in her tone that is different now, something barbed. Although we are in her hot little kitchen, I feel suddenly cold, a chill running down the nape of my neck.

Jenny wasn't even supposed to know about Callum. No one was.

We met at work, as so many people do: 34 per cent, according to a survey I read online on a day when I'd nothing else to do. It was a Monday, and my old boss, Darren, was overly excited because his publishing house had 'the television people' coming in. I'd been invited to the meeting because I'd illustrated the book they were interested in, a children's book about a little girl with anxiety who changed into a chicken whenever she got too nervous. The editor, Lucy, grabbed me as I came in. I'd made an effort for the television people, worn a nice patterned shirt and extra mascara. It was a couple of months after I'd gone freelance and I was spending too many days in tea-stained pyjamas as it was, but that morning I'd told myself that this was important. This meeting could be life-changing. Turns out that it was, but not in the way I'd expected. The project was abandoned after a couple of months. It's tough to make it in TV, Callum always tells me. He's one of the talented ones. Or the lucky ones.

I'd been on my own for a while at that point, after my last relationship had blown up in my face. For a while, I'd had a sense of being untethered, somehow, afloat from the world, and the freelancing actually made it worse. I was spending too much time on my own. Dad had called me a few times, but I'd stopped picking up. He only ever wanted to talk about Mum, and I found it too painful. So I was in a bit of a strange mood the day I walked into the meeting.

'They don't pay their taxes. You shouldn't buy from them,' was the first thing he ever said to me, nodding at the takeaway coffee I was clutching in my hand, wrinkling his nose at the branded logo on the side. His expression, when I glanced up at him, was deadly serious, and as he frowned at me I felt momentarily panicked.

'No, I know,' I said hurriedly, 'it's just it's the only place on my way in, you know, and I don't function very well without coffee! But you're right, I should make it at home and bring it in. It's just I've only started freelancing recently so I wanted to feel part of the real world again, you know, and...' I'd tailed off, blushing, wondering why on earth I was telling him all the boring elements of my sad little life. Around us, my former colleagues were bustling into the room in their smart office wear and heels, all of them a little bit more dressed up for this meeting than they'd normally be, all of them slightly on edge. Callum had grinned at me.

'Don't worry,' he'd said, 'I won't hold it against you. They do a good gingerbread latte at Christmas, so I'm as guilty as you are.'

I'm as guilty as you are. The words come back to me now, buzz in my head like flies.

He pulled out the chair next to me and sat down, placing a pile of papers on the huge boardroom table. We were on the fourteenth floor, the highest in the building, overlooking Ipswich. For a moment I felt a sense of dizziness, as though I was about to fall.

'Welcome, everyone,' the publisher was saying, his voice barely containing the obvious excitement he had that TV executives were actually in his building, in little old Ipswich, here to talk about one of his books. It so rarely happened for an independent house. There were plates of chocolate biscuits in the centre of the table, which I knew from experience nobody would actually touch. Under the table, I picked at my fingers, pulling off the skin around my nails.

'So you're the illustrator, huh,' Callum said to me, his voice low as the publisher began with the niceties. Despite the large room, I felt something intimate in his voice, as though he and I were the only two people at the table. I could feel myself growing hot under his gaze, because by now I'd realised that the man next to me was, in fact, inordinately attractive. And a television exec, too. I know it sounds silly, but to me, with my little flat in Ipswich and my oh-so-fledgling freelance career, it seemed glamorous. It seemed like something I might be able to tether myself to.

We looked at their pitch for the book, and eventually someone did cave and take a biscuit from the plate, and the whole meeting lasted for about two hours, but none of those things were really very important. What was important was the sentence Callum said to me at the end, catching me by the arm just as everyone was getting ready to leave.

'Can I buy you something other than coffee tonight?'

I didn't notice the wedding ring until much later. OK, that's a lie. I did. I was as guilty as he was.

*

'Caroline?'

Jenny's voice is edged with accusation and I take another sip of wine, even though I've barely eaten any of the pasta she's made and my head is beginning to feel fuzzy.

'I haven't seen him, Jen,' I say eventually, meeting her eyes. Her own gaze narrows and she tilts her head to one side, as though trying to work out whether I'm telling the truth or not. In the background, I hear Eve begin to cry again, and the sound of Rick shushing her, his voice low and deep. *He's there for her,* I think, *he actually wants to be here with his family. I don't know what that's like.*

'When was the last time you saw him?' she asks me, and I feel a flash of anger. I'm not a naughty child, being held accountable for my every move.

'I haven't seen him for two weeks,' I say eventually, and the pain of the words is just as deep, just as fresh as it felt when I walked away from him. 'I just – I can't do it any more.' Of course, I'm not telling her the whole story. I'm not telling her the depths of his betrayal. I can't bring myself to talk about it.

Jenny's face softens, and she reaches out a hand to where mine is clenched on the table. My fist is tight, tense from thinking about our last encounter. The way he went back on his promise.

'Keep it that way, Caro,' Jenny says to me, stroking her thumb against the back of my hand. It feels nice, comforting. 'You've got to remember – he wasn't yours to have in the first place.'

I stiffen. 'I know that, Jenny,' I say to her. 'You don't need to remind me.'

Rick comes back into the room and we spring apart from each other as though we've been caught doing something illicit. I wonder how much she's told him, whether they discuss me when they're tucked up in bed at night. *You won't believe the mess Caroline's got herself into now...* Jenny takes her hand from mine. Rick kisses her as he walks past, and I feel it again, the pang of jealousy. I want to be like that – wholesome, motherly, someone *worth* something.

Things are slightly strained for the next hour of the evening, but gradually, we pull the conversation back around, and by the end of the night it's as though our chat about Callum hasn't happened at all. I force myself to let them talk me into the thought of a dating app, pasting a smile on my face so that they don't think I'm a bad sport. The sides of my cheeks begin to ache from the effort.

It's as I'm getting my things together that it happens. I'm slightly tipsy by this point, preparing myself for the walk home, struggling a little to pull on my left shoe. It's Rick who answers the phone, and at the sound of his words I tense, feel my breath hold still in my chest. People's voices change when they get bad news. Jenny has been stacking our wine glasses and plates into the dishwasher, but she stops suddenly as Rick turns to us, his face slack and white.

'It's my mum,' he says hoarsely, 'she's in the hospital. They think it's a heart attack.' He raises a hand to his eyes and I've never seen him like this, so untethered, so diminished. I know he and his mum are close; Jenny used to moan about it when they first got together. *We see more of his bloody mother than anyone else I know.*

Instantly, Jenny's by his side, her cardigan-clad arms stretching around his torso, holding him as though he might topple at any minute.

'We've got to go,' Rick says. 'They said this – they said this might be it.'

His eyes are staring past me, unseeing, translucent. I feel sick – I know what's coming even before she asks me.

'Eve's asleep,' Jenny says, and she lets go of her husband for a moment, comes over to where I'm standing sloppily in their porch, one shoe on, one shoe off. 'Caroline – you couldn't stay, could you?'

I stare at her, my heart beginning to beat fast and tight, like a drum. She reaches out and takes my hand again, squeezes it in hers. Her skin is soft and warm.

'I'll call you from the hospital, as soon as we know what's happening. It won't be long. I just—' She glances back at Rick, who is still ashen. 'I just need to be with him, and I don't want to wake Eve. It's – she doesn't often get to sleep so easily.'

'I don't know,' I say quickly, the words coming out in a rush. 'I don't know, Jen – are you sure you can't take her with you?'

She releases the pressure on my hand for a second as Rick begins to move, grabbing his mobile and shoving it into his jeans pocket, reaching for the house keys.

'Please, Caro,' she says, 'please.' Her eyes are big and wide and begging. I imagine it, little Eve and me, her relying on me if anything goes wrong. I don't know if I'm capable of it. I don't know if I trust myself. But oh, how I want to.

'I'll ring you as soon as I can, Caro,' Jenny is saying, and she is sliding on her coat and kissing me sloppily on the cheek, telling Rick that he will have to drive because she thinks she might be over the limit.

You definitely are over the limit, I think to myself, and then the door is slamming, the house reverberating from the noise, and their footsteps are hurrying away down the path and to their car.

I stand there, my breathing too loud.

And that's how I'm left alone in Jenny and Rick Grant's house with their baby, for the very first time.

*

The place feels very quiet without Jenny and Rick. I make myself a cup of tea, feeling skittery and on edge. Quarter to eleven, eleven o'clock, and still Jenny doesn't ring. It must be taking longer at the hospital than they thought; I picture his mother lying supine on a bed, the anxious beeping of machines surrounding her. My own mother died very quickly, a car accident on the A12. The car that hit her was a learner driver. I googled pictures of him for years afterwards, but he never looked like a killer, he just looked like a normal teenage boy. Proof that nobody ever looks quite what they seem.

Eventually, because I can't put it off any longer, I leave the kitchen and stand in the corridor outside Eve's room. The door is very slightly ajar, and a thin shaft of light from the window falls onto the floor, highlighting my socked feet on the unfamiliar carpet.

Carefully, I push open the door. The smell of baby hits me, the soft, milky sweetness of it. My stomach is churning. You see, I wanted a baby. Someone to care for. I wanted one so much.

Callum took that away from me, and I let him. It's something I don't know if I'll ever forgive myself for.

The cot is in the corner of the room, a pretty blue and white mobile dangling over it. If I stay very still, I can just about hear the sound of Eve's breathing, the shallow little breaths, the occasional snuffle. I take a step closer, feeling my way through the semi-darkness. For a few minutes, I allow myself to imagine what it would be like to hold her in my arms, her warm little body pressed against me. Me, not Jenny. I let myself feel what it might be like to pop her into a sturdy, expensive-looking pram and have strangers smile at me in the streets, watch their faces melt as they bend down to look at her.

These are not the sort of thoughts my brain normally lets me have. I don't think about babies any more because I don't let myself think about them.

Not after what happened.

Eve shifts slightly in her sleep, the thin pink blanket over her moving in the darkness. She must be hot; I am. I can feel sweat beginning to prickle along the back of my neck, despite the fact that Rick has left the window open, just a crack. It is silent apart from the sound of Eve and I breathing, and for a moment, I feel as though it is just the two of us against the world. There is no Rick, no Jenny, no Callum, and no Siobhan Dillon.

A buzzing sound disrupts the silence, making me jump. For a moment, I get the sense that somebody is behind me, waiting in the shadowy doorway, but then the moment passes as quickly as it came and I realise that of course, it's just my phone in my back pocket. My fingers trembling slightly, partly from the disturbance and partly from the adrenaline of being so close to Eve, I pull it out of my jeans and press the button to unlock the screen. I'm expecting it to be Jenny with an update from the hospital but it's not, it's from someone else. A number I don't recognise.

I know what you're doing, it says. *Don't take what isn't yours.*

I stare at the words, shining out at me from the screen, the bright light casting an eerie glow against Eve's bedroom floor. The wine I had earlier is churning around in my stomach, suddenly making me feel nauseous. Stupidly, I suddenly want Jenny to come home, for her and Rick to burst through the door, with their irritating habits and their warmth; I want them to come in and flick the lights on, boil the kettle, check on little Eve.

The phone is hot in my hand, as if it's on fire. *Don't take what isn't yours.* Who is it from? How did they get this number? And how do they know about me?

Chapter Five

France
12th August: One day before the arrest
Siobhan

OK, here's the truth. I've known about my husband's latest affair for four months, two weeks and three days. I've known that whenever we make love, he might be thinking of her, and I've known that every time his phone goes off, it's her who's texting him. *Caroline*. I even know her name. I'm pretty sure that's who he was with in Norfolk last month, when he told me he was with a client. Yeah, right. He even hid his suitcase somewhere in a feeble attempt to cover his tracks; it wasn't in the downstairs cupboard where it normally lives. Didn't want me to see any evidence of his dirty weekend away. He wheeled it out from somewhere on the day we left for France, thinking I hadn't even noticed its absence. He must think I'm stupid, and lately I've been thinking that maybe I am.

Here's what I don't know. I don't know exactly how long the affair has been going on, and I don't know exactly when they met, although I'm guessing it will be something to do with his work. It usually is – the first few *liaisons* were, anyway. He likes to impress people, does Callum, *I'm a TV executive, yes, that's right*. Cue smile, another drink. It works on the people of Suffolk; it might not wash in London, but here our lives are smaller somehow, there is less competition. It allows him to shine. It worked on me.

I've turned a blind eye to his multiple affairs, on and off for the past six years. Why? For the sake of our family. For Emma. For our house, for our life. The first time, all those years ago, I was heartbroken, of course I was. But over time, I've grown less so. Call it pathetic, subservient, whatever you'd like, but I watched my mother lose everything in our parents' divorce and every time I visit her, alone and almost penniless in that nursing home in Norfolk, I feel validated in my decision. I decided to be strong, decided that I could cope. And then I thought they'd stopped, that he'd grown out of it all. After Natasha the intern, there was a break of about two years, two years where I couldn't find any evidence, couldn't see any difference in his behaviour. His phone held no secrets, and I allowed myself to relax a bit, congratulated myself on sticking it out. It was over – he was mine, and I no longer had to compete. I'd won.

But then along came Caroline, and I realised it hadn't stopped at all. And somehow, that felt worse because I'd let myself believe it was over. Fool that I am. Yes, the affair with Caroline has hit me much harder than the others because she's proof that he gave us a go, Emma and I, that he tried life without any extras and found it wanting. He went back to his usual ways.

What I really didn't know was that my sister might know too.

She's staring at me now, and the look on her face is one of such pity that I feel the heat begin to sweep up my cheeks, coating me in shame.

I turn away from her, a spark of anger beginning to fizz inside me. Maria has no idea what it's like to be married, none at all – she thinks it's cumbersome, a burden, not to be envied. I'm reminded of what our mother always used to say, in her crueller moments: that Maria was alone because she wanted to be, because she didn't know how to be loved. It was a nasty thing to say, really, but then our mother did have a sharp tongue when she wanted to.

'Siobhan?'

Maybe it's the use of my full name, but I make myself turn back to look directly at her.

'How did you find out?' I ask her, and she sighs. It's a long, deep sigh and for a moment I feel my anger begin to wane, to fizzle out and be replaced by sadness. And embarrassment. Because it *is* embarrassing, to be caught out like this, to realise that another person knows how we are living a lie. I've always kept his infidelities a secret, a shameful little thing to be locked up tight.

'Find out?' she says, looking confused, and it's then that I start to realise I may have got it wrong. Quickly, I backtrack.

'Find out that we're – having problems,' I say, but my voice is faltering, and my sister, sharp as a tack, is narrowing her eyes.

'I mean,' I say, 'nothing major, just – you know, Emma makes everything very tense; it's meant we're not as close as we were, as we used to be…but Callum…'

My heart is thudding. I am desperate that nobody finds out about Caroline Harvey. It is my secret, held close to my chest until I know what to do with it. Until I know how to proceed.

'Siobhan,' she says, 'you're my sister. I can always tell. You're not yourself, neither of you are. There's so much tension—' she lifts a hand, slices through the air with her fingers, 'you could cut it with a knife.'

'You're exaggerating,' I say, 'you're blowing it all out of proportion. Callum and I will be fine.'

She stares at me, her gaze so penetrating that eventually I look away. I'm not fooling her; I'm not fooling anyone. The only other option is to get her on side.

'Please,' I say, and I let my voice break a little on the next word, 'please. Don't make this harder than it already is. Let me deal with it in my own way, Maria.'

She doesn't say anything, just nods at me slowly, then gets up from her sun lounger and takes a couple of steps towards the edge of the swimming pool. The water glistens invitingly and as she dives in, I imagine what it would feel like for the blueness to close over my head, shutting out the world, once and for all. I watch Maria's lithe body, a body that would make most 46-year-olds jealous, as it cuts through the water, and wonder what she meant by our conversation – whether she knows something I don't.

'Why don't you join me?' she calls to me, her dark head bobbing up above the blue. 'The water's lovely.' She stretches out a hand, beckoning me towards her. I hesitate, then get up from the sun lounger and step forwards, my toes warm against the tiles. Maria claps her hands girlishly, the sound echoing through the countryside. Despite myself, I smile. *I'm lucky to have a sister*, I think.

'I just want him to be good to you,' she says. 'All I've ever wanted is for you to get what you deserve.'

I reach for a croissant of my own, bite into the buttery pastry. It feels like a small act of defiance, somehow.

Callum and Emma return late, just as the sun is beginning to set. We have a lovely view of it over the horizon; it catches the French hills with an orange glow as the planes flit through the air towards Caen Airport. Maria has an app that can detect where they're coming and going from; she holds it up into the sky and it picks up their radars. 'Dubai,' she will say randomly. 'Athens.' Emma loves it, she is still young enough to find gadgets fascinating.

Callum's face is flushed slightly from the sun, and when Emma leans close to me, I think I can smell the faint tang of alcohol on her breath.

'Did you have a good day? Navigate the roads all right?' Maria asks, and, unusually, Emma begins telling us how beautiful Rouen was, how much she enjoyed it. I raise my eyebrows at my husband, and he shrugs his shoulders, as if to say *no, me neither.*

'Your car was a bit stuttery on the bends,' Callum says to Maria.

'It was fine this morning,' she says, 'don't blame your tools.' She smiles at him, but he looks away. He doesn't like people criticising his masculinity, does my husband.

Maria asks Emma if she'd like to help her prepare dinner, something she'd normally roll her eyes at, and to my surprise my daughter readily agrees. The pair of them vanish into the kitchen, Callum disappears for a shower (I tell him to put some aloe vera on his face) and I stay outside with a glass of wine, my body feeling strangely energetic after our swim in the pool earlier. Emma's happy mood continues all night, as we eat out on the terrace, a feast of fish that they have brought back with them from Rouen.

It crosses my mind that my daughter is today the happiest, the most relaxed I have seen her in weeks, and that this coincides with the fact that she has just spent an entire day away from me. The thought begins to nag at me as I sup my wine: is my daughter really happier when I am not around? Do I put too much pressure on her? Or is it just that she prefers Callum's company to my own, that he is able to reach her in a way I cannot? And then a quieter, crueller thought: *what would Emma say if she knew the truth about her daddy?*

As my family chatter away around me, I feel my own mood begin to sink, so much so that it's only when Maria nudges me that I realise I have not spoken in almost ten minutes.

'Are you OK?' she asks me, and I know she's thinking about our chat earlier; she's thinking that this is all to do with my husband, but in fact it's not, not this time. I'm thinking only about my daughter, and why it is that she is happier in the company of her adulterous father than she is in mine.

I watch her, my beautiful girl, across the table – Callum has his arm slung casually across the back of her chair, his fingers brushing the wrought-iron curves of it. Maria splashed out on the outdoor furniture – well, she splashed out on everything. *All of her money goes on herself,* our mother said once, *she's no one else to buy for.* But that isn't quite true, I think to myself, for Maria has bought us expensive gifts before – a gorgeous lamp for my bedside, designer perfumes for Emma. Nothing for Callum, of late. She has a good eye for detail, it comes with her job.

'Actually,' I say, 'I think I'm going to go to bed. I'm really tired.' I stand, feeling the wine hit me a little as I do so – I've drunk more than I thought. The energy I had earlier has disappeared as quickly as it came.

'Are you sure?' Callum asks, concern in his eyes, but my daughter barely looks up, gazing instead at her father, at his relaxed face, his open smile.

My husband is a world-class actor.

'I'm sure,' I say, waving Maria off as she attempts to come with me, 'I'm just going to put my head down. Too much sun!'

I smile but I know it's awkward, and the thought makes me feel unbearably sad. I was a part of this family, but when I glance back at the three of them, their silhouettes glowing under the wash of the vanishing sun, I feel left out, as though a pane of glass separates me from them all.

As I watch them, Emma does look up, just once, and her eyes meet mine across the stone flagged tiles.

'Goodnight Mum,' she calls to me, and I am reminded of how many times we have said those words to one another – me bending down to tuck her in when she was a small child, her begging for one more chapter of Harry Potter before bed, her little legs scurrying up the stairs ahead of me as she grew older. She used to like it when I read to her, I'd sit and stroke her hair, read her the poems of Edward Lear and the tales of Roald Dahl. She liked anything with magic in it.

'Goodnight,' I say back to her, 'I'll see you all in the morning. Sleep well.'

In the morning, of course, the police ring the doorbell at 09.03 a.m., and none of us ever truly sleep well again.

Chapter Six

DS Alex Wildy takes a sip of coffee, the taste of it burning his mouth. His wife Joanne has started packing him his own flask of freshly ground beans from home but he's usually drunk it by the time he gets to the station. He didn't sleep well last night, kept up with thoughts of the Ipswich murder-kidnap case. He can't believe they've already wasted almost three days trying to track down Callum Dillon. TV exec, local celebrity – and alleged boyfriend of Caroline Harvey. Buggered off to France for a jolly holiday, leaving a dead woman in his wake. He sighs: a woman found dead and a baby missing – it's not the norm for little old Ipswich. Last year, the biggest case the town saw was a burglary in the Wickham Estate, and even then they only took a TV worth less than five hundred pounds. It was hardly worth prosecuting, but they did anyway. Couple of youths ended up with suspended sentences.

'It's good for you to have something to get your teeth into,' Joanne had said when this case first came in on the night of the tenth, and Alex had nodded, not wanting to admit that he already felt a little bit overwhelmed. He can't help it – he always feels so desperately sorry for the victims in cases like this. Whenever a baby is involved, or any child really, the whole thing becomes so much worse. He's desperate for little Eve to be found alive.

Jenny Grant gave the police Callum's name straight away, sobbing down the phone as she told them about coming back to find her babysitter, a 33-year-old local woman named Caroline Harvey, dead and her daughter Eve missing. Tracking him down was another matter. They'd gone to the Ipswich house he shares with his wife and daughter, only to find it locked up, curtains closed and door firmly shut. The neighbours hadn't had a clue; Alex got the impression they weren't used to socialising with the family too much, though their interest was more than piqued at the mention of Callum's name. Eventually, a work colleague of Callum's had mentioned France, and once they'd got onto border control, it hadn't taken long to get the Rouen police on the line, send a couple of officers over to the villa in Saint Juillet this morning. Callum should be on a plane any minute now, making his way back to the UK, as the country crawls with police out looking for Eve. There's a search party combing Ipswich and the surrounding area, the dogs are working with officers in Christchurch Park and beyond, over towards the coast with its heaths and woodland. Every time a phone rings they are all on high alert, waiting for news, but so far nothing has been found – no clothing, no signs of life. No sign of the victim's mobile phone, either – they are working to the assumption that whoever killed her took it with them.

Alex wonders what will be going through the TV exec's mind as he sits on the plane – hopefully with minimal leg room. At least they know where he is now. But during these crucial few days, anything could have happened. He grits his teeth. No point getting annoyed, not now. There's a job to be done. A baby to be found.

His colleague, Dave Bolton, nudges him in the ribs, causing the caustic coffee to spill down the front of his shirt, freshly ironed by Joanne last night. Alex knows that his wife is keeping busy at the moment, trying to distract herself from the latest miscarriage. He's not one of those men who wants his wife to do all the traditional chores – cooking, cleaning, ironing – but lately he's had the uncomfortable sense that she *wants* to do it, wants to keep her mind away from babies. He's told her to go back to work, if she wants, but she keeps insisting she's not ready.

'Come on then, she's in Room 2,' DS Bolton says, nodding down the corridor to where they've got the mother of the missing one-year-old. Thus far, any questioning of the baby's parents has taken place in their own home by DS Bolton and the assigned DCI, Gillian McVey. They'd been anxious not to cause them undue stress, but as the hours have passed and missing Eve hasn't been found, the DCI has made the decision to bring Rick and Jenny in for formal questioning, and DS Wildy has been roped in.

'She's in a bit of a state,' Bolton adds, 'understandably.'

'I'd be worried if she wasn't,' says Alex, and Bolton nods.

'Still,' he says, 'you never can tell at this stage. I've seen enough waterworks shows to last me a lifetime.' He grins at Alex, and they walk towards the interview room. Alex can see through the glass panel in the door that there is a woman hunched at the table, her slim frame curving downwards as though broken somehow. Her hair is thin and lank-looking, and her hands are clasped together on the table, a silver ring with a huge rock on it clearly visible in the light. Someone has brought her a glass of water, but the polystyrene cup is damaged at the sides, as though she has been gripping it too tightly.

'Jenny Grant?' he says, pushing open the door, and the woman looks up, quick as a flash, her eyes meeting his. She has the desperate, hunted look of an animal, reminding Alex of a rabbit he once saw trapped in wire in the garden back at home.

'I'm DS Wildy,' he tells her, 'I'm here to talk to you about the disappearance of your daughter.'

Interview with Jenny Grant, 13th August
Ipswich Police Station
Present: DS Wildy, DS Bolton, Jenny Grant
10.05 a.m.

DS Wildy: *Mrs Grant, please state your name for the tape.*
JG: *Jenny Elizabeth Grant.*
DS Wildy: *Mrs Grant, please could you talk us through the events of the tenth of August, the night you went to collect your daughter Eve from the care of Caroline Harvey?*
JG: *[pause]*
DS Wildy: *It's OK. Take your time.*
JG: *I'm sorry. This is difficult for me. [pause] Being here like this, in this room – it feels like I'm in trouble.*
DS Wildy: *You're not, Mrs Grant. We are not accusing you of anything at this stage. We just need to get a clear picture of what happened that night.*

JG: *[takes a deep breath] I was coming home from the hospital, the Norfolk and Norwich hospital. Rick – my husband – Rick's mother was in one of the wards, she'd been staying there for a few nights. She'd had a heart attack, like I told you before, and they'd kept her in for observation. She's in her seventies, but she's never had great health, and Rick worries about her a lot. All the time, actually.*

DS Wildy: *For the benefit of the tape, the woman in hospital is Margaret Grant, mother of Rick Grant.*

JG: *I had asked Caroline—*

DS Wildy: *For the benefit of the tape, Caroline Harvey, the deceased.*

JG: *[pause] Yes. I had asked Caroline to look after our daughter, Eve, for the night whilst we went to see Margaret in the hospital. I thought – I thought it would be OK because she'd looked after her on the night of the heart attack, about a week before. [pause]. I hadn't thought of her as a baby person before that, but she'd come round for dinner, and it all happened so quickly, there was no one else to leave her with. [pause] I just wanted Eve to sleep. I didn't want to have to wake her up and for her to start crying. [pause.] I was trying to do the right thing for my baby. [pause, sobbing]. She's my first child, my only child. I love her so much.*

DS Wildy: *It's OK, Mrs Grant, you're doing really well. Take your time.*

JG: *I should have just taken her with us, I know I should. But I've known Caroline since university. For years.*

DS Bolton: *Mrs Grant, would you say you and Caroline Harvey had remained close since university?*

JG: *[pause] No. No, not really, not the whole way through. We've been closer recently, in the last few years. She – she'd told me about Callum. I thought of him straight away. He wasn't very nice to her, I don't think – something happened between them, something bad. They'd stopped seeing each other a few weeks ago, she said, but it was obvious he still had a hold on her. I'm worried she might have called him, that he came over and lost his temper. [presses a hand to her mouth]*

DS Wildy: *When you say something bad happened between them, what do you mean?*

JG: *I don't know. I really don't. I never found out, but I know there was something, a reason she stopped seeing him in the first place. She was angry with him.*

DS Wildy: *Why did you choose Caroline to look after your daughter?*

JG: *Like I said, there was no one else at the time, that first night, when Margaret was taken ill. And when we got home Eve was fine, she was sleeping, she was completely fine. I don't understand how any of this happened.*

DS Wildy: *Let's return to the night in question, then, August 10th. You took Eve over to Caroline's flat this time, didn't you? Where previously she'd been in your house.*

JG: *Yes. Yes. I would have preferred Caroline to come to ours because that's where all Eve's stuff is, you know, her cot, her things, but I'd already put Caro out on the night of the heart attack; I didn't want to be selfish. I was so grateful that she was helping us. Rick was – Rick was very upset about his mother. [pause] It was stressful. I wanted to make things easier for us all.*

DS Bolton: *And what time did you take your daughter over to Caroline's flat? For the benefit of the tape, this is location A, 43 Woodmill Road, Ipswich.*

JG: *It was about 6 p.m.*

DS Wildy: *And how did Caroline seem when you took Eve to her?*

JG: *She seemed fine. She was really happy to see us; I remember thinking she was so natural with Eve. [pause] I thought, she'll make a great mother some day. Sorry – I just, I just need a moment. [long pause]. I can't think straight, Detective, my mind is – it's all over the place. All I can think about is Eve, I can't really – I'm not really thinking about Caroline. I know that sounds awful but she's my baby, my only girl. I need her back. [pause, crying].*

DS Wildy: *Take your time.*

JG: *[takes a deep breath] Sorry. I'm OK now. Caroline seemed fine. I'd brought Eve's travel cot, we set it up in the bedroom when I arrived—*

DS Bolton: *In Caroline Harvey's bedroom?*

JG: *Yes. It's a tiny flat. There wasn't anywhere else.*

DS Wildy: *Please continue, Mrs Grant. You set up the cot. Was Eve sleeping when you dropped her off?*

JG: *No, she was awake. She's often awake until about seven, that's when I normally put her down. That's the right time, that's what all the books say to do.*

DS Wildy: *We're not disputing that, Mrs Grant. Please don't worry. So, you left Eve with Caroline. What time did you leave the premises to go to the hospital?*

JG: *I stayed for about twenty minutes, I think, just running through everything with Caroline, you know, everything*

Eve might need. I left her some formula, we put it in the fridge. And a change of clothes – I'd been changing her clothes a couple of times in the night, recently, because it's been so hot. She would get very hot in her cot; we'd started keeping the window open.

DS Bolton: *Did you run through all of the details with Caroline on the night of the heart attack, a few nights before, the first time you left Eve in her care?*

JG: *[pause] No. No, I didn't. There wasn't any time. I did text her from the hospital. I told her where everything was then. But I was rushing out the door, the hospital had said Margaret might be about to die. Rick was distraught. He's very close to his mother. [pause] He always has been.*

DS Bolton: *So you left Caroline Harvey's flat at around twenty past six on the evening of August 10th. And you went to the Norfolk and Norwich hospital.*

JG: *Yes.*

DS Wildy: *And where was your husband during this time?*

JG: *He was already at the hospital with his mother. He'd barely left her bedside since the heart attack. Like I said, they're really close.*

DS Bolton: *So would you say it had been difficult for you, for those past few days, looking after Eve alone whilst your husband was with his mother?*

JG: *No, I would not. I'm her mother. I didn't find it difficult. Why are you even saying that, what are you suggesting?*

DS Wildy: *And what time did you leave the hospital to come back to collect your daughter from Caroline Harvey's flat?*

JG: *It was just after ten. We'd stayed at the hospital until visiting hours stopped – Rick wanted to. Then we both drove back. I dropped Rick at home and then I went to get Eve.*

DS Bolton: *Why did you drop your husband off first?*

JG: *[pause] He was exhausted and upset. I knew he wanted to be at home. So I said I'd go get Eve. I was worried I'd end up talking to Caroline for a while, and that it would get late. I wanted Rick to be able to relax and go to bed. He'd had a really long day. We both had, I suppose.*

DS Bolton: *And can you tell us what happened when you arrived at Ms Harvey's flat?*

JG: *[pause]*

DS Wildy: *We understand this is difficult to think about, Mrs Grant. But it's important, for your daughter's sake, that you are as detailed as possible in your recollection. Any small detail could be crucial to our investigation at this stage.*

JG: *I – I took the lift up to her flat. She's on the fifth floor, at the end of a long corridor. As I walked down the corridor, I could see that her front door was open, just a bit, and I was confused. I worried that I must have left it open, when I left for the hospital, and that Caro hadn't noticed. I reached the door and knocked on it quickly, then pushed it open and went inside. I didn't think she'd mind, you know, I was calling out to her, hello, it's me. I thought she'd be expecting me because I'd texted her when I left the hospital, just to say I was on my way back. I asked her if she needed anything from the shops. I wanted to say thank you to her, for looking after Eve twice in one week.*

DS Wildy: *Did she reply to your message saying that you were on your way?*

JG: No. No, I told DS Bolton yesterday that she didn't.

DS Bolton: *What time was the message sent? Remind us, if you could.*

JG: *It was about ten past ten, I think. I said I was dropping Rick home and then I'd be straight over. I offered to get her a bottle of wine as a thank you. Asked if she needed any milk, that sort of thing. I felt guilty for being quite a long time, and I wanted to make it up to her, make sure she knew I was grateful. Eve isn't always an easy baby.*

DS Bolton: *What do you mean by that?*

JG: *Nothing out of the ordinary – just that she's a baby, Detective. She's one and a half – she cries sometimes – well, she cries a lot, she can be tricky to put down to sleep. That sort of thing. I just – I just didn't want Caroline to think I was taking advantage. I got the impression that she sometimes felt – I don't know – different to Rick and I. I didn't want her to think we were just using the fact that she was single and didn't have any other ties, you know, getting her to babysit for nothing.*

DS Bolton: *So you didn't pay Caroline for babysitting?*

JG: *I – no. I offered to, but she's a friend. Was a friend. It would have been odd for me to give her money. Why does this even matter?*

DS Wildy: *What happened when you walked into Caroline's flat, Mrs Grant? Can you tell us about that?*

JG: *At first I couldn't see her. It was really quiet, and I felt myself begin to panic because the whole flat just had such a strange air about it, you know. I thought I could smell cleaning fluid, something chemical. [pause] Sorry, sorry. I'm OK.*

DS Wildy: *Take a deep breath, if you can.*

JG: *I went into the kitchen, to see where Caroline was, and she – she wasn't in there. She was gone.*

DS Wildy: *What happened next?*

JG: *I ran into the bedroom – it's a tiny flat, very small, but I had to check. I thought Caroline might have had to go out, an emergency or something, and that she'd taken Eve with her so as not to leave her alone. I wouldn't have minded, you know, as long as she was safe, as long as she had her. But in the bedroom – I found – [pause] the cot with...with...*

DS Wildy: *Do you think you're able to continue?*

JG: *[silence, sobbing]*

DS Bolton: *Interview paused at 10.45.*

Chapter Seven

France
13th August: The day of the arrest
Siobhan

The morning they come for him, there isn't any time for Callum to pack. The French police stand at our door, looking horribly out of place in the hot sun, their dark uniforms a stark contrast against the bright blue of the sky and the deep pink roses that climb up along the door frame. *They must be hot*, I think stupidly. Maria speaks to them in rapid French as Callum and I stand there, dumb, and I feel a stab of jealousy at how cleverly my sister can interpret their words. Emma has for once followed my instructions to remain downstairs, or so I think, but as Maria invites the police inside, I see the flash of her blonde hair disappear out of sight, proof that she has in fact been listening in. I reassure myself that she can no more understand the French than I can.

'Callum, they want to take you back to the UK,' Maria says to him, her words quick and urgent as the police look on. I try to meet the policewoman's eyes, but they gaze past me, flat and deadened in her face. I wonder what she thinks of us – the half-dressed English tourists linked to a dead woman back at home.

'I've done nothing to Caroline, what's happened to her?' Callum is saying, over and over. His eyes are welling up, tears threatening to spill over, but the police officers ignore him. I stare at him, wondering how real his reaction is. Crocodile tears, or the real emotion of a grieving lover? How much did this woman mean to him that he's prepared to risk admitting their affair? Or is he playing us all for fools?

'*Suivez-nous*,' the man says, and Callum swallows, looks at me, his face suddenly like that of a little boy. '*Come with us.*' I stare back at him, feeling sick with dread.

'You'd better go with them,' Maria says, 'they can handcuff you otherwise. This way, you're cooperating.'

All at once, I am immeasurably grateful that she is here, taking control – she speaks again to the police and they nod, apparently satisfied.

'Get him some clothes, S,' Maria says, and I run into our bedroom, where Callum's clothes are scattered across our unmade bed and a little on the floor on his side. He has always had bad habits when it comes to tidiness; I scoop up the clothes he was wearing yesterday, shorts and a white shirt that still has a splash of aloe vera aftersun lotion on the collar. His shoes, brown loafers, are discarded by the wardrobe and I grab those too, hurrying back into the hallway where the little group stand waiting.

'Siobhan—' Callum says to me as I hand them to him, my hands beginning to violently shake, 'I didn't have anything to do with this, I mean—' he swallows, 'I know Caroline, I do, but I didn't hurt her. I'd never hurt anyone! I know you'll be angry but please, Siobhan, you have to believe me.'

I look up at him, and in that second, I feel as though I don't know him at all.

'*Allez, vite,*' the policewoman says, her accent thick, and Callum struggles into the clothing, in front of us all, pulling the shorts up over his boxers. The police avert their eyes. I stare at Maria, willing her to tell me that this is all a joke, an elaborate trick designed to unnerve us – for what purpose, I don't know. But she doesn't. She doesn't say anything at all. I wonder if she is embarrassed, by my family coming to her beautiful house and causing all this upset. Shame curdles in my stomach.

'Emma,' Callum says to me, and I step forward, place a hand on his, grip onto him as tightly as I can.

'We'll come home,' I say, 'we'll get the next flight. I'll speak to Emma. Don't worry, Cal. Just do what they say, for now at least.'

'I'm sorry,' he says, 'I'm sorry.' His eyes look desperate, hunted, but is it all an act?

For a moment or two, I feel the younger of the two police officers look at me, but I avoid their gaze. I don't want anyone looking too closely.

'Can I pack my things?' he says to Maria, and she translates quickly, before shaking her head and wincing.

'They want everything left as is,' she says, 'for now, anyway. But you need your passport.' Carefully, she reaches out a hand and touches my husband's shoulder. I watch as she gives it a squeeze, so tight that it almost looks painful. The male police officer says something else, and Callum looks around, grabs his iPhone from where it sits on charge on the top of the bookshelf near the door. He hesitates, the phone in his palm, before giving it over to the policeman without complaint. Maria raises her eyebrows at me and I run back into our bedroom, fumble for Callum's passport, which is sitting nestled on top of mine in the drawer where I've put my underwear. My fingers are shaking as I bring it back to the hallway, hand it to my husband. The policeman takes it from his grasp.

'Things will be easier in England,' says Maria, and I watch in horror as Callum steps towards me, kissing me and whispering that this is all nonsense, lies and rubbish, that it will all be sorted in no time at all, that I am to tell Emma not to worry. He smells stale, of our twisted up sheets and of the sun. I stare at him, uncomprehending, and then he is walking away and the police are smiling grimly at Maria as she says something else that I don't understand, and then the front door is closing behind the three of them and the bright patch of sunlight is shut out, gone.

For a moment or two, my sister and I stand in silence in the darkened hallway. The main shutters that cover the huge sliding doors are still closed, none of us had got round to opening them yet. We had all slept in. I think of the bright red numbers on the alarm clock next to my bed – it feels like a lifetime ago now that the doorbell first rang, although in reality – I glance at my watch – it has only been twenty-six minutes.

'Do you know who she is? Caroline Harvey? Callum obviously does,' Maria asks me bluntly, and as I watch her mouth move, I feel the bare flagged stones of the hallway rise up to meet me, feel the world swimming in front of my eyes.

'Put your head between your legs, S,' Maria says, and her hand is on my lower back, guiding me gently towards the sofa in the large open-plan living room. The soft padding is comforting, and I sink down, Maria's reassuring voice in my ear, rubbing my back as she sits down next to me, telling me that it's all OK, that it's all going to be OK.

But it isn't, I want to scream, *it isn't*.

Outside, there is a loud splash, and despite my dizziness, I lift my head. Maria is swearing, running to the doors. Emma has jumped into the swimming pool.

*

I sit on the large double bed, the windows to our bedroom still closed against the sun. Callum's belongings are scattered around me – his wallet, his keys for our house in Ipswich. *What will he do without them*, I wonder, then realise there probably isn't much call for shopping inside a police station and that they're not likely to let him go home first anyway. Maria is on hold to the airline whilst she sits at the table, trying to book us all onto the next flight back home. None of us want to stay here – how can we, when this has happened?

Getting up, I pull back the shutters on the bedroom window and see Emma emerge from the pool at last, dripping wet. Hurriedly, I rush out, bringing her a thick, fluffy towel to the side of the water.

'I wanted to feel something,' she says, by way of explanation, and I nod as though I understand.

'Dad is going to be fine,' I tell her, watching as she dries herself off. I bite the inside of my mouth to try to calm my anxiety, and taste the rusty tang of blood.

'It's a misunderstanding,' I say, 'but we're going to go home and sort things out, straight away, OK, Ems?'

She stares at me; her blue eyes look huge in her face. She has Callum's eyes.

'Who is she?' she asks me. 'Who is the woman they're talking about, Mum?'

I hadn't realised she'd heard.

Chapter Eight

Ipswich

3rd August: One week before

Caroline

'Caro? We're home!'

Jenny's voice startles me. They're home from the hospital. Quickly, I back out of baby Eve's bedroom and close the door behind me, leaving her sleeping in the warm little room. The blue and white mobile spins as I shut the door, fluttering above her head like a bird.

I slip my phone back into my pocket and go to greet them, pasting a smile on my face even though that horrible text message is still burning in my mind. *Don't take what isn't yours.* They must mean Callum, mustn't they? I was hardly about to take little Eve! But then, who knows about the two of us, apart from Jenny?

'Hi,' I say, 'hi. How is she, how's your mum?'

Rick sighs. He looks shattered; the pair of them do, but he especially. His face is strained, as though he might've been crying. It's funny, you don't often see grown men cry, but he and his mum are close. Jenny's told me enough times. He runs a hand through his hair, bends down to start untying his shoes.

'She's stable,' he says, 'they're keeping her in for at least a few nights, maybe more, they said. I'll go back first thing in the morning. Christ, I'm knackered.'

'Is Eve all right?' Jenny asks me, bustling past me before I can even answer. She goes into the bedroom, and I hear her murmuring gently to her daughter.

'Of course she is,' I say, 'she slept the whole time. No trouble at all.'

'Thank you so much, Caro,' Jenny says, reappearing in the hallway, putting a hand on my arm. 'We really appreciate it. God, I don't know what we'd have done if you weren't here! She'd have screamed the place down if we'd woken her up. They probably wouldn't have let her into the ward.'

She smiles at me, and her eyes are warm, warmer than they were earlier in the evening. She looks relieved, and grateful – properly grateful, as if I really have saved her from something rather than just looked after a sleeping baby for a couple of hours while she rushed to her mother-in-law's bedside. I wonder if she's coping with motherhood quite as well as I thought she was, as the cute pictures of baby Eve dotted around the house would have everyone believe.

I glance at my watch, surprised to see that it's almost midnight.

'I'd better be getting home,' I say, 'it's pretty late.'

'You could stay over?' Jenny offers, 'sleep on the sofa? I'm so sorry it's got so late. We didn't realise the time.' She yawns, not bothering to cover her mouth with her hand.

'No, no,' I say, because although I'm tired, the thought of waking up surrounded by their busy, happy space is almost more than I can bear. The text message has really shaken me up, and I have a sudden longing to be in my own bed, with the duvet pulled over me like when I was a child, the door bolted shut behind me. I always bolt the door before I go to bed, and usually end up getting up ten minutes later to double-check that I've done it. I've never got used to sleeping alone, which is ironic really, given that most of the time I have to.

'Rick can run you home?' Jenny says, and he nods immediately, but I wave her away, anxious at the thought of spending even a few minutes cooped up with her husband and his pity.

'Don't be silly, I'll walk. It's only ten minutes.'

She looks worried. 'Are you sure, Caro? It's late.'

'It's only Ipswich,' I say, forcing a little laugh, 'I'll be fine.' I hesitate, wondering whether to say what's been on my mind, the words I was drafting in my head as I stared down at Eve in her little cot. 'And listen, Jenny, if you need me to look after Eve again, any time, I'm very happy to. Honestly.' I pause, swallow. 'It would be my pleasure.'

It's only brief, but I catch the look of surprise that flits across both of their faces. I try very hard not to mind. *It's fair enough that they don't think I'm a baby person*, I tell myself, *because I've never told them what happened*.

'Thank you, Caro, that's really kind of you,' Jenny says, rectifying the awkward moment, and she reaches out and gives me a hug, wrapping me tightly in her arms. It feels nice, and with a sharp pain I realise that no one has properly touched me like that since the night Callum and I broke up. And even then, it wasn't particularly nice. Over her shoulder, I look at the photos of Eve on the wall, then notice Rick watching me, and flick my eyes away.

'No problem,' I say to Jenny, hugging her back, and she smiles at me again, rubs her eyes with the knuckles of her hand. 'You must be tired,' I say.

'It *is* tiring,' she says, 'this baby malarkey – no one ever tells you how hard it's going to be.' For a moment, it's as though the shiny, happy armour she usually wears slips a little, and through the chink I see something else – how exhausted she is, how frustrating it might sometimes be to cope with little Eve. But as soon as the moment arrives it is gone, and she's leading me to the door, waving at me as I leave the house. Wondering if she's as happy with her choices as she makes out.

I can feel Rick's eyes on me all the way down their little garden path.

*

I walk quickly back through the town – it's much cooler now; England can never retain heat in the way mainland Europe does. I bet it'll be boiling in France next week. It's dark now, the only light provided by the lamps on the thoroughfare. The quickest way would be to take the side street and walk along near the harbour. Wrapping my cardigan more tightly around me, I hesitate for a second – there is something about the water that looks slightly menacing – but then I tell myself to stop being silly and set off for my flat, tucking my hands into my pockets, one hand gripped around my mobile. It's quiet – most of the pubs and the few clubs that there are in Ipswich are only really busy on Saturday nights, and even then, it all calms down by about eleven, last orders. It's a world away from the all-night noise of Leeds; the cacophony of traffic and party-goers that I got used to back at university.

As I walk, I start to feel a prickling sensation along the back of my neck, as though I am being watched. I'm imagining things, I think to myself, that stupid text message has freaked me out, but even so I walk a tiny bit faster, counting my steps – fifty-five, fifty-six, fifty-seven – to stop my thoughts from spiralling. As I round the corner onto my road, I pass someone walking – wearing a dark coat, the gleam of white headphones peeking out from their collar. I can't see their face and my breathing increases as I approach them, but it's just a woman, and she doesn't even glance at me. Feeling stupid, I ignore the odd sensation and gratefully tap my fob against the little sensor outside my block of flats, hear the reassuring beep of the system letting me inside. I'm glad they've fixed the security – there was a period where it kept breaking, giving anyone access to the main door. I think a few of the residents complained, not that I actually got round to doing so. The defunct CCTV camera stares blankly at me, its screen shattered into jagged pieces the same way it's been since last year when the kids from the Warwick Estate threw stones at it. Still, at least the lift is working today, something that's not always a guarantee. In the lift mirror I stare at myself – my cheeks are flushed and my eyes a bit glittery. *Too much time with Eve, playing the babysitter*, I think.

Back in my flat, I turn on all the lights and plug my phone in to charge, setting it on my bedside table as I pull off my clothes, my body sticky, sweat lingering from a day in the August heat. I open up the text message again. *I know what you're doing. Don't take what isn't yours.* The words blur, the angry little letters bouncing into themselves beneath my gaze. Frowning, I copy and paste the mobile phone number and put it into Safari, but all that comes up are random streams of 'who called me?' sites that don't give any help at all.

I try to think calmly, logically. I think of Jenny's face, the coldness in her voice when she asked me about Callum earlier, but then I think of the way she hugged me just now, the way she let me look after her child, and the fact that I have both her and Rick's numbers saved in my phone, and that as far as I know, they don't have another one used for threatening friends on special occasions. Why would they?

It's almost one in the morning. My sad little *how are you?* to Callum, sent all those hours ago, sits resolutely at the top of my WhatsApp screen. I stare at the page. Last seen at 22.04. He hasn't even looked at his phone for hours, he's probably in bed with Siobhan and has left it on charge like a normal person. Like someone who isn't obsessing over their mistress. Like someone who hasn't given me a second thought at all. Like someone who doesn't care that he's ruined my life. I hate the last seen function on WhatsApp, designed to make us feel ignored. *Us.* The mistresses, the after-thoughts. A group of women I wish I didn't belong to.

It's then that the thought occurs to me: Siobhan. And I can't believe I haven't thought about it before. The person who has the most obvious reason for threatening me is Callum's wife.

I've seen her a couple of times. Once, when I followed him home one night, keeping my distance, my hands shoved deep in my pockets and a big scarf across my mouth because it was Christmas time, and cold. It's not as bad as it sounds; I just wanted to see her, see where they lived. Their big house by the park was all lit up, a Christmas tree in the window, golden lights glittering along the roof. She was in one of the upstairs bedrooms, her figure illuminated by the light of the room. I watched as Callum went into the house – we'd been drinking mulled wine; she thought it was after-work drinks with his colleagues. I could only see her outline, really, the sway of her long hair, but it was enough to confirm that she was better than me. I stood there for about ten minutes, watching the house, my hot breath pushing into my scarf.

I lie down on the bed, fully clothed, staring up at the ceiling, so familiar to me now with its whorls and stains. I think of all the times Callum and I have lain here together, kissing and laughing and talking. After a moment or two, I get up to check that the door is locked, run my fingers over the bolt, slide the chain across. I think of Callum with Siobhan, of her long hair tumbling over her shoulder, touching him on the arm. *Don't take what isn't yours.* Could the message be from her?

I fall asleep with the phone clutched in my hand.

Chapter Nine

France
13th August: The day of the arrest
Siobhan

I lie to Emma, tell her that I've no idea who Caroline Harvey could be or how her dad knows her. My stomach twists as I do so – haven't there been enough lies? – but at this stage, I don't know what else to say. I've never told my daughter about Callum's affairs; I've always prided myself on shielding her from it. In the background, Maria swears – she is still on hold to the airline company, trying to change our return flights and get the next ones possible back to the UK. I can hear the sound of their holding music, very faintly, the noise of it tinny in the large hallway.

Suddenly desperate for some fresh air, I pull back the blinds from the large French doors, still in my nightie. The dazzling sunlight hits me, bright and unrelenting, and I twist the door handle, stepping outside onto the patio. There's a bottle of wine, empty, standing at the foot of one of the comfy chairs, and I stare at it, imagining us all grouped out here the other night, with no idea of the shock this morning would bring. But then I think of Callum on the plane, his odd jitteriness, and I wonder if he knew exactly what this holiday might bring, had been counting the hours until the dreadful sound of the doorbell, clanging through the house. Surely not, I reassure myself, surely my husband isn't capable of a crime. Adultery is one thing, but murder? I think of the tears in his eyes as he learned of Caroline's death. Real or false?

The lack of internet here, once a blessing, is now a curse – I want desperately to google her name, search the British news websites for any sign of what might have happened. Surely someone will call soon, the police will come back and tell us this has all been a big mistake. Not knowing is torturous.

'Siobhan!' Maria is calling me from inside the house, the cordless landline phone pressed to her ear. 'They're saying the next flight they can get us on is tomorrow.'

I stare at her through the open French doors. 'Tomorrow? Isn't there anything today?'

She shakes her head. 'We can get the 7.20 from Caen in the morning. They'll move the booking for us. That way you won't lose the money. Or we could drive, I guess.' She taps her fingers against the plastic casing of the phone, raising her eyebrows.

'Got to let them know now, S.'

'OK,' I say, 'OK.' The thought of a six-hour drive in this heat is unappealing, and this way, I have some time to collect my thoughts. 'OK, yes, yes please. If that's the best we can get.'

She nods at me and turns her attention to the person at the other end of the phone line. Anxiety courses through my veins. Part of me can't bear the thought of returning to England, of all this becoming real, but then staying here feels almost as bad. None of us can enjoy the holiday now, can we? The thought is absurd. And all the while we've no idea what is happening to Callum, where he is, what they're actually accusing him of.

'Done.' Maria appears on the patio beside me – I didn't even hear her come outside. 'We'll be home by lunchtime tomorrow, I'll leave the car here and fly back with you. I can pick it up another time. I'll let the police know, too.' Gently, she wraps an arm around my waist and I shiver slightly; my sister and I don't tend to show much physical affection, not now that we're adults. When we were younger, we did – we shared a room until I was almost fourteen – but I feel slightly stiff under her touch.

'What am I going to do?' I whisper to her, my voice cracking a little as I think of the next twenty-four hours stretching out in front of us.

She sighs; I can feel her breath warm against my neck. 'S, look, I bet they're only wanting to talk to him at this stage. Those officers weren't charging him. Not yet.'

There's a beat of silence. We both know that they wouldn't come all the way out here, track him down like this, if there wasn't more to it all than meets the eye. They wouldn't arrest him for nothing. I need to know more – when they think she was killed, where my husband was at the time. How much they have already pieced together. I need to be a step ahead.

'Not yet,' I say to her, 'but what if they do? What if he's done something, Maria?'

She doesn't answer me, and when I look at her again she won't quite meet my eye.

*

We don't eat breakfast – I can't stomach it and Emma says she's not hungry either. Maria makes a pot of coffee, black and steaming, and the three of us sit outside on the terrace for a little while, mobile phones on the table in front of us, even though it's relatively pointless due to the lack of signal. Above us, the rock towers into the bright blue sky. The crickets continue to chirp. The sun feels like it's mocking us, and eventually I tell the others I'm going inside to pack. I step inside, past the pile of rugs, the ornate lamp and the beautiful bookcase, the shiny life of my sister, untouched by an adulterous husband who may or may not be a killer.

In our room, I pick up my suitcase from the bottom of the wardrobe and place it on the still-unmade bed. I always unpack fully upon arrival whenever we come away; I hate the way my clothes feel after being crumpled up inside a suitcase for days on end. I run my fingers over my dresses, sliding them from their hangers. As I do so, I find myself wondering what *she* wears – or wore. Caroline Harvey. I try not to think about her, have tried not to for four months now, pushing away the thoughts of what she might look like, what she might sound like. I googled her name, of course, when I first found out, but reams of them came up. I had no way of knowing which Caroline was the one my husband had decided to screw. I've been thinking what to do for all this time, if I'm honest – debating whether to leave, whether to stay, whether to confront or ignore. I've ignored for so long, let all these women pass me by for the sake of our family, but Emma is sixteen now, older. I feel differently to how I used to. Somehow, him starting another affair after a period of fidelity feels much worse. I suppose I let my defences come down. I paw through my clothes, wondering whether my daughter and I could weather a broken marriage. But what has happened today

79

will change everything, won't it? The same options are no longer available.

A red dress slithers through my hands, one Callum bought for me on our anniversary, a few years ago now. He'd presented it to me with a flourish, and that night I'd put it on for him, feeling giggly and young, even though I was well into my thirties, my stomach marked with the scars of Emma's birth. A difficult birth; torturous almost. My daughter still tortures me, I think wryly, just in a different way. Callum used to buy me things a lot earlier in our relationship – clothes, jewellery, trips away. He hasn't bothered for years. Too busy with other things – or other people.

In spite of what's happened today, of the stab of pity I felt when he walked out of the door, I feel now a splash of rage against him, and in quick, decisive moves I yank the rest of my dresses from their hangers, begin stuffing them into my suitcase, taking none of the care I normally exhibit when it comes to my belongings. I scoop up my jewellery from the dresser, catching sight of myself in the large, ornate mirror – I look like a mad woman. My hair is all over the place, my nightie clings to me oddly and the clutch of bright jewellery in my hands glitters strangely against the pale of my skin. For a second, I stare at my reflection, as though it is someone else, and then I resume my frantic packing, shoving everything into my case, leaving only my toothbrush, my passport, and a change of clothes out on a chair for tomorrow.

Then the sound comes again – the clang of the bell. My insides freeze. Pulling on the cardigan I'd left out, I make my way back into the hall and see Maria and Emma standing at the door with the female police officer who was here before.

For a moment, my heart leaps – she's going to tell us it has all been a mix-up, and any second now, Callum is going to appear behind her – but even as I walk towards them, I know that isn't the case. Maria is nodding, Emma biting on her lip beside her, a strand of blonde hair falling over her face.

'What?' I say quickly, 'for Christ's sake, Maria, what is it now?'

'Your husband's things.' The policewoman surprises me by speaking in English, her heavy accent distorting the words. I feel a flicker of anger, wondering if their refusal to speak anything other than French this morning was designed to unnerve us all, intended to purposely confuse.

'They want us to leave everything as it is,' Maria says, 'they'll need to search the villa.'

'Can we take our own things?' I ask, stunned, and the policewoman shakes a head. 'Just yourselves,' she says gruffly, 'leave everything else. Including the car. We need to check it.'

She looks at me, and emboldened, I take a step forwards, pulling my cardigan over my breasts. She isn't better than me, this woman with her uniform and her orders.

'What will happen to my husband?' I say to her, ignoring the way Emma is anxiously watching me, and the nervous energy radiating off my sister.

'Your husband is being flown to England,' she says, her words short and sharp. 'He with English police.' She sniffs, as though the thought of the English constabulary is distasteful to her somehow. Maria, as if sensing my annoyance, steps forward and puts a hand on my arm, pulling me gently towards her.

'*Bien sur, nous laisserons tout comme* ça.' She turns to me. 'We will leave everything as it is.'

Chapter Ten

Rick Grant is sweating. Droplets of moisture dot his brow; they've had to give him a tissue because the sight of it is so uncomfortable. Alex Wildy watches as he dabs at the beads on his face, blows out his cheeks in a futile attempt to create a feeling of air in the stuffy interview room.

He's not as good-looking as his wife, but they make a believable pair – mid-thirties parents, perhaps slightly older than the average, pleased with themselves for having got on the property ladder, coupled up, produced a baby. A baby who is now nowhere to be found. There's something about Rick that Alex doesn't quite trust yet.

Sitting opposite him, Alex sips from his water, grateful for the cool relief in his throat, thinks longingly of the back garden at home, of his wife Joanne setting out the barbecue. Beside him, Bolton coughs, a sign that he's getting impatient, and Alex forces himself to ignore the summer heat, to focus on the task at hand.

'Rick Grant,' he says, 'let's get started, shall we?'

Ipswich Police Station, Interview Room 3
11.40 a.m.
Present: DS Wildy, DS Bolton, Rick Grant

DS Wildy: *Mr Grant, you are aware we have been speaking with your wife this morning, and that you are now being questioned on the record as part of our inquiries into the disappearance of your daughter, Eve Grant.*

RG: *Yes.*

DS Bolton: *Mr Grant, what can you tell us about your wife's relationship with Caroline Harvey, the woman found dead on August 10th?*

RG: *[clears throat] They met at university, up in Leeds. Must have been around 2005, first year.*

DS Bolton: *Where you were also a student at the time?*

RG: *Yes, the three of us were. Jenny and Caroline were on the same course, they both studied art. They became friends in the first year, and then flatmates in our second year.*

DS Bolton: *By which time you and Jenny were a couple?*

RG: *[pause] Yes. But I don't see how that is relevant. I want to find my little girl.*

DS Wildy: *We understand, Mr Grant. There are officers out looking for Eve as we speak, and police are currently going door to door, questioning anyone in the neighbourhood who might have seen what happened on August 10th. But the more information we can gather from you the better. All of it will help us in piecing together the events of that night.*

RG: *You think she's dead, don't you?*

DS Wildy: *No one is saying that. There is a good chance that your daughter is alive.*

RG: *Have you got any actual leads yet? Do you think Caroline's boyfriend has got my daughter? Christ, if I could get my hands on him…I can't stand that I'm just sitting here, when our little Eve could be chopped up somewhere. [puts head in hands].*

DS Wildy: *Mr Grant, we are currently pursuing several lines of inquiry and I can guarantee you, we will leave no stone unturned when it comes to finding Eve. There is no evidence as yet that she has come to any harm.*

RG: *You and I both know it's only a matter of time. I'm not stupid, Detective. [sighs, sniffs]. God, this is all too much. My mother's ill too, did you know that? My mother's about to die and my daughter's gone missing. I don't know how much more I can deal with.*

DS Wildy: *We're very sorry to hear about your mother, Mr Grant.*

RG: *Sorry. [pauses, collects himself, takes a deep breath and wipes sweat from his brow]. Is there anything else? I want to help. I'll tell you whatever you need to know.*

DS Bolton: *What was your own relationship to Caroline Harvey?*

RG: *[hesitates] Erm, we were friends, I guess. I mean, she was Jenny's friend, mainly, but we got on OK. We haven't seen her that much since we got married, since Eve was born. [pause] I don't think they were as close as they used to be. I didn't know much about her – tell you the truth, I always felt a bit sorry for her. Never seemed to have a man. Her life struck me as a bit—*

DS Wildy: *A bit what?*

RG: *Empty. Yeah, I always thought her life was empty. I don't think she and Jenny were really that good mates any more.*

DS Bolton: *And yet she was the person you chose to leave your daughter with?*

RG: *[pause] To be honest, I was a little surprised that Jenny wanted to. I've always thought Caroline was a bit—*

DS Bolton: *A bit?*

RG: *Unstable.*

Chapter Eleven

They haven't named Callum on the news. Not yet. I catch sight of screens in the airport as soon as we land, snippets of bulletins, but nothing that looks as though it mentions the murder of a woman in Suffolk, nothing that hints at my husband. A teenager has been knifed to death in Tottenham, the screen shows crime-scene tape flapping in the breeze. A political party has come under fire from one of their own, and a member of the royal family has been made a patron of a new charity. Her smile beams down on us. None of it is connected to whatever horror Callum is caught up in.

Emma is glued to her phone, finally back in full signal now that we're on English soil. I am wearing dark blue jeans and a sweat-stained top, without a bra. The material is beginning to chafe against my chest. I didn't sleep last night, lay awake in the room Callum and I had shared. I hadn't got out of my nightie all day, hadn't seen the point. The three of us had watched as the clock ticked on, ignored the sunshine, the delights of France well and truly over. We rose this morning at 5 a.m. to get to Caen for the first flight home. My eyes itch and sting with tiredness, and my stomach growls with hunger. I haven't eaten since a couple of cheese crackers last night that Maria forced on Emma and I. *You're setting a bad example for your daughter, Siobhan*, she'd hissed at me, semi-kindly, and I'd made myself nibble on the edge of the cheese, the cracker turning to sawdust in my mouth.

The airport in Southend is humming; after the quiet of the villa it feels surreal, as though someone has turned the volume up on a television set, inordinately loud, horribly bright. We are ushered into security, through a side gate, Emma, Maria and I. Our faces are bare; my daughter still has flecks of yellow sleepy dust in the corners of her eyes. Only Maria looks anything like her usual self; her dark hair is swept back neatly, her handbag, with only the essentials in, is over her arm. I have left the majority of my belongings at the villa, as requested. My arms feel empty and bare; I clutch my passport tightly, terrified of losing it.

All around us there are holiday-makers; I catch sight of a large group of women, probably in their early twenties, older than Emma, all wearing bright pink. One of them has a sash draped across her shoulders, silver glittery letters spelling out the words *Bride To Be*. As I watch, they laugh, almost en masse, their hair spilling over their shoulders, their tipsy faces swimming with excitement even though it's still early in the morning. I wonder where they're headed: Malaga, probably, or Ibiza. Up early to make the most of the trip.

The security guard tells Emma to relinquish her phone.

She drops it into the tray and I see the tweets lining up, flashing on and on and on. The first thing I did when we landed was to google it – 'Caroline Harvey Ipswich' – but her name mustn't have been released yet because no torrid news articles come up. We are scanned, because we are not normal, we are suspicious, suspicious by default. If Callum can be a murderer, any one of us could be guilty too. That is what they will think.

Given the all-clear, we are ushered out of a side door, and immediately the cooler air hits me. I shiver a little, cold without the heat of France, and tell Emma to put her cardigan on.

There are two police officers waiting, ready to take us home. Two men this time, and I almost weep with relief for the simple fact that I can understand what they are saying, in contrast to yesterday morning's horror, and the antagonism of the French police-woman. One of them, the older of the two, has a Birmingham accent and he half smiles at us as he opens the car door. The three of us squash into the back, Emma in the middle, her warm body closer to mine than it's been in days. I want to put my arm around her, pull her head onto my shoulder, cuddle her like I used to when she was little, but her body language is stiff, spiky.

'When can we see Dad?' Emma says abruptly, and I glance at Maria, unsure of what to say. I'm saved by the Brummie policeman.

'Your dad is in police custody today,' he says, almost cheerily, 'they've taken him to Ipswich station. Our job now is to take you ladies home. All being well, you'll be able to see him in the next few days.' He exchanges a glance with his colleague as we pull away from the airport, out onto the roundabout. The British road signs whizz past us as we drive, heading towards Suffolk. Beside me, I see Maria reach for Emma's hand, hold it gently in her own. My own hands remain clenched in my lap.

'What night do they think this happened?' I ask urgently, and the police officers exchange glances in the mirror.

'I'm afraid we can't discuss the case with you, Mrs Dillon,' one of them says, and I fall silent, defeated, my thoughts spinning round and around like a washing machine of anxiety.

At least they are letting us go home. Maria hasn't yet mentioned going back to her own flat, twenty minutes away in Woodbridge; an unspoken understanding between us that she will stay with me, for now at least, until we know what is going on.

'We should telephone Mum,' I say softly to her, in the back of the car, 'or at least warn the nursing home. In case she sees something on the news.'

Maria shakes her head. 'There won't be anything on the news, S, not at this stage. Not until he's charged.' She looks out of the car window; the motorway rushing past us, car after car, relentless and unstoppable. 'I'll call her later on anyway, see how she is.' I nod. We both know our mother doesn't know what day it is from one moment to the next, now, but if any news of this sort were to somehow permeate her consciousness, it would be terrible.

One of the policemen switches on the radio, fiddles with it until he finds the football. Arsenal vs Man United. The commentator's voice fills the car, and I force myself to take deep breaths, in and out, in and out as the motorway begins to give way to countryside, the flat, familiar planes of Suffolk starting to come into view. My phone lies on my lap, switched to silent. The messages pinged in as soon as we got back into signal; emails from the school about various fundraisers, a text from my friend Helen wanting to go for a drink next week, the usual nonsense in the mothers' WhatsApp group. Emails from work that for now I can ignore: they all think I'm on holiday for at least another five days, and my contributions are limited anyway. It's the mothers' group that get to me the most. We've lived in Suffolk too long – the women I met when Emma was little still cling to me, only now the big drama is sixth-form applications rather than the primary school catchment madness. I don't know how to talk to them about my marriage, about my daughter. None of them are going to understand this.

'I'll make up the spare room for you when we get back,' I say to Maria, just for something to say, and my voice surprises me; it is flat and dull. One of the policemen turns round and offers Emma a KitKat, and she reaches for it, starts unpeeling the silver foil and shoving little pieces of it into her mouth.

'It's good for shock,' the Brummie one says, and my own stomach grumbles with hunger. Someone on the radio scores a goal, and for a second the atmosphere in the car lightens as the policemen grin. Callum loves football; he always wanted a boy to take to the games. Years ago, when we were still trying for a second baby, we used to talk about it, a little boy, someone he could don in miniature football kit and bundle along to matches. A mini-Callum. But there again, I failed.

By the time we reach Ipswich, we are all silent. The police officers are surprisingly kind, and I watch numbly as they remove our small amount of bags from the back – Maria's coat and handbag, the bag containing all of our passports, and a rucksack containing the random things I had time to throw together this morning, the things I reasoned the police couldn't expect us to leave without: our toothbrushes, my hairbrush, a couple of paperback books to zone out my thoughts on the aeroplane home. I imagine the villa now, eerily untouched, abandoned in the early hours of the morning, Maria's empty car in the drive. A modern version of the *Mary Celeste*. Our arrival at the villa seems like decades ago now; the sense of relaxation I'd allowed myself to feel at the poolside seems ridiculous, something I didn't deserve in the first place. Over before it began. As the police said, there was no reason for us to stay in France. It was here where it happened. It's here where they need him.

*

As we pull up outside the house, I keep my eyes resolutely down, refusing to look up at the windows of our neighbours. Have they heard? Do they know? I don't feel ready to find out. The policemen leave us and I shiver, force myself to keep going, unlock the front door.

Inside our house, Maria boils the kettle, the sound loud in our quiet kitchen. Everything is exactly as we left it: cups on the draining board that I didn't get round to putting away before we left for France, a little pile of unopened mail sitting on the doormat. My eyes flick over the letters, as if there will be evidence of my husband's wrongdoing tucked amongst the NatWest paraphernalia. The air feels stuffy, as though we have been away for weeks rather than mere days, and Emma and I set about opening windows, letting the fresh air into the house. My skin itches; I am desperate for a shower, but I know we don't have long. In the next few days, the police will no doubt be here with a search warrant. The thought makes me sick to my stomach.

The three of us convene with mugs of tea. Emma is the first to speak.

'He didn't do it,' she says, her voice loud, pulsating with anger, as though being back on home turf has invigorated her. 'He didn't do it, Mum. He can't have done, can he?'

'Emma,' Maria says, giving her a warning look, 'we don't have all the information yet. We have to keep calm. Whatever happens, we need to stick together. As a family.'

I manage to find my voice, as though dredging it up from a well. 'Maria's right,' I say, 'we're all exhausted. Things will look clearer tomorrow.' I pause. It is so hard, so very hard, to know what to say, but for now I know that my priority must be my daughter. My precious girl.

'We all need to get some sleep,' I say, 'because the police are going to want to talk to us too. You know they are. And whatever Daddy did or didn't do, he loves you very, very much.' The words taste bitter on my tongue. Emma is sixteen, not six, but I don't know how else to play this.

Emma begins to cry for the first time since the doorbell rang in France; the tears trickle down her cheeks towards her mouth, dripping onto her chin. I take a step towards her and Maria does too, and then the three of us are holding each other, standing there in the kitchen, our arms tightly wrapped around one another, forming a wall against the rest of the world. I want to stay like this for the rest of the day, but Maria begins to bustle around, making something for us to eat, boiling the kettle for endless cups of tea, phoning Mum in the nursing home. I hear her talking to her, her voice low and sweet, and I know I should say hello too, but I'm so exhausted and really, what is the point when she can no longer even tell the two of us apart.

*

Of course, I don't sleep that night. I lie awake, staring up at the ceiling, alone in our huge double bed. It was nice to finally shower; I stood under the hot water for far too long, feeling it beat against the top of my head, wishing it could drown out the thoughts that are swirling round and around in my mind. I can't stop picturing Callum at Ipswich Police Station – is he in a cell? Is he being questioned? Maria says they should let him have a phone call but the phone hasn't rung yet. I wonder if the police will have told him that we're back. I wonder if I ought to be researching lawyers for him, making his case to a solicitor, but I don't have the energy. After all, I think, he has been lying to me for months. *Years.* Years and months and weeks and days and hours and minutes of lies. And I've let him.

I wonder if they will question me too.

Emma went up to her room very early on, claiming a headache and telling Maria and I that she wanted to be left alone. I thought about following her, but Maria told me to leave it. 'Let her be for a bit, S,' she said, 'it's been a very long day.'

I stretch my limbs out in the bed, feeling the ache between my shoulder blades. Callum usually takes up so much space, but now I spread my arms wide, feel the soft rub of the sheets beneath my skin. We have been married for fifteen years; I am so used to being part of a couple that the sensation of being alone is odd. My mind can't seem to reconcile the fact that he's not brushing his teeth, he's not crashed out in the spare room, he's not finishing work in the studio outside. He's in a police station, suspected of murder. The thought is so bizarre that for one awful, inappropriate moment I almost want to laugh.

I reach for my phone. There is a text from one of the ubermothers, something about a meeting next week, and a photo from Callum's cousin Rosa containing a picture of her newborn baby. I cannot bear to reply to her, to tell her what has happened. It won't be long before she finds out, after all.

Although I know I need to rest, I pull up the Safari app and search again for anything that might tell me what on earth is going on. The brightness of the phone making my eyes hurt, I google 'Ipswich murder August' and hold my breath as it loads. I'm not really expecting there to be anything but this time the pages pop up, one after another, and my hands begin to tremble as my eyes scroll down the page. The headline jumps out at me, the words clear and nightmarish in black and white.

WOMAN FOUND DEAD IN IPSWICH
FLAT: BABY MISSING

My heart flips over in my chest and I sit up straight, abandoning all thoughts of sleep. My hand scrabbles for the bedside lamp and I flick it on, the golden glow illuminating the bedroom. *Baby missing?*

The first link I click on is the *East Anglian Daily Times*, our local paper covering Norfolk, Suffolk and Essex. They love Callum, the TV exec – every so often they drum up some sort of feature on him, when there's not much else going on – some piece about his latest project, a glossy photo of him smiling into the camera. They once did a piece on all of us, took photos inside our home, one of me and Callum together, grinning into the camera. They made me look like a housewife, only just stopped short of popping a pinny on me. Didn't mention my own career at all.

I wonder how quickly the tide against my husband might turn.

The article is short, but I read every word twice, checking I haven't missed anything, any tiny important detail that would release me from the hell of my thoughts.

WOMAN FOUND DEAD IN IPSWICH
FLAT: BABY MISSING

Police are searching for missing baby Eve Grant, who has not been seen since around 6 p.m. on 10th August. Eve was last seen in the care of a woman in her thirties, who was found dead in her Ipswich home on Saturday night. The woman has not yet been named but a source close to the investigation said she was a friend of one-year-old Eve's mother. Eve is believed to have blonde hair, and was wearing a pink Baby-gro on the night she went missing. Members of the public who may have information pertaining to this case are asked to call 0845 54 54 54 to speak anonymously to the police.

August 10th – the night before we flew to France. I think quickly, my mind spooling back, coming up with my lines. *I was at my book club all evening, I left Emma and Callum at home.* Yes, I remember now. I am breathing heavily, too fast, and I stare at the words, feeling sick. This can't be right. This can't be what they want Callum about, surely. Not a child. Immediately, an image of Emma comes into my mind – Emma at one year old, a tiny, happy little baby, playing on Callum's stomach as he lay back on the bed. Emma adored him, she always has. *But will she still*, I think, *now that this has happened?*

I click through to various other sites, my heart thudding

– there is a picture of Eve on the BBC website now, last updated ten minutes ago; she has chocolate brown eyes and bright blonde hair. I suck in my breath sharply – she's a beautiful child, angelic. *Grant*. I run it through my mind, trying to think straight. Someone from school, someone from his work? But none of it rings a bell. The surname means nothing to me.

I go through page after page but the news story is the same on them all – there are no further details about what happened, and Callum isn't mentioned anywhere. Frowning, I'm about to reach for the light switch when I think of Twitter. Emma's always saying that everything breaks on Twitter first – perhaps she's right. I never use it, the pharmaceutical company has its own account, with a twenty-something in charge to respond to our clients or disgruntled customers. But how hard can it be?

I navigate to the site and type in '#Ipswich' – and there it is. The internet is loving it. They always do when a child is involved.

@BBCBreaking: Woman found dead in #Ipswich flat; baby missing. The victim has been named as Caroline Harvey, and it is believed that the baby was not her biological child. More news as we have it.

@Sarah124: So was she looking after someone else's baby? God, imagine. I'd never leave my child with someone else. Just shows you what happens! #Ipswich #CarolineHarvey #Suffolk

@Mumma49: @Sarah124 Well sometimes you have to, don't you? Not all of us can afford not to work! #princess

@EastAnglianDailyNews: The woman, believed to be in her mid-thirties, was found dead at the scene. Suffolk Police are asking for anyone who saw anything between the hours of 6 and 9 p.m. on 10th August to please call 0845 54 54 54.

@Mick101: How do you think she died? People do sick stuff these days. Too much influence from TV and video games. #disgrace

@RandoTweets: Whoever killed her took the baby with them, it's obvious. Question is, who? #RIPCaroline

On and on they go, Caroline's name darting out at me like an arrow. My heart is bumping so fast in my chest that I can barely breathe. Caroline is dead, murdered, gone. But how an earth does the baby fit in? And who does little Eve Grant belong to?

Chapter Twelve

Ipswich
14th August
DS Alex Wildy

So they've finally got him in. The boyfriend, Callum Dillon
– hauled unceremoniously back from the French coast to talk
to the Suffolk Constabulary. Bit of a change of climate, that's
for sure. It's raining today, thick heavy drops that spatter
the windows of the station, providing small relief from the
heatwave. Callum isn't being particularly helpful – God knows
why the French police decided to bring him in in such a state.
He hasn't showered; it looks like they grabbed him on the
spot, and he's angry about it, too, after spending a night in the
station following an afternoon of questioning at the hands of
the French yesterday, which wasn't part of the plan. A young
French police officer called Adele has emailed them over the
transcripts, pages of *no comment*, Callum's anger at being held
there bouncing off the page. She'd telephoned too, to make
sure they'd received everything. Adele is a junior, Alex can
tell by her tone, subservient yet eager in her halting English.
It reminds him of how he used to be when he first joined up,
desperate to rise through the ranks. Only now that he's here,
he's not so sure he likes it. Alex has brought Callum three cups

of coffee already this afternoon, but none of them have made him any less pissed off.

The image of the woman's body is still paramount in Alex's mind, and that's what is fuelling him today, even though he knows he needs to focus on the missing child. He's been a police officer for six years now, long enough to have seen his fair share of bodies, but not long enough that he's become completely numb to them. And a young woman too, a young woman with so much to live for. A woman like his own wife, Joanne.

Alex didn't like the way Rick Grant had called Caroline's life 'empty' – from what it sounds like, he didn't know the half of it. And neither did Jenny. He keeps wondering about them, the parents, finds himself thinking about the sweat on Rick's brow and the diamond on Jenny's finger. They have called Norfolk and Norwich Hospital, wanting to check out the alibi that they were visiting Rick's mother on the night of the murder, but as yet nobody has been able to confirm it. A harassed receptionist had told them they'd look into it straight away, find the CCTV of the entrance and the ward. 'As soon as you can,' Alex had said, 'this is a murder investigation, after all.' He needs Rick and Jenny either out of the picture or in it. He wonders what Caroline saw in them, what the friendship was really like. The thought of Caroline makes him shudder inside – it's the way she was laid out, that's the bit that is sticking in his head, her body positioned so strangely over the child's cot; that is the part that he cannot forget.

At first glance, you might have thought Caroline was bending over to tend to a baby, her dark hair hanging over her face and her arms reaching down into the cot. Well, not reaching, dangling, but they didn't know that at the time.

It was only when they lifted her up and saw the blood all over her chest, the gaping knife wound and the vacancy in her eyes, that they realised the cot underneath her was completely empty, spotted with blood. The covers were there, but the material was cold; cold and slightly damp, too, even the parts that weren't drenched in blood. She must have been trying to protect the child, even in her very last moments.

'Wildy?'

DS David Bolton is knocking on his office door, a sheaf of papers in his hand.

'Ready to go again?' he says. 'I might sit this one out. Watch him from the monitors.' He pauses. 'Don't be too nice, Alex.'

Alex stands, pushes the thought of Caroline's body and the blood-soaked baby covers out of his mind, and makes his way to the interview room where they have left Callum Dillon waiting for a quarter of an hour. The DCI likes doing that, says it's a good technique – let them sweat (quite literally, in this heat) and make them anxious enough to want to talk to you.

But Callum Dillon doesn't look like the anxious type.

Interview Room 2
4 p.m.
Present: DS Wildy, Callum Dillon

DS Wildy: *Mr Dillon, please state your name for the tape.*
CD: *Callum Dillon.*
DS Wildy: *Mr Dillon, we appreciate you cooperating with our request to return to the UK and to give up your time to answer some questions.*

CD: *It's not like I was given much choice, is it? The French police arrested me.*

DS Wildy: *As I say, we appreciate it. Apologies, I gather you had rather an abrupt end to your holiday.*

CD: *Can someone just tell me what the hell is going on? Or is that too much to ask? I haven't even been home, I've been brought straight here, I haven't showered and I'm exhausted. I spent hours being questioned in France by people I could barely make sense of, and now I'm here and you're acting as if I've just wandered in of my own free will rather than being dragged here in handcuffs! It's a joke. I've just had someone close to me die in the worst way possible and you're treating me like a criminal.*

DS Wildy: *The sooner we get our questions out of the way, the sooner you can be done with all of this and go home to your family, safe in the knowledge that we won't bother you again. How does that sound?*

CD: *Obviously I want this over with. I don't even know why I'm here; it's some sort of ludicrous misunderstanding. I don't mind telling you that I'll be putting in a complaint to the IPCC.*

DS Wildy: *Let's hope I can help clarify things for you a little. Mr Dillon, when did you begin your relationship with Caroline Harvey?*

CD: *[sighs] I – OK. Fine. I'm not here to lie to you, I'm not making a secret of it. I'm devastated by Caroline's death, of course I am. We began seeing each other about eighteen months ago.*

DS Wildy: *Devastated, hmm. So would you say yours was a happy relationship, Mr Dillon? It's fair to say it wasn't* a conventional relationship, isn't it, given that you are in fact still married. Is that correct?

CD: Yes, I'm still married. You know I am. My wife is – [breaks off]. When can I speak to my family?

DS Wildy: Your family returned to Southend Airport yesterday morning, Mr Dillon, and were escorted home by two Suffolk Constabulary officers. They are all perfectly fine, so there is no need to worry. You'll be able to speak with them once we've finished chatting, if that's OK with you. At the moment, we'd rather there was no communication between you which might contaminate the investigation, but you are by law entitled to one phone call. Would you like to make that now?

CD: [silence]

DS Wildy: Mr Dillon?

CD: No, no, just get on with it, will you?

DS Wildy: Certainly. So, Mr Dillon, would you say your relationship with Caroline was a happy one?

CD: Look, we'd broken it off. She'd broken it off, a while ago – she wanted to put a stop to it all and I thought she was probably right, so we called it a day. [sigh] I'm not proud of it all, Detective, but I promise you, I know nothing about her – about her death. The first I heard of it was the police at the door of my sister-in-law's villa. I don't know who would want to do that to Caro. She's – she was a lovely girl.

DS Wildy: So you yourself had no reason to be angry with Caroline, to wish her ill? You weren't a bit annoyed that she'd, as you say, 'broken it off'?

CD: No! Like I say, it was the right thing to do. It had been coming for a while. I was – we were – it was difficult, you know, I've been married for a long time. I made a mistake, you know how it is, how these things can be. I'm not saying I didn't care for Caroline, because I did – obviously, the officers saw how upset I was at the news – but it wasn't supposed to be a long-term thing. I was – I suppose I was relieved when she wanted to call time on it. I wasn't angry.

DS Wildy: When was the last time you saw Ms Harvey?

CD: [pause] I don't know – a while back. Probably a fortnight ago. We'd agreed to leave things, and then there'd been a few text messages. Nothing much. She'd calmed down with the incessant phone calls.

DS Wildy: Incessant phone calls?

CD: Oh, they were nothing really. Just wanting to talk, but she'd call at odd times, you know. [rubs his head] I did my best. Like I say, I cared about her.

DS Wildy: Did the phone calls anger you, Mr Dillon?

CD: No, they didn't. As I said, they'd slowed down anyway.

DS Wildy: What is your relationship to Rick and Jenny Grant, and their daughter, Eve Grant?

CD: I don't know them at all! I've never met them. Caroline mentioned Jenny, very occasionally, but look, you know how it is – we weren't really that involved in each other's lives.

DS Wildy: Because you were having an affair.

CD: Well, yes. Christ, what is this? Having an affair doesn't make me a murderer!

DS Wildy: Did your wife Siobhan know about your affair, Mr Dillon?

CD: [pause] No. No, I don't think so.

DS Wildy: Do you know where Eve Grant is, Mr Dillon?

CD: *Of course not! [pause] I've never seen that baby before in my life. Christ, the poor parents. If anything happened to my Emma I'd be destroyed.*

DS Wildy: *Can you tell me where you were on the evening of August 10th, four days ago, Mr Dillon? What were your movements that day?*

CD: *Jesus, you can't really think I did this to Caroline. Can you? God, OK, OK, August 10th. I was home for most of the day. I had quite a bit to do for work, I work in TV—*

DS Wildy: *Yes, we're aware of that, Mr Dillon.*

CD: *OK, then you know that something like this is completely ridiculous. I'm well known around here, I have a family. I'm not some murdering junkie who took a kid from its parents for the fun of it and bumped off the babysitter whilst I was at it. And I don't like being treated as though I am. [pause] Sorry. I'm just – I'm very stressed.*

DS Wildy: *We understand, Mr Dillon. So you were working at home on August 10th? All day?*

CD: *[runs a hand through his hair] Pretty much, yes. I was at home, we live over near the park, Christchurch Park, although no doubt you know that anyway. I was working in my studio at the bottom of the garden, I work there a lot. The company has a big project on, we're bidding for a new script. It's easier to concentrate out of the office sometimes. [pause] My daughter was home too, we had lunch together at the house.*

DS Wildy: *And then?*

CD: *Then, I – God I don't know, I just stayed at home. Working in the studio. Siobhan – my wife – went to her book group in the evening, and Emma and I stayed in. She was upstairs,* and I was head down trying to get things finished before France. I wanted to be able to relax with my family. I might have popped out for half an hour at some point to the corner shop; I went to get something for dinner, we didn't have much in the house.

DS Wildy: *The studio you mention, you can see it from the house, can't you?*

CD: *Yes, mostly. It's at the bottom of the garden, gives me a bit of peace and quiet. But yes, you can see it from the upstairs windows.*

DS Wildy: *But nobody can confirm you were actually in it that night?*

CD: *Well, my daughter knew I was, I'd seen her earlier that evening. She'd have seen the lights on in the studio, I think.*

DS Wildy: *But she wasn't actually with you?*

CD: *No.*

DS Wildy: *So you didn't go anywhere near Caroline's flat, then? You didn't go to say goodbye to her before your holiday?*

CD: *No, how many times, we'd stopped seeing each other! It was over.*

[DS Bolton enters the room]

DS Bolton: *Afternoon, Mr Dillon. Now look, I'm sure you're as tired of these questions as we are, but until we get a straight answer from you, they're not going to stop. I will be straight with you if DS Wildy here won't – we currently have you pretty high on our list for the murder of your girlfriend. You've got motive, you've no doubt got means, and we want to know whether you had opportunity. Jenny Grant certainly seems to think so.*

CD: *Jesus, I've told you a million times, Detective. I did not kill Caroline Harvey. I did not abduct Eve Grant. I've never met Jenny Grant. I was nowhere near the property that night.*

DS Wildy: *So where were you at 6 p.m. exactly, then?*

CD: *[sighs] God, it's like Groundhog Day. I've told you. I was at home in my studio. And I went to the shop.*

DS Bolton: *Can anybody verify that?*

CD: *I – no, not directly. My wife had gone out to her book group, like I said, and at 6 p.m. my daughter Emma was upstairs. She was listening to music, but she knew I was around because she'd seen me earlier at lunchtime. It's the school holidays, we'd got into a routine of having lunch together on days when I wasn't in the office.*

DS Bolton: *So to recap: you saw your daughter at lunchtime, around, what, 1 p.m.? Following that, she went up to her bedroom and you went outside to your studio. Is that a usual occurrence in your household, Mr Dillon? For two people to be in entirely separate rooms without speaking all night? What about the dinner you'd gone to get from the shop?*

CD: *[pause] Sometimes. And I ate the dinner, downstairs by myself. I did call out to Em but she said she wasn't hungry. And then I went back out to my studio, in the garden as I had to finish some work before going on holiday. My daughter would probably have heard me coming in and out of the house. Then I went to bed. It was late by the time I came in from the studio, so rather than wake Siobhan, I decided to sleep in the spare room.*

DS Wildy: *Had you and your daughter had any kind of argument, Mr Dillon?*

CD: *No. We – my daughter's a teenager. She's been a bit moody, lately. Stays in her room a lot. My wife and I have been trying not to push her buttons. It's why we booked the holiday in France, we wanted to try to give her a break, have a nice time, change of scenery, you know. My sister-in-law offered us the villa in Saint Juillet. She was very keen that we visited.*

DS Bolton: *Ah yes, the holiday. It's interesting to me that you left for France the day after Ms Harvey was killed.*

CD: *We'd been planning a holiday for a long time. It was all booked in.*

DS Bolton: *I see.*

CD: *Look, I don't understand why you're keeping me here. What actual evidence have you got? Just because two people are shagging doesn't mean one of them has to be a killer! Jesus, I've had enough of this. I want a lawyer. I'm not answering anything else until I have one.*

Chapter Thirteen

Ipswich
15th August
Siobhan

There's someone in the hallway. The sound wakes me from an already-troubled sleep, and my eyes flit to the digital clock: 3 a.m.. I can hear footsteps coming down the corridor, towards our bedroom, and my heart gives a little flutter. My phone is still on my chest; I must have fallen asleep still scrolling through Twitter, looking desperately for news of what happened on the tenth.

'Mum?'

Emma pushes open the door to my room, still wearing her night clothes. For a second, her figure is silhouetted in the doorway, ghostly and white.

'Jesus, Em. You scared me.'

'Sorry.' She comes and sits down on the edge of the bed, her body weight indenting the mattress. I push myself up against the pillows, fumble for the bedside light. It is strange not having Callum beside me, the heat of his body. Groggily, I put my phone on the bedside table, face down, even though she's surely been doing the same as me, scrolling through news websites, no doubt with more agility.

'Are you OK?' I ask, then internally admonish myself for what is a fairly stupid question. Her father's just been taken away on suspicion of murder; she's not really OK and neither am I.

'What d'you think's going to happen to Dad?' she says, and there's something in the tone of her voice that makes her sound so much younger than her years, and I feel a huge wave of love towards her; despite how far apart we have drifted of late, she is suddenly a little girl again, wanting reassurance, wanting Mummy to make it better. It's been a long time since she's looked to me for guidance.

'I don't know, darling,' I say truthfully, and I see her face start to crumple, to turn in on itself. Anxiety radiates off her.

'Do you think they've got the wrong person?' she asks me, and I take a deep breath, trying to think how best to respond.

Do I think they've got the wrong person?

'I don't know,' I say eventually, 'I don't know any more than you do, my love.'

'Why would Daddy know that woman?' she asks me, and I meet her eyes, those blue-violet eyes that startled me when she was born, and pleased Callum because they were so like his. Strangers used to stop me in the street about Emma's eyes, peer into the pram and come up beaming.

'Your baby has the most gorgeous peepers!' they'd say, 'aren't they unusual! Gosh, how gorgeous. She'll be a stunner one day.' I used to wheel her around the Ipswich docks, around Christchurch Park, showing her the trees as they changed from winter to spring to autumn and back again.

She looks back at me now, unblinking. For a second I find myself wishing that she were younger, that I could smooth this all over with milk and a biscuit, and keep her in the dark about what her daddy did or didn't do. But she is sixteen; she's not a child.

'The police think he was having an affair with her, don't they?' she whispers, and mutely, I nod. She will find out anyway, there's no doubt about it. I can't keep Callum's secrets from her any more.

'Do you think that's true? Did you know? Did Maria? Has he done it before?'

'Emma,' I say, 'it's very late. We both need to sleep. Things are going to be difficult over the next few days, you know they are. Us both being exhausted won't help.'

'Are you really not going to tell me?' Her voice hardens, just a little.

'Emma,' I say, 'of course I didn't know.'

She stares back at me for a few seconds, the lie hanging between us like a spider's web, gossamer thin. One poke and it would break. Eventually, she gives in, lowers her lashes and gets up to leave the room, moving silently back down the corridor to her own bed. I lie back on the pillows, my heart beating fast at the small act of deceit.

I can't keep Callum's secrets, but I can keep my own. It's him who taught me how to.

*

My sister is up first in the morning, bustling around the house as if it is her own. We live in a three-bedroom Victorian house on the outskirts of Ipswich, Suffolk's county town, splayed across the River Orwell. Our house is one of a row of detached houses behind Christchurch Park; we bought it fifteen years ago, right when we were first married, before these properties became more than we could've hoped to afford. Maria has been sleeping in the spare room – the room that was always intended for the second child, the child that never was. The imaginary boy at the football games. It wasn't as though we didn't try.

When I poke my head around the door, I see that she's opened the window, letting the fresh air in, and her clothes are draped over the chair. On the bedside table are the earrings she was wearing in France; it feels as if she has claimed the room already, the way she used to when we were kids.

'Breakfast,' she says, pouring me a glass of orange juice as I shuffle down into the kitchen in my dressing gown. There is something comforting about being back here, away from the stifling heat of France, away from those police with their incomprehensible questions. I pull my gown more tightly around me. I'm going to tell her; I've been thinking about it all night. I've got to tell someone that I knew.

'Where's Emma?'

'Not up yet.'

'Maria,' I say, before I can lose my nerve, 'I knew about Caroline. I knew about the affair.' The words rush out at me, and there is a certain relief in saying them, at telling someone what I have kept inside me for months.

My sister freezes for a second, her hand still clutching the carton of juice.

'How long has it been going on for?' she asks me, and I shrug helplessly.

'I found out four months ago.'

There is a beat and I see her assessing me. Then, 'Has he done it before?'

I pause, then nod. 'Yes, but this one – Caroline – felt – I don't know, different. Worse.'

'Worse how?'

'Because I thought – I thought he'd stopped.'

Slowly she shakes her head, and I can see the anger on her face, the anger which I know is on my behalf, though she quickly tries to mask it. 'You're better than this, S,' she says, 'you don't deserve the way he's treated you.'

'I don't know what to tell Emma,' I say desperately, 'I don't know how much she already knows, what she suspects. And—' I hesitate, scared to put into words the next confession, the deeper one, the one that I keep shoving to the back of my mind. 'And I'm scared that if I tell her I knew, she might – and the police might – think I had something to do with it.'

I am keeping my voice low for fear of my daughter hearing, my words strained and urgent across the kitchen table.

Another beat. 'And did you?' she says eventually, her eyes never leaving my face.

'Did I what?'

'Have something to do with it.'

'Maria!' I'm shocked at the coolness of her tone. 'Of course not. Of course I didn't!'

'Well, then.' She pours orange juice out into a glass, a steady smooth flow of it. My heart is beating a little bit faster, but I take a deep breath and force myself to keep calm.

'Tell Emma nothing,' Maria says firmly, 'and let's keep it that way.' I watch as she splashes milk into a cup of coffee and pushes it across the table towards me.

'Did you sleep?' she asks me, and I shrug, shake my head. She nods, and gets out a carton of cereal from the cupboard. The conversation appears to be over; it's as if I haven't told her anything at all, as if she hasn't just asked me whether I might have killed my husband's lover.

'Not much. I was looking on Twitter, searching for news.'

She almost laughs. 'Twitter? You?'

I roll my eyes at her. 'I'm not a total dinosaur, Maria.' Pulling out my phone, I google again to check if anything else has been said overnight, my stomach sinking as the words load. Maria comes to stand behind me, looks over my shoulder. I can feel her breathing, the soft push of air against the back of my neck.

POLICE QUESTION MAN
OVER IPSWICH DEATH

Suffolk Police are holding a man in his mid-forties in connection with the death of a woman in the dockside area of Ipswich. The woman, named as Caroline Harvey, believed to be in her thirties, was found dead by a friend on the evening of 10th August. A child in her care is also believed to be missing, and police are conducting a widespread search for one-year-old Eve Grant, who was last seen wearing a pink Baby-gro. Eve has blonde hair and brown eyes. Anyone who has any information regarding the case is urged to call 0845 54 54 54. All calls will be treated anonymously.

Feeling sick, I move over to Twitter. Maria puts a hand on my shoulder, squeezes me twice. I can see the glint of her nails out of the corner of my eye: perfectly polished. My own are bitten and ragged now, the skin around the nails is pink and angry as a result of my worrying at them.

@SimpsonLily How can a baby just vanish like that? It wouldn't even have been dark yet. Someone must have seen something.

@JessR7 Do we think the woman was trying to protect the baby, and that's why she was killed? The baby was the target?

@TomPugh I bet the man they've arrested is the baby's father. Mark my words. It's always someone close to the case. Her parents probably staged the whole thing. Wouldn't be the first time, would it? Remember that kid last year. Some people don't deserve to be parents.

'Christ,' Maria says, 'it's everywhere. That poor baby. Can you imagine?' I think of Emma perched on the edge of my bed last night, looking as pale and wan as I feel. My baby, all grown up. If everything unravels now, I have spent the last sixteen years in vain. The idea of this baby Eve being out there on her own, alone, or hurt, makes my stomach churn.

'Do you think they're right?' I say to Maria. 'Do you think the baby's parents might be involved?' The thought is, to me, bizarre – I can no more think of harming Emma than I can think of harming myself.

Maria shrugs. 'God knows. You do see it, don't you? People holding their own kids to ransom. Or custody disputes gone wrong. Maybe that Grant couple weren't as happy as they seemed.'

I go silent, trying to imagine it, my mind racing with the possibilities. I wonder what the police are thinking, whether they're on the right track, or even close. I think about that night, trying to remember it as clearly as I can. I came home from book group a little tipsy, I admit. I wasn't *drunk*, I was OK to drive, but still the memories are a bit hazy. I stopped at the shop for a bottle of white wine and some milk – I knew we were about to run out from that in-built instinct that anyone trying to keep a household afloat has. I remember pouring myself another glass of wine when I got home, checking in on Emma and finding her asleep. Digging out my passport from the drawer, ready for the flight the next day. Going upstairs, doing my teeth and getting into bed, alone. I looked out at Callum's studio, I know I did. Was the light on? Or was it off? Was my husband out that night? Did he come into our room? If the police ask me, I don't know what to say.

The first car pulls up outside the house just as I'm trying to force down some muesli. It tastes strange in my mouth, dry and ashy, and I manage only a few spoonfuls. Emma seems to be skipping breakfast. Maria finishes her own muesli then puts on some toast, and I wonder how she can manage it, but then she always has been able to cope in tough situations. It's her who dealt with Mum when she needed to go into the nursing home, it's her who helped me once when I got into trouble at school, lying to the teachers on my behalf. And after all, it's my husband who's suspected of murder, not hers. My clever sister, free from the clutches of cheating men. Jealousy scratches at my throat.

'It's the press,' my sister says now, going over to the large bay window that looks out onto the road. 'There's a couple of them. Get Emma to come down, now. We need to make a plan.'

But it's too late – there is a knocking at the door and the sound of rattling at the letterbox.

'How do they know?' I say helplessly, and Maria gestures at my phone on the table.

'Same way we do, I guess. It's only ever a matter of time until these things come out.'

My phone pings with an email from work – one of my associates, asking me to call her. *As soon as you can manage.* Shit. Does that mean they all know too? Have they somehow got wind of the fact that my husband is the man in the article?

'Mrs Dillon!' The reporter's voice is loud and clear, slightly nasal as it echoes through our hallway. No one has moved the pile of post just inside the front door that built up whilst we were in France, and there's a vase of dead flowers on the table to the right. I should have thrown them out before we left, but we were in a hurry to get to the airport. The water will be smelly and stale.

'Ignore them,' Maria says. 'God, they need to send someone to help us, advise us or something. I'm going to call the station in Ipswich. This is ridiculous – they can't just leave us in the dark like this, not with Callum in custody and none of us knowing what the hell is going on.'

'How do they know my name?' I say to her, panic beginning to flutter inside me, and I could have imagined it but I think my sister rolls her eyes.

'S, they're reporters. It's their job to know your name.' She pauses. 'One of them probably saw Callum going into the station and recognised him.'

'What's going on?' Emma appears in the kitchen, her hair pulled back off her face, her phone clutched in her hand. 'People on Twitter are saying they've arrested the baby's father, it's all over everything.' She looks at Maria, a panicked expression on her face.

I shake my head. 'There's an article saying a man in his forties,' I tell her, 'but the press seem to know it's Callum. They're outside.' As if on cue, there's another shout through the door and Emma jumps, fear flitting across her features.

'Go get dressed,' Maria says, and I think she means Emma but then I see she's directing her words at me, that my daughter is already wearing jeans and a T-shirt with the *Friends* logo on it. Not knowing what else to do, I do as she says, pulling a long-sleeved cardigan from the wardrobe, my fingers brushing against Callum's shirts, ironed and ready for his return to work after our holiday. He always dresses smartly for the office, as if he's some sort of New York media mogul. I think momentarily of the villa, of the crisp blue of the pool, the sound of the crickets rubbing their legs together. It feels a million miles away, another lifetime. I think of Callum sitting beside me out on the terrace, his arm around my back and his phone buzzing with a message.

I need to know what happened that night.

Chapter Fourteen

Ipswich
15th August
DS Wildy

Alex Wildy is biting into a much-needed bacon sandwich when his mobile rings, the vibration alerting him through his jacket pocket. He's barely eaten in the past twenty-four hours but nonetheless he drops the food quickly, presses the phone to his ear. A Northern accent, female, starts talking before he can even say hello.

'DS Wildy? This is Jackie, calling from the Norfolk and Norwich hospital. Just calling to say we've got that CCTV tape you requested, sorry for the delay. One of our security lads showed it to me this morning and Mrs Grant *is* on there, fair and square, visiting her husband's mother Margaret. August 10th, wasn't it? Tape shows all three of them in the ward. Rick Grant was there most of the day and then Jenny came in that evening, stayed a few hours. I'm sorry we couldn't confirm it before, we've been up to our necks, had a patient pass on this morning and it's all been a bit…' The voice trails off, then picks up again and Alex can almost imagine the woman on the end of the phone giving herself a mental shake. 'I've asked the lad to drive it over to you lot, is that all right by you?'

Alex is nodding. 'Yes, that'd be great. Jackie, did you say? Thanks very much. We really appreciate your help.' He hesitates. The nurses were so good to Joanne over the latest miscarriage. The NHS always brings a lump to his throat. 'Take care Jackie,' he says, 'I'm sorry to hear about your patient.'

He hangs up, replaces the phone in his pocket, his appetite forgotten. So the parents are in the clear. Heartbroken, frantic, but probably not responsible. He sighs, frustration bubbling through him. The search team looking for Eve Grant have been up all night, and still there is no sign of a body. A call in the early hours of the morning about blood spots found in an alleyway near the harbour had momentarily created a flurry of activity, but they had quickly turned out to be coming from the cut hand of a drunk man who'd wandered the wrong way home from Isaac's Bar on the waterfront, clutching a broken bottle and a half-eaten kebab.

So far, the door to doors have turned up nothing – the PCs have been up and down Woodmill Road, knocking on doors, and the hotline published by the paper has had dozens of calls, none of which contain any viable information. Eve has been missing now for four days and already, Alex has begun to dream about her – that little blonde-haired face staring up at him from all manner of horrific places: the depths of a river, a disused building site, the boot of someone's car. He feels sick at the thought of it, not that he'd ever let on to the team.

Alex can feel the tension settled in firmly across his shoulder blades; Joanne is forever on at him to visit a chiropractor but quite honestly, he doesn't know when he would find the time. His priority now has to be finding Eve – and getting to the bottom of who put a knife into Caroline Harvey's chest. The weapon, too, is missing. The wound in her chest would suggest a kitchen knife, non-serrated, but it is nowhere to be found. The PCs are searching the parks, the nearby drains, the lift shaft in Caroline Harvey's block of flats.

Callum Dillon is flatly denying all involvement, and without any evidence, they can't yet charge him with anything. But despite his claim that he was working in his studio all night, he has no concrete alibi, which doesn't work in his favour. At least if Callum had been the one to kill Caroline, it would make a bit of sense. But why take the baby? It isn't as if a one-year-old would ever be an incriminating witness. Alex thinks about the wife, Siobhan. Callum claims she was out at her book club on the evening of the 10th, but Alex still wants to check this out. He thinks it over – clearly, she'd be upset to learn of her husband's affair, the betrayal of it. But would it lead to murder? Statistically, it feels unlikely that she'd have hurt baby Eve, but they cannot rule it out. Then there is the daughter, Emma, in the family home that night with only her father to verify her whereabouts. Just sixteen but by all accounts, a troubled girl. Could she be covering for one of her parents?

The only other option is a random attack – a kidnapping with Caroline as an unfortunate bystander who got in the way. But there has been no contact, no sign of a ransom. Jenny and Rick's phones have been wired, in case whoever has Eve gets in touch, but as the clock ticks on, the possibility of it becomes more and more unlikely. DS Bolton has pulled up a list of sex offenders in the area, but so far all are still in prison, or dead. *Best place for them,* Dave had said unpleasantly. And then there is Caroline's phone, missing from the scene and untraceable via the masts. Why take the phone unless it was something personal?

Alex flips again through the photographs of the scene, wincing at the splatters of blood, the angle of her body. The images are vivid and unrelenting. The fifth-floor flat, now sealed behind crime-scene tape and crawling with SOCOs, is very small. He imagines Jenny Grant pushing open the door to that awful sight, the panic she must have felt as she raced through the tiny rooms. Compared to what they've seen of Callum Dillon's house, Caroline Harvey lived in a shoebox.

He turns to the photograph of the deceased. Shoulder-length brown hair, hazel eyes. Attractive-looking woman. Thirty-three. Lived alone; no siblings, one elderly father living alone in Stowmarket. They sent a family liaison officer over to the father – a Christopher Harvey, in his eighties now. His wife, Elsie Harvey, died in a car accident along the A12 years ago – one of the PCs pulled up the old report. Jesus, what a life. Alex feels a shudder run down his back. By all accounts, Caroline Harvey was pretty lonely – no children, no husband, no mother, no wife. They have considered the idea that it was some sort of break-in, or a planned abduction with Eve the target and Caroline as collateral damage. Now, Alex is wondering if it was the other way around. Nobody seems too heartbroken at the loss of Caroline Harvey, despite Callum's claims of devastation.

Pissed off would be the overriding emotional state to describe him now – he's a big-shot exec, used to getting his way, and being questioned about a messy murder case, not to mention a baby that seems to have vanished into thin air, isn't exactly good for his profile. Alex doesn't like him – doesn't like the way he left the country the morning after Caroline's death, doesn't like the way he kept their affair a secret from his own wife for eighteen months, doesn't like the angry way he's reacted to being questioned. Someone like Callum could've had very good reason for wanting Caroline dead – perhaps she'd threatened to go to his wife, or worse, go to the press. Ultimatums are thrown around in love affairs more often than you'd think.

Alex thinks Callum Dillon might crack soon enough. In his experience, cases like this are often fairly cut and dried, more so than you'd imagine. He's having an affair with her; she starts to want more than he can give. She gets obsessive, maybe – what was the word Rick Grant used to describe her – maybe a bit *unstable*. She puts pressure on Callum to leave his wife and daughter, break up his marriage. Maybe she starts threatening to tell Siobhan Dillon the whole thing. And Callum doesn't want that to happen. So on the night of August the tenth, he walks over to her flat – it is only a twenty-minute walk, they have paced it out – and he tries to talk to her. She's resistant. And then he loses his temper. He picks up a knife. A knife they still haven't found.

Alex groans under his breath and runs a hand through his hair. It's all fine, he thinks, it's all fine, but what about the sodding baby? Where does little Eve Grant fit into the equation? And more to the point, *where is she?* They have to find her. Time is running out.

*

'The press are onto Callum Dillon's family. Someone must have leaked it.'

Alex is momentarily taken aback at Dave Bolton's words. 'What, they've named him?' Callum is still in custody; they have applied for an extension. Soon enough, his lawyer will arrive – no doubt some expensive-looking twat in a suit that the TV exec is paying through the nose for.

David shakes his head. 'No, course not. They're not that stupid, not yet. But the Twitterati are catching on now too. They had the wrong end of the stick earlier, lots of folks saying we had Rick Grant in. Keen to pin it on a family member, like that Amy Willis case in Norfolk a few years back. Remember the one?'

Alex nods. 'Course. Parents covered the whole thing up.'

'Exactly. The good people of the internet want Rick Grant banged up.'

Alex sighs. 'The CCTV puts him at the hospital, fair and square. Unless someone else was acting on his orders, I think we can rule him out. To my mind, anyway.'

David nods. 'The search team have been out all night looking for Eve. A search of Christchurch Park has brought up nothing, and we haven't got CCTV from the back of the Woodmill Road flats either – turns out the cameras were smashed by kids last year and nobody's got round to doing anything about it. Council cuts, happens all the time in little old Suffolk. So anyway, I'm thinking it's time to do an appeal from the parents. OK by you? The DCI is keen.'

'Are they up for it?'

'Seem to be. Jenny is, anyway. Rick less so. I think he knows he might come under fire. On that note, I've got the warrant here – finally – to search the Dillon house top to bottom. And I want to talk to the wife, as well. See how much she knew about her husband's affair. In my experience, it's pretty rare for the other half to be completely in the dark.'

Alex nods, pulls up the photograph of Siobhan Dillon that they have on file. A beautiful woman, there is no doubt about it – long brown hair, almond eyes, pale Irish colouring. He wonders how she must be feeling, now that the speculation about her husband is out there. Pretty shitty, he imagines. He glances to the door, back down the corridor to where Callum Dillon will now be ensconced with his lawyer, a London guy who David says arrived ten minutes ago. Callum Dillon doesn't deserve a woman like Siobhan, and he certainly didn't deserve poor Caroline Harvey as well. *Why don't women ever fall for the nice guys*, Alex thinks to himself, then remembers Joanne's smiling face, pictures her waiting for him back in their bed. *Sometimes they do, I guess.*

Chapter Fifteen

Ipswich
15th August
Siobhan

I cannot stop myself from reading the articles, over and over, as though they are going to suddenly tell me something new, something that will make all of this nightmare go away. But of course, they never do. Each one makes it slightly worse.

POLICE SEARCH MARINA IN HUNT FOR MISSING BABY

Police searching for missing one-year-old Eve Grant this afternoon began the process of dredging the Ipswich marina. Eve was last seen on the night of 10th August at a flat in Woodmill Road, Ipswich, where she was in the care of a woman who was found dead at the scene. Eve's parents, Mr Rick Grant and his wife Jenny, will tonight make an appeal on BBC One to anyone who might know the whereabouts of their daughter.

Christ, the marina. I imagine baby Eve floating, the sight of a little body bobbing beside the boats, that blonde hair dragged through the water like weeds. My stomach turns. I am filled with a sudden, bizarre urge to go out there, join one of the search parties, wade through water to try to find that little girl. How will she survive out in the world at such a young age? Defenceless, alone, or worse? Tears prick my eyes and I swallow hard, try to control my breathing. Panicking isn't going to help anyone.

'Mum, look.'

I glance up from my phone at the sound of my daughter's voice, and see immediately what she's gesturing at.

Jenny Grant's face fills the television screen. She is younger than I thought she'd be; I suppose she's Caroline's age. At least ten years younger than me.

The three of us, Maria, Emma and I, sit huddled together on the sofa in our living room. Maria is holding Emma's hand, her thumb gently stroking the back of my daughter's knuckles in slow, comforting movements. Again, I feel left out – I have swapped Callum for Maria, usurped once again as the favourite parent. How has it happened? What is it I have done? I wish someone would stroke my hand, calm the anxiety that shifts and stirs inside my stomach day in, day out.

The street outside our house is, for once, quiet. Only two reporters remain, lingering in the hope that one of us will emerge. The rest of them are at this press conference; as the camera pans over their faces I actually recognise a few of them – they've been camped outside here for the last twenty-four hours. Pale, sharp faces; they remind me of racing dogs, whippets. God knows what it's like outside the Grant home – it must be hell. I imagine being separated from Emma, not knowing where she might be, not knowing whether she is alive or not, and the thought is so viscerally terrifying that I feel my vision tip and blur. I force myself to take deep breaths, in and out. My daughter is right here, safe and sound. I am not the one having to go through this.

But then we are going through our own form of torture, aren't we?

A couple of police officers visited this morning, told us Callum was still being held at the station, that he'd requested a lawyer. The thought made me feel worse, not better. Innocent people don't need lawyers, do they? I wondered if I was supposed to perform some sort of wifely duty and contact lawyers for him, but they told me he'd already done it. Callum knows lots of lawyers through his work. I've never met any of them.

'Mrs Dillon,' the first officer had said this morning, a woman with short blonde hair and sharp, wolf-like features. 'I'm DCI Gillian McVey. We apologise for cutting short your holiday.'

I'd almost laughed at her – as if that was what I cared about. But I could already see the impression they had of me, of us all – rich spoiled family, husband playing away. It was the wife in the pinny thing all over again – they'd probably even dredged up that article. I'd stood strong, back ramrod straight, whilst Maria made the officer an unnecessary cup of tea.

'Mrs Dillon, you were at your book group on the night in question, that's correct, isn't it?' the DCI had asked, and I'd nodded, swallowed hard.

'And your daughter was here.'

'Yes, that's right. I checked in on Emma when I got home.'

'And your husband, was he in when you came back that night?'

127

As she was speaking, Emma appeared in the kitchen, at the side of my vision. I felt my body tense up under her gaze.

'He was working that night,' Emma said, her voice clear. 'He was in the studio in the garden. I was upstairs, but I heard him come in and out, the sound of the door. And the TV, for a bit. He gives himself little breaks from work. But he never left the garden. I'd have heard the gate.'

'Is that so?' the DCI said, and my daughter nodded. Maria handed her the cup of tea, steam curling up into the room, adding to the heat. The policewoman accepted it without much of a thank you.

'And he was upstairs when you got in a bit later?' Her gaze was back on me. I could feel Emma watching me too.

'No,' I said, 'I got into bed alone, but – Callum came up later, slept in the spare room. I was already asleep, he didn't want to wake me. But I heard him come in from the studio.' The words had felt strange in my mouth.

'Right, thank you. Well, we'll be asking you to come to the station to answer a few more questions this week, Mrs Dillon,' Gillian McVey had told me. 'I'm sure you won't be opposed to assisting our enquiries.' She raised her voice at the end of her sentence, as though she was asking me a question, but I knew she didn't really need my answer.

Her companion, a younger, male police officer who looked almost too young to be on the job, had been scanning our kitchen as Gillian and I talked, his eyes darting around. I don't know what he was looking for, but I doubted he was going to find it in amongst my toaster and kettle or Emma's stash of Haribo.

'And we are in the process of obtaining a search warrant for your property,' DCI McVey had continued, taking a sip of her tea. 'We will aim to keep this as non-intrusive as we can, Mrs Dillon, but it's necessary for us to complete a search as part of the official investigation.' She'd paused, reached a hand into her jacket pocket. 'If you want to talk to me at any point, Mrs Dillon, this is my direct line. I hope you'll give me a call.' She'd put the tea back down onto the table, barely touched. I saw a flicker of annoyance pass across Maria's face; she's never liked being rejected, not even in tiny ways like that. 'We know you want to protect your husband, Mrs Dillon,' the officer said, softening her voice a little, 'but if you do think of anything that we ought to know about, it's in his best interests if you ring us at once. In a case like this, time really is of the essence.'

I'd nodded at her, taken the card without looking at it. My fingers felt cold and numb, as if I'd been sitting on them for too long and got pins and needles.

'Don't you think you ought to be out looking for the baby?' I asked suddenly, the words bursting out of me, too loud in our kitchen. 'A one-year-old can't survive all this time without her mother. You should be out looking for her, not wasting time here.'

The officers had exchanged glances, and embarrassment had flooded my face.

'I'm sorry,' I'd said quickly, 'this is an upsetting time.'

My daughter disappeared after that, shying away from any more attention. I went up to see her after they'd left, stroked her hair for a bit.

'This is all going to be over soon, Ems,' I told her, 'you'll see.' She and I haven't mentioned Callum's affair since the night I confirmed it – sometimes I think I dreamed that entire conversation, but of course I didn't. My dreams now mainly consist of Eve, of that little face, those conker-coloured eyes. They haunt me. Every hour that ticks past, every minute makes things worse. I've seen the TV dramas. I know how these things so often end.

'What's going to happen?' she asked me, and I didn't answer, couldn't think of the right words.

'Did you actually see Dad in the studio that night, Ems?' I asked her, and she paused before answering.

'I saw the light on,' she said, 'which is almost the same thing.' There were tears in her eyes. 'I just want us all to stay together,' she'd whispered, 'I want to stay a family.'

'We will,' I promised, bending down to kiss her on the top of her head, much closer than she usually lets me get, 'we will.'

'Do you promise?'

'I promise.'

'She's scared,' Maria told me, 'she's too young for all this. She doesn't know what to think.' My sister had looked at me reproachfully, as if I'd been forcing Emma to stare at pictures of Caroline Harvey's dead body for hours on end. There aren't any, of course. I've looked online. I am desperate for news of little Eve.

*

'God, they're making a meal of this,' Maria says now, and I refocus on the TV screen, where Jenny Grant is speaking, cameras flashing in front of her, distorting the image a little with white spots of light.

'All we want,' she is saying, her voice filling the living room, 'is for our baby to come home.' A picture of Eve fills the screen and I lean forward; she really is a beautiful child. That curly hair, the cherubic features. I steal a sideways glance at Emma but she too is riveted, her eyes fixed on the screen. In her lap, her phone vibrates, and I catch sight of Twitter updates along with the green roundel of WhatsApp. I don't know whether Emma's spoken to anyone about what's been happening. Her friendship circle seems to have dwindled over the last few months. She goes out occasionally, but tells me nothing about where she has been or who with.

Thank God we're in the summer holidays, I think, not for the first time. I cannot imagine Emma going into school at the moment, I cannot imagine what people might be saying. Well, that's not true. I *can* imagine, I just don't want to. I still haven't called work back, ignored the email asking me to phone. I've messaged Bridget, one of the HR girls, telling her to redirect any correspondence to a senior colleague for now. She didn't ask questions – I find HR tend not to, despite it being part of their role. Callum would say that's me being cynical.

'It's as if everyone's forgotten that that woman is dead as well,' Maria remarks. She's drinking vodka and tonic, the glass cupped in her free hand. She's on her third top-up. My sister doesn't usually drink spirits, but we're out of wine and nobody wants to risk going to the shop for fear of being accosted.

'It's like being under house arrest,' Emma mumbled earlier, then seemed to regret her choice of words. After all, Callum is under actual arrest, and with every hour that goes by when he isn't released, the stakes grow higher.

'Eve is the light of our life,' Jenny is saying, tears beginning to form in her eyes. One of them escapes and makes its way down her cheek, tracking through her foundation. I wonder if they made them up especially, as though they were celebrities about to go on camera. Next to her, her husband puts an arm around her shoulders, squeezes her gently. He's a thick-set man, not as attractive as she is, and not as attractive as Callum either. His voice, when he speaks, is strangely gruff, and his eye contact with the camera is nowhere near as good as hers. I lean forward, closer to the television, watching to see if there is any chance the noise on Twitter could be right. Could the police think the whole thing is a cover-up, engineered by the parents crying on the TV screen?

'Will Dad have to do one of these?' Emma says suddenly, at the same time as my sister says, 'Do you think they give them media training before this sort of thing?'

'No,' I say to Emma, and, 'I don't know,' to Maria.

I focus on the band of text running across the bottom of the screen, giving the details of the case once again, then find myself recoiling as a photograph of Caroline Harvey flashes up. I haven't been expecting it – so far the media haven't shown her picture, focusing instead on little Eve, and the sight of her takes me by surprise. Maria too stiffens beside me, and Emma gives a barely audible gasp.

'Suffolk Police have today released an image of Caroline Harvey, believed to be the resident at Number 43, Woodmill Road. Miss Harvey was found dead in her flat on the night of August 10th, and baby Eve is thought to have been in her care when she was taken. The incident has provoked a new report on safety surrounding babysitting, with MP Nicola Roland speaking out about precautions young women should be taking when alone in their houses with children. On average, it is thought that...'

The newsreader's voice is echoing around the room but to me it seems blurry. All I can focus on is the woman: her huge hazel eyes, the way her dark hair falls to her shoulders.

'She looks a bit like you, Mum,' Emma says, and Maria takes a long sip of her vodka before standing, presumably in order to get a refill.

I cannot stop the mental images from coming: Caroline and Callum, their bodies twisted together, him holding her, kissing her, whispering in her ear. The image on the TV changes to a still of the harbour, the newsreel across the bottom now talking about divers in Ipswich marina and the timeframe; about how concerns for Eve are growing by the minute. There is footage of them draining the water, of men in white suits and waders, the muddy banks of the Ipswich docks. It is nightmarish, surreal.

But all I can see is Caroline. Caroline and my husband. Have I made a mistake, keeping quiet all these years? If I'd confronted him years ago, would it ever have gone this far? Would baby Eve be missing?

Without warning, my stomach contracts and vomit rises in my throat. I clap a hand to my mouth and Emma turns to me, horrified, as sick spills from between my fingers.

'Maria!' she shouts, and my sister comes running, takes one look at me and rushes back to the kitchen, re-emerging with a tea towel and a bowl, the big wooden one I chop salads in. That seems like a different life now – a life in which I chopped salads and drank tea and made love to my husband. My husband who had an affair with Caroline Harvey. My husband who may or may not have killed her. My husband who may know where baby Eve is.

I vomit again, not caring when the liquid splashes onto my shirt. My sister leans over me, dabs at the mess with a wet towel, her hands gently pushing against the fabric and my skin.

'It's all right, Siobhan, it's all right,' she is murmuring gently, as sweat beads along my brow and my hands go clammy. 'It's all going to be all right.'

But it isn't going to be all right. I know it isn't. Not even my big sister can fix this one, can get me out of the hole I am in.

Chapter Sixteen

Ipswich
10th August: The night of the murder
Caroline

I don't know why but I'm nervous about tonight, about babysitting little Eve again on my own. Even though I said I didn't mind, even though I do want to help Jenny, I can't stop my eyes from flicking to the clock every couple of minutes, as six o'clock draws closer and closer. I think it's the thought of the night stretching ahead of us, just me and Eve, of all that responsibility. What if I drop her and she hits her head? What if I feed her the wrong thing? What if she falls asleep and doesn't wake up?

I know I looked after her on that first night at Rick and Jenny's, but that was different. I didn't have time to worry about it, I didn't have a choice. Whereas this time I've had all of today to obsess over it, all of yesterday too, ever since Jenny phoned and asked me for the favour.

'Rick's driving me mad,' she'd hissed down the phone, her voice low, as though maybe he was in the next room. I don't know why she didn't just go upstairs – their house is big enough. There's nowhere to have a private conversation in my flat, literally nowhere to go.

'He's distraught about his bloody mother, keeps saying he doesn't know what he'll do if she dies. I mean, Caro, she's in her late seventies. He's got me and Eve. And she's a miserable old bag anyway, truth be told.' She'd sighed heavily.

'Well,' I'd said, 'some people are really close to their parents, Jen. And seventies isn't that old.' I think of my dad, rotting away in the house in Stowmarket, unable to talk about anything he's feeling, and my mother, buried six feet under in the local churchyard. *Some people*, I said. Not everyone. Not me.

'I know, I know. I suppose it's because I never have been, I can't understand it. I'm a bitch, I already know, you don't have to tell me.' She gave a little laugh. I gripped the phone more tightly.

'Anyway, it was lovely to see you the other night. We're so grateful to you for staying and watching Eve.'

There was a pause, and I knew what was coming.

'We were wondering – we've got to go to the hospital again, tomorrow night, they're running some tests and Rick wants to be there. I said he should go on his own but – I don't know, he wants me with him, I guess. Says hospitals freak him out.' I could almost feel her rolling her eyes down the phone.

'Is there any way – and do say no if you want to, Caro – that you might take Eve for the night again, babysit her for us? I mean, not for the whole night, of course not, just for a few hours? Say two or three? Maybe an eensy-weensy bit longer?'

I'd hesitated, thinking of that moment alone with her in the bedroom, of the beat of my heart in the darkness.

'I could bring her over to you!' she'd said quickly, and I could sense the pleading tone in her voice. 'She'd be so easy, I promise, I'd make sure she had everything with her, everything she needs, all you'd need to do would be to pop her in the cot and check on her every now and then. You probably wouldn't even need to change her nappy! Well, not unless it got really bad. I'd bring you wine as a thank you! Good wine, not that cheap stuff we used to drink at uni! What do you say?'

'OK,' I'd said, feeling the fizz of excitement go through me even as my stomach began to fill with dread, 'OK, sure. I'll do it. I'd like to.' Immediately, I wondered whether I'd made the right decision, but I pushed the thought away, focused on what Jenny was saying, her gushing words of relief.

'Amazing! God, you're a lifesaver. Thank you, Caro. Honestly. Hey, I thought you were really good with her the other night.'

I snorted. 'I didn't do anything, Jen – she was asleep the whole time.'

'Well, I know, but often with new people she gets really agitated, wakes up. It's as if she can sense them in the house! But she was good as gold, you must have been a calming presence.'

It was the next words that got to me.

'You'll make a good mother some day, Caro. You know that, don't you?'

Those words went round and around in my head for ages.

Anyway, so now I'm sitting watching the clock tick towards six, having a very small glass of red wine as I wait for Jenny and Eve to arrive. I'll brush my teeth before they get here – I don't want Jenny to worry. My phone buzzes and I reach for it; ever since the other day I've been scared of getting another of those creepy messages, telling me *they know what I'm doing*. But there's only been the one.

Speak of the devil.

My family and I are going to France tomorrow. When I get back, I think it's best we don't speak any more. Please, stop calling me. Take care of yourself.

My heart gives a giant lurch because it's him, it's him in my phone, sending me a cruel little message before he jets off with his wife and daughter. I stare at the words, not quite believing them. Before I can stop myself, I am typing out a reply, my fingers hitting the keys too hard, making typos because I'm writing so quickly.

I don't send the reply; I type until I cannot type any more and then I screenshot it all, all the things I want to say to him, and then I delete the text. The cursor blinks at me knowingly. It's healthy, I think to myself, what I've just done is *healthy*. I've written down my feelings, all the things I want to say, but I haven't inflicted them on anyone else. I haven't sent the message. Good girl, I think.

I read about that trick in an online therapy thread. Some people said you're meant to actually write a letter, but surely a text is just as good.

The worst part, though, is his final line: take care of yourself. So patronising. So estranged.

I have been calling him, I think I may as well admit that now. Not a lot. Not as much as that message makes out. But in the last week, the week since I saw Jenny, I have a few times. I think it was seeing her and Rick, and Eve of course. It reminded me of what I'd lost. Or of what I'd never really had. And it reminded me of what he did to me. It made me angry. So I rang him, just a couple of times, usually late at night. He picked up only once, hissed at me down the phone. I was going to tell him about the text message, the threatening one telling me to keep away. But our conversation never really got going.

'Is your wife there?' I said, and that was when he hung up. I thought about going round to his house, forcing him to listen to me, though I don't know quite what I wanted to say. I even thought about taking Eve with me, holding her on my hip, showing him what a good mother I could have been. Anyway, in the end I didn't do either of those things, I just stared at my phone for a really long time after he'd hung up, reading and re-reading the message that I didn't send.

There's a knocking at the door and with a start I realise I've lost track of the time – it's five to six and Jenny is here with Eve. Well, at least it's a distraction. A focus.

I can't wait to see Eve.

I get up, and go to open the door, realising too late that I haven't brushed my teeth. Hopefully she won't come close enough to smell the wine on my breath. I might have another one once Eve is down to sleep.

Chapter Seventeen

Ipswich
16th August
DS Wildy

The TV appeal went well, is the general feeling in the force, but these things are always a double-edged sword. They got coverage on the BBC and on the local news. Rick wasn't great, a bit stiff and awkward, and he didn't look quite as *bothered* as he should have, he was more on the robotic side, but Jenny Grant's tearful face generated a lot of coverage, you can't argue with that, and ever since they've been inundated with people thinking they might have seen little Eve. Malaga, one woman said, holding hands with a dark-haired man, but at the same time a teenager thought he'd seen her in Brighton.

'She's unlikely to be in both,' Dave Bolton had said wryly, but they'd agreed to follow up both the sightings anyway, given the circumstances. On the down side, if Caroline's killer is still out there, the appeal yesterday might have spurred him on. In Alex's experience, appeals from the relatives either prompt a response from the kidnapper – a reaching out of sorts, or they lead to total silence and almost certain death for the missing person. There aren't many other ways this thing can go.

Caroline's flat has been thoroughly dusted by forensics,

and the only prints coming up are those of herself, Callum Dillon and Jenny Grant. There are, however, traces of bleach around the surfaces; the kettle has been wiped clean, as has the sink and parts of the floor in the kitchen. Could be normal cleaning, could be someone covering tracks. The prints they have found are not enough – Callum freely admits to being in Caroline's flat on multiple occasions over the course of their affair, and they know Jenny Grant dropped baby Eve off that night. If there was another intruder, they were very careful about where they put their hands. But Alex's money for the murder of Caroline is still on Callum. They've been granted an extension to hold him in custody for another twenty-four hours, which his lawyer is not happy about, but part of the reason he knows the DCI doesn't want to let him go is out of concern for Siobhan Dillon's safety. Eight months ago, the Norfolk police across the border had let a suspect out on bail after a day and a half, and that night he'd strangled his girlfriend. Alex doesn't like thinking about it. Nobody does.

His wife Joanne had asked him about the Eve Grant case last night; she'd watched the appeal and Alex could see a couple of crumpled up tissues stuffed down the side of the sofa on her side. She'd always been a very empathetic woman, but the idea of someone losing their child was unbearable to her. Alex had gone to sleep wondering if they were, in fact, perversely lucky not to have a child to lose in the first place. And then he'd hated himself for that thought.

*

Jenny Grant is back in the police station, without her husband this time. She is there voluntarily, claims she cannot bear to sit at home whilst Rick sits listlessly on the sofa, lost in a stupor of grief.

'Has anyone come forward?' she is asking one of the duty officers desperately. 'Has anyone seen the appeal and come to talk to you?'

Alex can see her wringing her hands together, tiny hands, like a bird. Her cardigan hangs off her shoulders; even in the last few days she looks to have lost weight. DS Bolton approaches and puts a hand under her elbow, guiding her towards Interview Room 1, where they can sit down. For some reason, he doesn't like her – said as much to Alex last night after the appeal went out.

'There's something weird about her,' he'd said, frowning, 'all that perfect yummy mummy stuff, and then leaving her daughter with someone she barely knows any more, someone she admits she wasn't that close to. Someone even her husband thought was unstable. It doesn't sit right with me.' He'd sighed. 'I don't think she did it, clearly she wasn't there, but I wonder if she's keeping anything from us. About Callum, or Caroline.'

Alex stares now at Jenny's fragile frame, the paleness of her skin. He follows his colleague into the interview room, and sits down, his eyes never leaving Jenny's face.

'I'm keen to have another chat with her whilst she's here,' Dave says under his breath, 'find out what else she knows.'

Interview with Jenny Grant, 16th August
Ipswich Police Station
Interview Room 1
Present: Jenny Grant, DS Wildy, DS Bolton
16.30 p.m.

DS Wildy: *Mrs Grant, what can you tell us about Caroline Harvey's relationship status at the time of her death on 10th August?*

JG: *She was single.*

DS Wildy: *Indeed. And to your knowledge, she had no permanent partner, and hadn't done for the last few years?*

JG: *[pause] Not a permanent partner, no. Not to my knowledge. But she had Callum, they were sleeping together. I told her it was unhealthy. That man is a misogynist. He was cruel to her. He might be dangerous. [pause] Detective, how is any of this helping to find my daughter? Do you think he did it?*

DS Bolton: *Mrs Grant, as you know, there is an extensive search team out looking for Eve as we speak; that investigation has taken up a large part of our resources and what DS Wildy and I are trying to do is establish any kind of motive for the individual who may have taken your daughter and murdered Ms Harvey. We are at present working with the assumption that this was one and the same person.*

JG: *So you're saying it was him? Callum Dillon? You think he's got my daughter? Did someone say that after watching the appeal, did someone see him?*

DS Wildy: *The appeal has turned up a few lines of enquiry, but nothing concrete so far, I'm afraid. However, there is still time. As for Callum Dillon, he is currently being held in police custody, Mrs Grant, but we are attempting to question him to find out if he knows anything about the whereabouts of Eve. Anything you tell us about him and his relationship to Caroline might help us to form a clearer picture about the sort of man he is.*

JG: *Have you actually asked him? Have you asked him if he's got my daughter? [voice rising] I don't want to sit here talking about him, I want you to ask him! I want you to make him tell you! Whatever he did to Caroline, I don't understand how it can have had anything to do with my baby. She's an innocent child. She's a baby! [wrings her hands again, several times].*

DS Bolton: *Please, Mrs Grant, we do understand that this is very distressing. But we also do need you to try to answer our questions today as best you can.*

JG: *[pause, quietly] OK.*

DS Wildy: *Is it correct that Ms Harvey and Mr Dillon had been conducting a sexual relationship for the past eighteen months, and that you found out about this relationship by accident approximately six months ago?*

JG: *Yes, that's right.*

DS Wildy: *Had you ever met Mr Dillon, or seen him and Caroline together?*

JG: *[pause] No. I'd never met him. I only knew about their relationship because I'd seen them together one night, round near her flat. I thought I recognised him, so I asked her who he was and she didn't want to tell me. I got suspicious, and eventually she told me his name. At which point, I looked him up on Facebook and discovered he was married to*

Siobhan Dillon. And that the reason I recognised him was because I'd seen him in the local paper, some TV thing.

DS Wildy: *You looked him up on Facebook?*

JG: *[pause] Yes.*

DS Bolton: *Do you make a habit of looking up your friends' love interests on social media, Mrs Grant?*

JG: *Why are you saying it like that? No, I don't, but I was curious. Caroline knew I didn't approve of her seeing a married man – my parents divorced over a similar thing, back when we were at university. I was looking out for her. I didn't want her – I didn't want her to get hurt. [pause] Why are you speaking to me like this, anyway? I'm the victim here. I'm the mother who's lost her baby. [pause, crying] I'm sorry, I can't – I can't do this…*

DS Wildy: *We're not trying to upset you, Mrs Grant. We wanted to chat things over with you, seeing as you came in to see us. We thought it might help. Would you like a glass of water?*

JG: *[beginning to hyperventilate] I can't breathe, I can't breathe – I can't, why are you – please don't –*

DS Wildy: *[glares at his colleague] I think that's enough for now. Interview terminated at 16.50. Mrs Grant, we're going to fetch the doctor, OK? You stay there. You stay right there until I come back.*

Chapter Eighteen

Ipswich
16th August
Siobhan

Callum looks awful. His face is covered in stubble and he looks as though he hasn't washed since he got off the aeroplane back from France two days ago; perhaps he hasn't. There is a strange smell as I move closer to him, a musty tang that even his expensive aftershave seems unable to mask.

DCI Gillian McVey telephoned this morning, asked me if I could come in to the station to answer a few more of their questions. At her words, my heart began to beat faster; I could feel the blood rushing up and down my limbs, making me feel almost light-headed. I don't know why. I'm not the one who's done anything wrong, am I? They don't know anything about me. I'd told them already I'd been at book club that night, with some of the uber-mothers.

'We do it every month,' I'd said, 'a group of us. I came straight home afterwards, went to bed. I was tired.' I'd smiled at that, made a joke of it. 'I'm a mum, I'm always tired. You know what it's like.' I left out the extra glass of wine I'd had when I got in – there was no need for them to know

The DCI told me that I'd be able to see my husband, that

he'd been asking for me. For a moment or two, I thought about refusing to come, imagined the look on my husband's face when he was told in no uncertain terms that actually, his wife didn't feel like seeing him right now, seeing as he'd spent most of his marriage lying to her about his extra-marital affairs and God knows what else. But of course, I didn't refuse. I told DCI McVey that I'd be there as soon as I could.

'Don't delay, Mrs Dillon, will you,' McVey had said, 'I'd really like to speak to you as soon as I can.'

After she'd hung up, I stared at the phone for a minute, replaying her voice in my head, searching for anything untoward in what she was saying. I thought about what I'd said to them, about hearing Callum come in that night, creeping into the spare room. About Emma, promising her that everything would be OK. *You're being paranoid*, I told myself, but then, if I'd been more paranoid in the past, perhaps none of this would have happened at all.

I got my bag together, the house keys, my mobile phone. A book, in case they planned on keeping me waiting, although I don't know how I'll ever be able to face the book club women again after all of this. I could feel myself dithering, delaying the moment I had to actually leave the house and go talk to them.

Maria and Emma stayed at home, listlessly completing a jigsaw puzzle in the kitchen. None of us know what to do with ourselves – our lives are in limbo.

'What did the police say they want you for?' Maria asked me, concern in her eyes, and I told her what the DCI had said.

'Do you think I should come with you?' she'd asked me, and I told her no, asked if she could stay with Emma.

I walked to the police station; it isn't far. My legs felt like jelly the entire way – both at the thought of seeing Callum, and the thought of that DCI with her laser-beam focus on me. At the front desk, I announced myself to the duty sergeant, who nodded straight away, as though he'd been briefed to expect me. As though I was a person of interest.

'We'll take you through to see Mr Dillon first,' he said, and he led me down a long corridor, walking too quickly. I struggled to keep up. I felt my breath catch in my throat as he pushed open a door, nodded at me, and left me alone with my husband for the first time since France.

Now I stand in front of him, my mouth dry and my palms sweating. I wish I had my handbag to hold onto but they wouldn't let me bring it in. I don't know what they thought it contained – it's mainly lipstick and tissues.

'Siobhan,' Callum says, the minute I step further into the room, the room of the station with its dingy white walls, nailed-down plastic seats, and stark yellow lighting. It is horrible; depressing and bleak. For a second when I see his face I forget what has happened and on instinct, feel as if I should reach out to him, wrap him in my arms, but I cannot, I don't want to, and besides there's no doubt several police officers are watching us from behind the safety of camera screens in the next room. And the man in front of me is someone I don't know any more. Plus, there is the smell.

'I'm sorry,' he says hoarsely, 'I'm so sorry about Caroline.' There is a pause, as he waits for me to speak.

'I didn't do this, you have to know that, Siobhan, you have to believe me.' He is staring at me, his eyes slightly wild, his lips chapped and sore. I swallow, hard, and sit down on one of the chairs, not trusting my legs to hold me up for the duration of our conversation.

'Where were you that night, Callum?' I ask, and he lets out a noise, a sort of sob in the back of his throat.

'You sound like them. Jesus, Siobhan, I've had three days of questioning, first the French and now the idiots here, and that's the first thing you say to me! I was at home in the studio. Like I told the police. It's the truth.'

I don't say anything.

'Where is Emma? How is she?'

'She's at home with Maria,' I say, 'she's OK. In the circumstances. But I can't imagine this has done her any good, Callum, can you?'

He looks pained. 'Why would I do this, Siobhan? How could you possibly think me capable of what they're accusing me of? Jesus, we've been married fifteen years.'

I just watch him as he almost writhes before me, tying himself into knots. I prepared myself for this meeting, you see. I told myself not to waver. I promised I'd be strong. My husband's powers of persuasion can be powerful; remarkably so.

'How could you have an affair?' I say coldly, and the look on his face is, for a moment, sweetly satisfying. It's a moment I've imagined many times over, ever since I found out – the moment where I confront him about sleeping with Caroline Harvey, but in all my imaginings it's fair to say I never thought it would happen quite like this – in a police station, with a dead woman and a missing baby all over the news in connection with our family name.

'It just – it just happened,' he says, and he's beginning to cry now. He is so very, very different from the confident, careful man I pledged myself to fifteen years ago. It's funny how people change. I force myself to look straight ahead, not to let the tears that are lurking just behind the surface of my own eyes make their way to the top. I feel foolish, embarrassed and ashamed for letting him walk all over me for all this time.

'But it was over, Siobhan,' he says, and the tears are turning into sobs, awkward and embarrassing, not suitable for a TV exec with an over-inflated sense of self. 'It was over! You can check my phone if you don't believe me, you can check my emails. I finished it; I wanted a fresh start. I wanted to focus on you, on Emma. Our family.'

'I can't check your phone, Callum,' I say, 'it's in police custody. Remember?'

The chair I'm sitting on is so uncomfortable; the plastic digs into my skin. My mouth feels dry and sand-papery. There is no air in the police station, or at least none left for me.

'Siobhan,' he says, taking a deep breath, obviously trying to pull himself together, 'please. You can't honestly think this is something I'm capable of doing. Someone killed her, Siobhan. They stabbed her with a knife, she bled to death. Presumably they took her friend's baby too. Is that something I'd do? Are you telling me seriously that that's something you think I'd be able to carry out?'

And now he is doing what Callum always does: he is becoming angry, he is beginning to turn the blame onto me. The tears are slowing to a stop, replaced with something darker. I can feel it happening, feel the balance of power shifting. I steal a sideways glance at the camera in the corner of the room, wondering if they really are watching us, and I grip the sides of my chair a tiny bit tighter.

'I don't know,' I say to my husband, through gritted teeth.

'I don't know what to believe. I don't know what you're capable of any more. When I married you, Callum, I didn't think you were capable of having an affair, not at first, and I didn't think you were the kind of man who'd be able to lie to me, time and again. But you are. Not only once, but multiple times. Did you think I never knew, Callum? About any of them?'

His face changes, paling even further as the impact of my words sinks in. Good. It is hard to hold back, now. I carry on speaking, the words rushing out of me like a dam that has been broken.

'I didn't think you were the kind of guy to ignore his teenage daughter in favour of some no-strings shagging down the road, but you are. I didn't think you were the type of guy to enlist a hot-shot lawyer at the first inkling of trouble, but you are. I didn't think you were the kind of guy to text their mistress whilst on holiday with your family, but you are. And the minute I found out about you and Caroline, do you know what I did? I went through your phone. I became *that* woman. You turned me into someone I never wanted to be.'

I don't add that I've been going through his phone for years; there's not really any need. I'm slightly out of breath now, almost panting, but Callum is looking at me strangely.

'Wait a minute,' he says slowly, 'so you knew?'

Too late, I realise my mistake.

But he's quick. 'You knew about me and Caroline before this – before all of this happened? You knew whilst we were in France? *Before* we were in France?'

I can see his brain ticking, the realisation dawning on him. I bite down on the inside of my mouth, furious with myself for giving this nugget of information away.

'I – no, I didn't know for sure,' I say, backtracking slightly, 'I didn't know who she was.'

'But you said you went through my phone,' Callum says, quick as a flash, 'just now, you said you'd become "that woman". Which means you did know who she was, because you saw our texts, you saw her name. Didn't you, Siobhan?' He leans forward on his plastic chair, and he's stopped crying now.

'Yes,' I say quietly. 'Yes, Callum, I knew you were having an affair. I've known for months.'

I raise my head to look up at him, expecting to see more sorrowfulness in his eyes now, more regret at what he has put me through. But that isn't what I see at all. His gaze is hard, and his words, when they come, make me gasp.

'You've known for months,' he repeats, and I nod, thinking back to that awful day in April when I'd found the receipt in his jacket pocket – dinner at the Blackbird in Norwich. It's where he always used to take them, his little bits on the side. As soon as I saw it, I knew it was happening all over again. I'd been a fool to think it was over, a fool for thinking I'd won, that my patience and virtue had kept our family together and stopped him looking elsewhere.

That afternoon, I'd answered his phone for him whilst he was in the shower, heard her purring down the line. The hideous embarrassment of it all, when I realised I was right, when I looked back through his call history, his messages. It was like being in a time warp, backtracking eighteen months. When she'd phoned, I'd thought it was the plumber. Tragic, I know. I may as well have been wearing my pinny at the same time. I've always wondered whether she *wanted* me to find out, calling him so brazenly like that in the middle of the day. I hung up at the sound of her voice.

'So if you've known about Caroline all this time, who she was, what she was to me,' he says, 'what I want to know is, where were *you* on the night she died, Siobhan? Where were you on the night little Eve Grant went missing?'

Oh, for God's sake.

'I was at book club,' I say slowly, 'you know where I was.'

'That's where you *say* you were,' he says, 'but how do I know you're telling the truth? We slept in different rooms that night, after all.'

Chapter Nineteen

'He's a real dick,' Dave says, stuffing a Malteser into his mouth as the two of them watch Callum try to implicate his wife in Caroline's death.

Alex nods, reaches for the bag of chocolates which are steadily melting in the heat. 'He is,' he agrees, 'but look, maybe he's got a point. Don't you think? I've been thinking we need to look at the wife more closely.'

Dave makes a face, getting to his feet with a sigh. 'Personally, I can't see it. Siobhan Dillon? Look at her, she wouldn't hurt a fly.'

They both look, taking in the way she's staring her husband down. She appears tired, with dark circles around her eyes, which is unsurprising given the circumstances. Her hair is pulled back from her shoulders, tied neatly with a few strands escaping. She looks younger than her forty-four years.

'McVey wants to chat to her now,' Dave says, 'woman to woman. Think she's got a bit of a thing about it.'

Alex nods, wiping a smear of chocolate off his hand and onto his jeans. 'What McVey wants, McVey gets.' He pauses. 'Has anyone checked out Siobhan's book group alibi?'

Ipswich Police Station
Interview Room 3
Present: DCI McVey, Siobhan Dillon

DCI McVey: *It's nice to see you again, Mrs Dillon. Thank you for coming in. Please state your name for the tape.*

SD: *Siobhan Elizabeth Dillon.*

DCI McVey: *Thank you. Mrs Dillon, as you know, we are currently holding your husband in custody in connection with the murder of Caroline Harvey, and the potential involvement in the disappearance of Eve Grant. We are nearing the end of the maximum period of time for which we can hold him in regards to this offence, meaning that it's of paramount importance that you answer my questions honestly, to avoid us wasting any further time. Is that clear, Mrs Dillon?*

SD: *Yes. [pause] Can you call me Siobhan, rather than Mrs Dillon?*

DCI McVey: *Of course. Siobhan. Did you know that your husband Callum Dillon had been conducting an extra-marital affair with Ms Harvey?*

SD: *[pause] I did learn of the affair very recently. Yes. I did.*

DCI McVey: *That must have been upsetting.*

SD: *Yes. It was. Of course.*

DCI McVey: *How did you find out about the affair, Siobhan?*

SD: *[sighs] Do I have to go into that here?*

DCI McVey: *Well, it would help if you did.*

SD: *[pause] I found a receipt in his jacket, for a place he – a place he used to take women. And then I answered a phone call meant for him. From her. I thought it was the plumber, the boiler was on the blink and we were waiting for him to call. Callum was – he was in the shower. I guess he'd got complacent, he left his phone on the side and I picked up without thinking. I wouldn't normally. [pause] But after I heard her voice I looked through the phone, saw a message from her.*

DCI McVey: *What did the message say?*

SD: *I can't remember the details of it. But it was obvious. Kisses and everything.*

DCI McVey: *Lots of people put kisses after their texts. What made you so sure that this was indicative of a sexual relationship?*

SD: *[sighs] Trust me, Detective, it was obvious. [pause] I'm sure you've been through his phone records anyway. It isn't exactly the first time he's done any of this. He doesn't really care about getting caught. I usually turn a blind eye – I'm sure I'm not the first woman you've heard say that in your time.*

DCI McVey: *[inclines her head] Siobhan, can you tell us a bit about the days leading up to you and your family's trip to Saint Juillet, France?*

SD: *Yes. My sister owns the villa, she was driving out there anyway to take over some furniture, bits for the house. She's been doing it up for the last two years, she's a designer. So she asked if we wanted to come this time, fly out and see the place for ourselves.*

DCI McVey: *And it was your husband who booked the flights, sorted out when you'd be going.*

SD: *Obviously, yes. But we all wanted to go.*

DCI McVey: *Siobhan, do you think your husband arranged the holiday in advance to remove himself from the country*

following the premeditated murder of Caroline Harvey?
That he knew what was going to happen that night and
wanted to ensure he had an escape route in the morning?

SD: *I – no. I don't know.*

DCI McVey: *Siobhan, please don't be afraid to tell me the*
truth when I ask you this next question. [pause] Has your
husband ever been violent towards you?

SD: *[pause]*

DCI McVey: *Siobhan?*

SD: *No. No, he's never hit me. Nothing like that.*

DCI McVey: *Are you sure about that?*

SD: *Yes, I… Yes, I'm sure. [knots her hands together in her lap]*
Please, Detective. I'm sure.

DCI McVey: *You say he's had affairs before. Have you ever*
confronted him about them?

SD: *No, I haven't. I was trying – I wanted to keep things*
together. I wanted to remain a family. And I thought –

DCI McVey: *You thought what?*

SD: *[speaking more softly] I thought the affairs had stopped.*
He seemed to stop. I thought it meant I'd done the right
thing, you know, keeping quiet about the other women. For
about two years it all calmed down, he was around more,
I didn't think he was seeing anybody else.

DCI McVey: *So you're understandably angry, then. You were*
angry to find out that he'd begun a relationship with
Caroline.

SD: *[pause] I was upset, Detective. Not angry.*

DCI McVey: *OK. Siobhan, have you ever met Jenny and Rick*
Grant before?

SD: No. *Their names meant nothing to me until – until all of this. I don't know them, and neither does Callum, as far as I know. He's never mentioned their names to me.*

DCI McVey: *How can you be sure about that, Siobhan? When up until a few months ago, you had no idea your husband was sleeping with Ms Caroline Harvey?*

SD: *[pause]*

DCI McVey: *Siobhan? Answer the question, please.*

SD: *I suppose I can't. I can't be sure.*

DCI McVey: *No. You can't be sure, Siobhan, can you?*

SD: *[silence]*

DCI McVey: *And on the night Caroline died, you say you were with your book club, is that right?*

SD: *Yes. It's not far, we meet at a pub in the town. The Horse and Crown. There were about six of us, they'll all tell you I was there. We were reading* White Teeth. *The Zadie Smith.*

DCI McVey: *And you got home at what time?*

SD: *Eleven, I guess. Maybe a bit later. We stayed for a few glasses of wine; it was light until quite late. When I got back I knocked on my daughter's room, popped my head around the door to say goodnight. She was sleeping already. She's a teenager, as you know, they need a lot of sleep. Anyway, I looked in on her, and then I went to bed.*

DCI McVey: *And your husband was already there?*

SD: *[pause] I…*

DCI Mcvey: *Siobhan? Was your husband home when you arrived back from book club that night?*

SD: *I think he was still working in the studio. I mean, I was very tired, as I've said.*

DCI McVey: *You and your husband usually share a room, that's correct?*

SD: *Yes, of course. But sometimes, if one or other of us came in late, we'd go into the spare room instead, it wasn't uncommon. We tried not to disturb each other.*

DCI McVey: *So your husband didn't sleep in the spare room because you'd had a row, then? Because, say, you'd found out about his affair and confronted him?*

SD: *No, that wasn't it.*

DCI McVey: *[leaning forward, closer to Siobhan] Look, Siobhan. [voice softens] I know how you must be feeling. On top of everything else, you're feeling betrayed. Sad. Hurt. [sighs] I was married once, you know. Years ago, now. He left me for his secretary. [laughs] What a cliché, but it happened. I was humiliated. Eventually I moved here, became a police officer. Never looked back.*

SD: *[silence]*

DCI McVey: *I understand the desire to protect your husband, Siobhan, I do. I understand your wanting to keep your family together, protect your daughter. But you need to tell us the truth now. If you're not sure whether your husband was home that night, my officers need to know. [leans forward] We can help you, Siobhan. We can help you and Emma. Get you somewhere safe. But I need you to work with me, not against me. Did you check to see if the studio light was on? Did you see him in there? And did you actually hear him enter the house, like you said you did?*

SD: *I –*

DCI McVey: *I'm on your side, Siobhan. I've been in your shoes. [pauses] Aren't you angry with him, just a little bit?*

SD: No.

DCI McVey: *No, you're not angry?*

SD: No, *I didn't check. I don't know what time he came home, OK? That's the truth. But it doesn't mean he did it, Detective, does it? Does it?*

DCI McVey: *Thank you, Siobhan. I really appreciate your being honest with me. It's very helpful, very helpful indeed.*

Chapter Twenty

Jenny barely knocks on the door before inserting herself into my flat, Eve in one arm and a huge, unwieldy-looking travel cot tucked under the other.

'Helloooo,' she calls out, in that way people who are very comfortable living with other people do, and then she appears in the doorway of my living room slash kitchen, her hair piled on top of her head and looking – well, a bit frazzled to be honest. Quickly, my eyes dart to the sink but the tell-tale wine glass is hidden from view. I wish I had some gum, or a mint, something to mask it on my breath. Still, hopefully she'll be gone soon, and it'll be just me and Eve. And Eve isn't likely to notice, is she!

'Thank you so much again for this, Caro! You're becoming my star babysitter!' she says, setting the cot down in the middle of the room with a loud 'ooph.' To my surprise I see that Eve is awake, her mouth silenced with a little pink dummy, her eyes wide and blinking at me.

'Hello Eve,' I say, standing up from where I've been sat on the sofa and coming to help Jenny, who is looking around my flat as if suddenly realising for the first time how un-baby proof it is. I see it through her eyes: the sharp edges, the gaping plug sockets, the little balcony with a sheer drop down to the concrete below. The wine bottles stacked in the rack by the cupboard, the glasses that might shatter. The many, many ways that something could go wrong. My heart skips a beat, but I'm committed now, aren't I? It's all going to be fine.

'Is she OK on the sofa?' I ask awkwardly, 'just while we set up the cot?'

'Yes, yes,' Jenny says, disentangling Eve's little arms from where they're wound around her neck, and placing her daughter gently onto my sofa. Callum laughed when he first saw my sofa – 'It's tiny! It's more like a big armchair. How are we ever going to shag on that?' – but then again, he comes from a life where plush four-seater sofas are the norm. A different life to mine.

Eve's brown eyes are huge, they stare around the room, and I wonder how much one-year-olds can really take in. Can baby Eve sense my loneliness, the emptiness of my life from just a scan around my living space? I notice Callum's suitcase, stuffed away near where I keep my unused ironing board, and hope Jenny doesn't notice the name tag, start on at me again. I wish he'd come and get it, the sight of it reminds me of our mini-break and how happy we were, or how happy *I* was, anyway.

Eve blinks at me, and I long to touch her, to pick her up and cuddle her close, but it feels awkward with Jenny here, huffing and puffing over the travel cot.

'Honestly,' she says, 'this bloody thing is meant to be "portable and easy to use, any time, any place". It's a sodding nightmare! It weighs a ton for starters and I can never get it to pop up the way they said it would in Mothercare.'

Her cheeks are flushing red and quickly I grab the other side of the cot, pull on it so that the mechanism expands. I did it! I've never even set foot in Mothercare, and I feel a tiny, silly burst of pride.

'There,' I say to Jenny, 'we're all good. Shall I put it in the bedroom for now?'

She looks disproportionately relieved, and nods. I drag it through to my room, which thankfully looks a bit tidier than usual.

'God, well done,' Jenny says when I return, distractedly stroking the top of Eve's head. 'Thanks for helping. Ugh, sorry if I seem a bit stressed, it's doing my head in, this constant carting back and forth to the hospital. Rick's insistence that I'm always there to help. I mean, why can't he go on his own? It's ridiculous. And then when we *do* get there to see Margaret, he sort of clams up, just sits there like a shell-shocked little boy who can't believe his mum isn't bustling around putting the fish fingers in, you know? He goes all quiet and then I'm left to make conversation with bloody Margaret, who to be honest, Caro, has never really liked me all that much anyway. We sit by her bed for what feels like an eternity, with all these sick people coughing and spluttering around us, and the nurses virtually ignore us, and then eventually they throw us out and I have to drive back here, listening to Rick bang on about her.'

She stops, out of breath.

'Sounds rough,' I say, and she starts laughing, and despite myself, I join in.

'God, listen to me, I'm a barrel of laughs. Sorry, Caro. It's just getting to me, I suppose. I'd rather be home with Eve. Well, I'd rather be here with *you* and Eve, drinking wine and gossiping about the old days.' She smiles, nods to the wine rack. 'Nice collection, by the way.'

She bends down and reaches into her bag, pulling out various items – bottles of milk for Eve, a blanket, a pack of nappies.

'Just in case,' she says, 'everything you need should be in here, I'll leave you the whole bag, look. But let me just pop these in the fridge.' She glances around and I direct her to the corner, where my rather bare fridge feels embarrassing in comparison to their full-to-bursting family Smeg.

'You need to get some proper food in Caro, gosh!' Jenny says, and although I've started to feel quite warm towards her, a flicker of annoyance bubbles inside me. She sounds like my mother – well, if I still had one.

'Now, are you going to be all right, princess?' Jenny asks, bending down to Eve who is still sitting in a vaguely upright position on the sofa, her head lolling against the grey cushions.

'Shall I take her dummy out? I don't like to leave them in too long really,' Jenny says, and without waiting for an answer she whips it out of the baby's mouth and pops it into a small Tupperware box, produced from the depths of the Mary Poppins bag.

Almost immediately, Eve starts to cry – I don't know what sparks it, but she's staring at me as her eyes begin to fill and her mouth opens.

'Ohhh, dear,' Jenny says, picking her up whilst simultaneously glancing at the clock. 'I'm going to have to go, I'm afraid – it's OK, darling, Mummy's here, and this is Mummy's friend, Caro, who you met the other night. She looked after you then, didn't she? Yes, she did, shh, shh. It's all going to be fine.' She smiles at me and her daughter reaches out, grabs her finger tightly.

'I don't think she wants you to go,' I say, and even though I know, I *know* it's stupid I feel a little dart of disappointment, of inadequacy that this tiny child is rejecting me too.

'Oh, she'll be fine, she'll settle down. Have you got anything you could read to her?'

And then I remember: I keep a little shelf of competitor books in the next room, to look at when I'm doing illustrations. Not to copy, as Callum not-so-kindly put it, but to use as inspiration for my own drawings.

'I think they're a bit above her reading age, though,' I tell Jenny, but she waves a hand.

'I told you the other day, we're trying to get her used to books as early as possible. It's good for her to hear the sound of the words, you could read a couple to her? If she doesn't settle? And show her the pictures?'

Another glance at the clock – it's almost twenty past six.

'I really do have to go, Caro, but you'll be OK, won't you? Just call me if you need anything; I've got my mobile, of course.'

Eve is still crying, and the cries worsen as Jenny holds her out to me.

'Here, take her. She'll get used to you in a few minutes, and if she carries on crying, walk her around the flat a little bit – oh, I suppose there isn't much room – but still, a bit of movement normally helps to quieten her down.' She glances at the windows. 'Don't take her out on the balcony though, will you? It's so high! I don't know how you stand it.'

I grit my teeth at the dig; she doesn't mean it. 'Of course not.'

I reach out and she puts Eve in my arms. The sudden weight of her makes me gasp, but Jenny doesn't notice. She's gathering her handbag to her, and I feel a splash of panic.

'What if she gets sick?' I say quickly, and Jenny stares at me.

'Sick? She won't get sick. She's been fed already, and you can give her a bit more bottle around eight if she isn't asleep by then. But she will be! Don't look so worried, Caro.' There's a buzzing and she pulls out her phone.

'Oh, God, it's Rick wanting to know what's taking so long. Bye, Caro. And thank you! Bye princess.' She leans forward, kisses her daughter on the forehead.

'See you in a couple of hours. I'll make it as quick as I can, promise. And I'll text you when I'm leaving the hospital.'

The door bangs shut behind her, and she's gone. It is 6.25 p.m.

*

The moment the door closes and Jenny is out of sight, Eve's cries intensify and I worry that Jenny will be able to actually hear them going down the corridor. Quickly, I use my foot to shut the living-room door, creating another barrier between the sound and the hall, and then I begin to pace, making small circles around the kitchen, from the fridge to the sofa and back again.

'Ssh, Eve, ssh. What's the matter? You're fine, we're fine, and Mummy will be back soon.' I clutch her to me, loving how warm she is, how alive. After a few minutes, she does begin to quieten and I feel a wave of elation – I *can* do it, after all. I'm not completely useless. I don't have to be the person everyone thinks I am – I can be someone else.

When I'm sure – well, as sure as I can be, with my total lack of experience – that she isn't about to burst into tears again, I gingerly sit down on the sofa, Eve in my lap. It's easier now; I turn her around so that she's facing me, her little feet balancing on my thighs. She has white frilly socks on, and a pale pink Baby-gro – not for Jenny any worries about gender stereotypes.

There are little bubbles of spit in the corner of her mouth, and her lips are pink, a proper pink that you don't see on adults unless they're wearing a very specific shade of lipstick called something hideous like Candy Heart.

'You're a good girl, aren't you, Eve?' I say to her, using that baby voice that I always hate hearing out in the street, grown adults cooing like pigeons, but somehow I can't help myself. She blinks at me. Her eyes are big and dark, and combined with her squiggles of soft blonde hair, the effect is angelic.

She looks much more like Jenny than she does Rick, I think, and the thought inevitably leads to another, darker one.

I wonder what sort of baby Callum and I would have made.

*

I remember so vividly the day I found out I was pregnant. I remember what I was wearing – a blue dress with little swallows on, and a cardigan because it was April and a bit cold. I'd been feeling a bit funny all week, but had put it down to working a lot, trying to make sure that being freelance didn't mean everyone forgot about me, and I thought the fact that I was feeling sick was just down to anxiety. Or because I wasn't eating that well now that I was freelance – I'd routinely forget to cook proper meals, exist on toast and avocado and yoghurt.

Things were already beginning to unravel between Callum and I, and I had the sense that I was clinging onto a sinking ship, my fingers clawing at the woodwork, trying to pull him closer when he was already moving away from me. Closer to Siobhan.

When my period didn't come, I didn't think much of it – I'd never been particularly regular and since changing pills I would sometimes bleed at random times, which was both embarrassing and unsexy if it happened at the wrong moment. But when it was over two weeks' late, I thought I may as well take a test, just to be sure. Just to rule it out.

I didn't tell Callum – he was at home that day for his daughter's birthday. We didn't talk about his daughter, Emma, very much – he'd occasionally open up, perhaps if we'd had more than usual to drink, he might feel able to be more intimate – but most of the time he was a closed book on the subject. I often wished he'd take his wedding ring off; I hated the way it would graze against my skin, a little reminder that he wasn't really mine. But he never did. The way Callum and I normally played things was to pretend that he didn't have another family, in as much as we could.

The result of the pregnancy test changed that.

I went to Boots on my own, coincided it with a trip to my old office, an excuse to get out of the flat, and perused the aisles looking for what I needed, feeling like a teenager in trouble. It was ridiculous, and I knew it was – I was a grown adult, but somehow the affair made things murky, shadowy. I thought of couples going to buy tests together, or women telling their partners excitedly what they were doing, and I began to entertain thoughts of what would happen if I *was* pregnant. I suppose, looking back, I let myself fantasise.

Callum would be a good father, I thought, as I went up to the counter to pay; after all, he was with his daughter today, wasn't he? He didn't want to miss her birthday, so he wouldn't want to miss our child's birthday either. And he wasn't happy in his marriage, not really – obviously he wasn't, or else why would he be with me? He said he'd never strayed from Siobhan before, that there was something different about me, something he couldn't resist. I pushed away all the things that Jenny would say, that he was a man who wanted to have his cake and eat it, that he didn't respect me and never would. I hated hearing those things. I didn't think they were true. Or at least, I didn't want them to be. I told myself that Jenny was being dramatic, that she might even be jealous, because she was stuck with boring old Rick and I was with someone exciting.

Looking back, I don't think Jenny was ever jealous of me at all. I don't think anyone's ever been jealous of me in my whole entire life.

Back at home, I thought about asking Callum to come over but his message had said he was with Emma all day, so I didn't. *Emma.* I tried not to think about her as a real live person with a name; it made me feel guilty. I pictured her as the sort of happy, healthy girl that might play hockey after school, the sort of girl that had enough going on in her life with friends and boyfriends that what her parents did didn't matter to her too much. The sort of girl that went for manicures with her mother. The sort of girl that could live without a father, if needs be. Who might have to, now.

I peed on the stick, hunched over the toilet, my fingers shaking just a little bit as I placed it on the side of the sink and waited. Three minutes felt like three hours. I thought about texting someone, but I didn't know who to text. Since going freelance and meeting Callum, I'd found it harder and harder to keep up my old friendships – only the persistent ones like Jenny managed to squeeze through, and even then I was nowhere near as close to my girlfriends as I'd once been. One by one they seemed to couple up, moving into the Suffolk countryside, away from Ipswich, buying houses because we weren't in London and they could actually afford them. And a couple of them had children now, children whose scans I'd beamed over and whose christenings I'd sat through. Maybe this will change everything, I thought to myself, maybe I'll be back in the club.

But I think I always knew, at the back of my mind, that my pregnancy wouldn't be like theirs. And I was right, because my pregnancy ended before it had even really begun.

The positive symbol stared up at me, bold and indisputable, though I took another two tests anyway, just to be sure. When I was finished, I lined them all up in a row and snapped a photo of them on my iPhone. For a split second, I wished I had a mother to call up, but I didn't, and my father wouldn't really care too much. He'd aged very quickly over the last few years, and while I cared about him, in a distant way, we'd never had the sort of close father–daughter relationship that Callum seemed to share with Emma.

I hesitated for a moment, before sending the photo to Callum. I captioned it 'Surprise!' and added a party face emoji. To this day, when I think about that emoji, I always want to cry.

On my lap now, Eve begins to wriggle, snapping me away from that cold April day and back to the present. She does a sort of jig on my legs, her little feet like those of a tap dancer.

I bring her close to me, my hands underneath her arms, and kiss her on the forehead like Jenny did, like a mother would. For a minute, I pause, inhaling her scent, that delicious baby scent of Johnson's shampoo and life.

I can feel my heart beginning to thud, already thinking about the moment I will have to give her back. I could hold onto baby Eve forever.

I wonder what would happen if I did?

Chapter Twenty-One

The crime scene, Flat 43, Woodmill Road, has the stale, strange air of a space that no one has lived in for a week. Alex makes his way past the blue and white tape, through the corridor into the kitchen, where a glass door opens out onto a balcony which runs along the (admittedly small) length of the whole flat. Caroline Harvey was lucky to have some open space, he thinks, before remembering that in actual fact, Caroline Harvey wasn't lucky at all.

Her body is in the mortuary, now; her next of kin identified it with DCI McVey two days ago. The father, Christopher, had come alone apparently, looking completely shell-shocked, but when McVey had asked him when he'd last seen Caroline, the old man had struggled to remember.

'Probably not for six, seven months,' Christopher Harvey had said at last, which DCI McVey said she'd found odd, considering Stowmarket is only a thirty-minute drive away from Ipswich, if that.

Alex continues into the flat. The cot is still there but the blankets and pillow inside are gone, concealed in an evidence bag back at the station. They've tested for DNA, of course, but the only match showing up is Eve's. He looks again at Caroline's things – the bathroom, a collection of shampoos and conditioners lined up on the side of the bath, half empty, the showerhead dangling drearily above. There is a water ring around the tub, as if it has been used relatively recently. An empty toothbrush mug, the toothbrush removed for DNA testing. The kitchen-cum-living room is quite sparse – there are a couple of paperbacks lined up next to the television, a candle – he sniffs it – lemon-scented. An ironing board propped up to the side of the fridge, no sign of an actual iron. Wine glasses in the cupboard, a mug with the letter C on the side, Scrabble-style. There is something sad about the feel of the place, other than the obvious. Orange markers denote the spots where bleach was found on the floor. Another one is placed next to the kettle.

He tries to imagine the night of the murder, of baby Eve alive and well in her cot. He's been hoping against hope that Eve is still out there, that whoever came to the flat had Eve as their target and Caroline merely as collateral damage that needed to be got out of the way. But the positioning of the body – he gives a little shiver. It suggests otherwise. It suggests that this was something personal. Perhaps even something planned.

'Wildy?'

DS Bolton appears behind him, and Alex is surprised. He'd come to the flat for another look on his own whilst the DCI interviewed Siobhan Dillon, wanting to get a better sense of a case that is, quite frankly, baffling him. He doesn't know why Dave is here; he'd left him helping the duty doctor calm Jenny Grant down after her inadvertent panic attack earlier this morning.

'What's up?' he asks, and Dave makes a face.

'I've sent Jenny Grant home with another family liaison officer. I couldn't get any sense out of her after you left. She was a bit of a wreck.'

'OK,' says Alex, 'well, perhaps we went in too hard.'

Dave makes another face. 'Yeah,' he says, 'well, that's the thing. Her husband's come to the station. Seems seeing Jenny in that state has snapped him out of his funk. He's pretty pissed off. Wants to talk to you.'

Alex stares at him. 'Pissed off with us, you mean? For upsetting Jenny?'

Dave nods. 'Yep.' He looks away, rubs the end of his nose, a sure sign that he's feeling guilty about something.

'What is it?' Alex presses him, and DS Bolton tells him that Rick Grant has just punched his fist through the station wall.

*

There are smears of blood on the white wall of the visitors' room at the station, accompanied by a bit of a dent in the plaster. A stressed-looking duty sergeant is currently filling in a long-winded form, detailing the incident. DS Wildy finds Rick Grant with one hand bandaged up, droplets of red spotting the dressing.

'Mr Grant,' he says, not reaching for a handshake, 'sorry to have missed you. I understand you'd like a chat.'

The man looks up at him, and the expression on his face is somewhat sheepish. 'Sorry about the…' He tails off, gesturing to the damaged wall with his un-bandaged hand.

'Well, it's not the first time,' Alex says gruffly, sitting down beside him, giving a nod to the duty sergeant who looks grateful to be relieved of what was obviously some sort of Rick-watch.

'Jenny's so upset,' Rick Grant says suddenly, and when Alex looks at him, he can see tears glinting in the man's eyes. Furiously, Rick wipes a hand under his nose, lets out a grim half laugh.

'I just lost it,' he continues. 'She came home in such a state, saying you lot had been asking her all sorts of stuff, accusing her of things, asking about Callum, and I saw red. I've been sitting at home the last few days, staring at nothing, wanting to help but not knowing how. Useless. I've been crap. I just wanted to *do* something.'

'Mr Grant,' Alex says gently, 'we do understand how difficult this is for you and your wife. Our intention was not to accuse Jenny of anything – she came to the station herself to see what the response to the appeal had been, and my colleague took it upon himself to ask her some questions whilst she was here.' He pauses. 'DS Bolton can be a bit – overbearing, at times.'

Rick doesn't reply.

'Is there anything you'd like to tell me, about that night, or about your wife?' Alex asks, careful to keep his tone measured for fear of another attempt at a hole in the police station wall.

'I shouldn't have made Jenny come with me to see my mum,' he says after a few moments. Alex can hear the station clock ticking on the wall, the rustle of papers as the duty sergeant pretends not to listen. They ought to go into an interview room, perhaps, but he is reluctant to break the moment, to risk Rick's temper reappearing and him choosing not to divulge something that could be important.

'She didn't want to come,' Rick continues, 'she never liked my mum, not really. If I hadn't made her come with me, none of this would've happened.'

'You can't know that,' Alex says. 'It's possible that whoever took Eve might have targeted your house, were she at home with Jenny.'

But Rick is shaking his head, speaking over him. 'No,' he says, 'no. I know that's not it. We should never have left her with Caroline Harvey. Never. That woman wasn't right in the head. I can't stop thinking about it, about her, the things Jenny said about her past. The whole thing is her fault somehow. I know she's dead, but – but we shouldn't have let her take care of Eve. Not my Eve. My daughter.' He looks at Alex, his gaze suddenly clear. 'The way she looked at those photographs…' he tails off. 'She wanted Eve for herself. I didn't trust my instincts. And now we've lost our baby.'

The gruff façade the man had when Alex first walked in has faded now, and the policeman watches as Rick Grant raises a bandaged hand to his face and sobs, the sound echoing throughout the room, drowning out the ticking of the clock until it is the only thing Alex can hear.

*

Rick Grant's words echo in DS Wildy's head as he sits back in his chair, staring again at the images of Caroline Harvey's body. He accepts the possibility that the poor woman was unstable, but she's dead, for Christ's sake – she isn't hiding Eve up her jumper. But Rick seemed so convinced that it was her fault, that somehow, despite her death, she was to blame. Alex sighs.

Could Caroline have *paid* someone to take Eve away, before she died? Could Callum or Jenny have killed her for that?

The wound on Caroline's chest is deep; disturbingly so. The angle of the knife is straight on, implying she was stabbed before falling forwards over the cot, but Luminos tests of the floor in Caroline's kitchen show blood splatter there as well – a small mark near the door of the fridge, and one near the doorway. He wonders whether someone might have moved her, or whether she was stabbed in the kitchen and made her own way to the bedroom in an attempt to protect little Eve. Or to take her for herself.

Alex groans aloud, runs a hand through his hair. He knows they are failing with every minute that goes by – failing Eve, failing an innocent child. Without evidence, they can't pin this on Callum, and he can't help but feel they are missing something, that someone close to this investigation is not telling the truth. The police in Rouen rang this morning, confirmed that the forensics had finished at the villa, found no DNA aside from that of the immediate family. The car belonging to Maria Wilcox was searched too, yielding nothing more than fibres from a rug matching one in the house, and the family's own DNA. The results were sent over by Adele, the junior officer, and there it all is, in black and white. *No further evidence*. Similarly, the search of Ipswich Harbour has brought up nothing, and the press are becoming more and more vindictive with every hour that brings no results, no charge, no conviction, and no Eve. Jimmy, the guy running the Suffolk Police Twitter account, has been looking increasingly stressed over the last few days, and a glance over his shoulder confirmed everything Alex had been suspecting about which way the civilian tide was turning.

@NorwichLad18: What are the pigs doing throughout all of this? Little babby goes missing right on their doorstep and they can't pull their finger out? #FindEve

@MB_Goodchild: @SuffolkPolice when are you going to admit that you've no clue what you're doing?

@Poppy29: Have they searched the Grant house yet? Bet it was them. The mother looks proper shifty.

@Tom03: Reckon @Poppy29 is right you know, I bet they know more than they're letting on. Maybe they wanted rid of the baby and saw a way out. Made it look like an accident. Thought they could pin it on someone else.

@RichGirl1: Nah, it's that TV guy. They'd have let him out otherwise. It's his wife I feel sorry for.

@MB_Goodchild: @SuffolkPolice any updates???

Alex printed a few of them out, not wanting to tell the DCI that he was turning to social media for the answers. Frustration brims inside him – they have a good amount on Callum Dillon, true: a possible motive if Caroline was going to tell his wife, the relationship with Caroline himself, and his fingerprints in the flat. But none of those things give them any idea where Eve is, and at this stage, the thing he cares about the most is reuniting her with her parents, or at the very least, giving them some closure. A body to mourn, a solution and an end to a nightmare that they probably don't deserve to be in. He sighs. Unless they do.

He thinks of the empty harbour, the fruitless searches of alleyways and parks and bins in Ipswich and the surrounding areas, that have all turned up nothing. Could Eve's body be in *France*, outside of the house? Surely not. He pictures it, a tiny pile of bones nestled underneath that beautiful villa. The place must be worth at least a million. Who owns a place like that, anyway? What kind of person can afford it in the current climate?

Well, Maria Wilcox can. The sister-in-law. Maria is an interesting one, he thinks. Very beautiful, unashamedly so, on the few occasions they have seen her. By all accounts she is the one taking care of the daughter, Emma – the daughter who is so obviously struggling under the weight of what her father may or may not have done.

She splits her time between France and England, it seems, having bought the Saint Juillet holiday villa two years ago. When they spoke to her, she was very forthcoming – the most forthcoming of them all, in fact – detailing her thoughts on Callum and his marriage to her sister. The picture she painted wasn't exactly rosy.

In the UK she owns a property in Woodbridge, the pretty market town in Suffolk, but somehow Alex finds it easier to picture her in France, sunning herself by that beautiful swimming pool. He has seen the photos of the villa, sent over by the Rouen police, and he can't imagine why anyone would bother with Suffolk when they could be over there. Still, it's good of her to stay with her sister. Siobhan Dillon is having a rough old time of it. Has had a rough old time of it for years now. Enough to push anyone over the edge.

Chapter Twenty-Two

Ipswich
16th August
Siobhan

I stand to one side as the police come into the house. Thankfully, it's not DCI McVey – I have no wish to see her again after the grilling she gave me this morning. Guilt eats at my insides; I wasn't going to admit to her that I didn't hear my husband come in that night – it feels like a betrayal of Emma, of everything I promised I'd do to try to keep the family together. Still, I think, they won't charge him without evidence. My words alone won't change anything.

They have an official warrant to search our property now, the property we bought together fifteen years ago, the property in which we've raised Emma. Now it is treated like another crime scene; gloved hands riffle through our belongings, fingers flick through my dresses and Callum's shirts, the ones that we weren't forced to leave in France. They are thorough, spending a long time out in the studio in the garden, where Callum likes to work, and where he keeps his computer – though they've taken that away now – and all our paperwork. I don't go in there very often, it has to be said. My husband doesn't like to be disturbed.

I've always felt this house was too big for the three of us. Its space gives us an excuse to be apart – to busy ourselves in separate rooms, to be ships passing in the night. Perhaps if we had managed another child, someone to be a companion for Emma, things might be different. Maybe a sibling would have rubbed off her edges, brought her out from her moodiness and into the world of the living. But then again, maybe it would have made things worse. She might have had to share Callum's attention, and I don't think she'd have liked that at all.

They search Emma's room too, even though I think this is ridiculous and I tell them so. They're very interested in the things we took to France, but I explain to them that most of our luggage is exactly where we left it, that the French police were eager to get us out of the villa and back to our own country. Back where we belong. *You should know that*, I think to myself, wondering not for the first time about the lines of communication between Ipswich and Rouen. But of course I don't say that, not in so many words. I offer to make them tea and hover in the kitchen whilst it happens, trying not to wince as their clumsy fingers rub up against everything I own.

The visit from the police only serves to reignite the presence of the press outside. I've barely left the house since we got back from France but we're running out of everything – milk, toilet paper, shampoo, wine – so that afternoon I brave it, putting on my big coat despite the fact that the August sunshine is showing no signs of letting up. It's not as hot as it was on the French coast, of course, but Suffolk is still muggy. The air clings to my face, making me feel claustrophobic.

'I won't be long,' I say to Emma and Maria, who have taken to sitting in front of the television at almost all times of day, watching the news for updates, occasionally doing jigsaw puzzles, shutting themselves away from the outside world. I've told my sister that she ought to go back to the Woodbridge flat, have a break from it all.

'You could take Ems with you,' I said to her, 'get her away from this circus a bit. It might be good for her.'

Maria had looked at me strangely, as though I'd suggested something completely absurd.

'I need to be here with you,' she'd said, 'I'm worried about you, Siobhan. I want to stay until this gets sorted out. Work are fine with it – I'm my own boss, remember.'

'Have it your way,' I said, 'but this could go on forever.'

I think of all the missing children that have never been found; their names circle in my head. I can't stand to look at the pictures of Eve Grant that they repeatedly show on the news, I can't bear to think of the pain her parents must be in. I can't bear to think that my husband might have caused it.

Part of me does want them to charge him, or at least that's the thought that entered my mind around 2 a.m. while I faced down another night of insomnia. For them to find something so insurmountable, so concrete, that there is no other option. At least then Emma and I might be able to move forward, to progress with our lives. Of course, I don't want Callum to be guilty. But living in this purgatory is fast becoming unbearable.

'Mrs Dillon!' The minute I leave the house, my coat wrapped around me, hood up, the reporter is in my face. There are vans halfway down the road, stretching down towards Christchurch Park – the neighbours must be getting sick of it. Not that I've heard from them. We never really socialised with people on the street very much; when we first moved in I thought we might, but as time went on it got harder and harder. All these people living these anonymous lives. Well, not that ours is anonymous any more. Ours is splashed all over the front pages.

TV EXEC CHEATING ON HIS WIFE was a headline I caught sight of the other day on one of those industry insider gossip websites. Callum has been suspended from the team, pending the outcome of the investigation. We don't have to worry about money, not yet anyway, but obviously it won't last forever.

The reporter is pushing a big, black microphone into my face, so close that for a moment I fear it's going to hit me. He is young, skinny-looking, and his breath smells of stale cigarette smoke. I didn't think anyone smoked any more, these days. None of the uber-mothers do.

'Do you think your husband will be charged soon, Mrs Dillon?' His voice takes me a second to place, then I realise that it's Brummie, the same as the policeman who brought us home on that first night and gave my daughter a chocolate bar. That night seems like a lifetime ago now.

'I have nothing to say,' I tell him, clenching my fists around my phone and house keys in my pocket. I am sweating in this coat, the sun hot on my back.

'How did you feel when you found out your husband was cheating on you?'

'No comment,' I say, pushing past him only to be confronted by another one, a woman this time. She's wearing short sleeves and a baseball cap to keep the heat off her face, and she smells faintly of sun cream. The scent makes me think of happier times – on the beach with Emma when she was little, crabbing at Walberswick on the Suffolk coast. Smearing the cream onto her little nose and the back of her neck to make sure she didn't burn. We used to take her every year, drink cold pints of cider in the pub afterwards. We haven't been for a long time now.

'Siobhan, how is your daughter coping with the news? Do you think this case could push her over the edge?'

The reporter's words cut through the hot afternoon air. I stop walking; I think I even stop breathing for a second. The male reporter has heard too and has backed away slightly, but the woman stands boldly in front of me, microphone outstretched, a cameraman no more than a few steps behind her.

'What did you just say?' I ask her, the words almost hissing out of my mouth. She doesn't even have the grace to look abashed, she just stands in front of me, woman to woman. She has auburn, flyaway hair that's escaping from underneath the cap, and a wide, red-lipsticked mouth that reminds me of a clown's.

'I said, how do you think her father's arrest will impact your daughter, Emma? There are rumours that she's becoming a bit unstable? Struggling to cope? Her school have reported antisocial behaviour over the last few months.'

I can't believe she has the audacity.

'That's not what you said,' I hiss at her, you said "Do I think this case could push her over the edge?" What is it you mean by that?'

'I know it must be a sensitive issue, Mrs Dillon. I want to give you the chance to share your side of the story. And Emma, of course. We can run a whole feature on you both. People don't like the fact that you're hiding away. It doesn't look good, you know that, don't you?'

Anger bubbles inside me.

'Do you have children?' I ask her, and although a large part of me wants to turn around and run away from her, run back into the house and slam the door, clutch Emma to my chest, I force myself to stand my ground, to look this woman, this *vulture*, in the eye.

'No,' she says, 'I don't.'

'Well then,' I say, keeping my tone as level as I possibly can, even though it takes every ounce of self-restraint in my body, 'perhaps you might reconsider your approach in the future. Perhaps you might educate yourself in these sort of things before you come here, to my house, and ask those sort of questions about my 16-year-old daughter.' I pause, fighting for breath. 'I don't know how you can live with yourself.'

With that I push past her, push past them all, leaving the cameras snapping and flashing in my wake. No doubt it's already on Twitter: *Mum loses her shit at reporter*, but this time, I don't care. It's not as though people aren't talking about us already.

I'm getting sick to the back teeth of all these people camped outside my house. It's a disgrace! They're blocking our driveway – my Sammy could barely get the car out this morning. The council need to move them, I'm telling you. –
Barbara Pinder, number 80, Christchurch Road

It's horrible living so close by to the Dillon house. I feel as though I ought to stop by, you know, ask them if there's anything they need, offer to be a friendly face, but at the same time one doesn't like to get too involved. If they need anything, surely they'd ask? I mean, we've never been close,

but I used to see the three of them from time to time, taking Emma to the park when she was younger, popping in and out, that sort of thing. The parents often came home late from work. I used to feel a bit sorry for the daughter, to be honest.
– Rachel Sanders, next door neighbour to Siobhan and Callum Dillon

God knows I've tried to be friendly to the Dillon family over the years. Went to a Christmas do at theirs once, a while back now. House is lovely inside, I'll say that, but that husband of hers is unbearable. Thinks he's such a big-shot, deigning to live in Ipswich when he obviously thinks he's destined for Hollywood. Ugh. I can't stand him. So yeah, I guess I don't bother with them that much now. Can you blame me? **– Simone Smith, three doors down from the Dillon family house**

There's something up with that Dillon daughter. She's always struck me as a troublemaker. Trust me, kids like that don't get like that by accident. There'll be something wrong at home. Something that's caused it. There always is. **– Brenda Miller, teacher at Ipswich School for Girls.**

Chapter Twenty-Three

Ipswich
10th August: The night of the murder
Caroline

I'm giving Eve some formula that Jenny's left in the fridge, even though I'm not one hundred per cent sure that she needs it. If I'm honest, I just wanted to have a go at feeding her, see what it was like to feel her sucking on the bottle, watch her little chest rise and fall as she fed. She's much quieter after she's finished, and she looks as though she could fall asleep. With a start, I realise that I haven't thought about Callum for over an hour, I've been so utterly and gloriously distracted by baby Eve.

'Do you want to have a little sleep now?' I ask her, using the silly cooing voice again, putting my index finger to her warm little cheek. Her skin is so soft against mine.

'Your mummy's so lucky, isn't she, Eve? Isn't she?' I say aloud, bringing my face down towards hers and rubbing noses, giving her an Eskimo kiss.

'You are the loveliest baby in the whole wide world. Yes you are, yes you are!' I tickle her tummy and she gives a little squirm, then makes a noise that sounds as though it could be a laugh. I feel a rush of adrenaline – I made her laugh! I make a mental note to ask Jenny when she gets back whether she's done that before. A tiny part of me almost hopes that she hasn't, that I'm the first one to have made it happen. Maybe after this Jenny might let me babysit more often, now that she knows I can do it, now that I've proved myself. In fact, I could look after her during the days, couldn't I, now that Jenny's back at work – I can stay at home all day if I want to, I can balance the laptop on the sofa next to me and keep Eve in my lap, multi-task. Make the most of being a freelancer, really embrace that lifestyle. They wouldn't even have to pay me. I'd save them a fortune on childcare.

Feeling energised by this thought, I get to my feet and go over to the cot because Eve's eyes are drooping a little and I don't want to tire her out. I picture Jenny coming home and finding us, Eve sleeping peacefully, me calm and relaxed in the other room, a scattering of children's books around me that I've been reading to her. She'll be so pleased, she'll stop thinking of me as her childless, husbandless friend, and start thinking of me as a capable woman who could be a very good mother. A very good mother indeed.

*

After I sent the photo of my pregnancy tests – all three of them – over to Callum that day in April, he called me straight away. I was pleased – he didn't usually call me that often, we stuck mostly to messages – but when I picked up, I could tell at once that his tone wasn't quite what I was expecting.

'We need to talk, Caroline,' he'd said, without even saying hello, let alone a congratulations. For a moment or two, I ignored it, and ploughed on anyway, talking over him excitedly, as though if I'm just buoyant enough, it will change his mind.

'Isn't it wonderful? I mean, I know we didn't exactly plan it but you know how much I've always wanted a baby, I told you right when we first met, didn't I? I know things can always be wrong so that's why I took the three tests, just to be sure, and now I am sure and I'm so excited, I'm so pleased, we must—'

'Caroline.' He'd interrupted me, that one word bringing me abruptly to a halt. 'We need to talk. Are you at home?'

I'd forced a laugh, trying to lighten the mood of the phone call. 'Well of course I'm at home, I don't exactly make a habit of lining up pregnancy sticks in other people's bathrooms! I don't think that's really the etiquette, do you?'

'I'll be over in an hour. Don't go anywhere.'

The line went dead before I could reply. I was wrong-footed, horribly so – although we didn't chat by phone much, our text conversations would usually end in streams of kisses, suggestive emojis, promises of tomorrow. We were in love. Weren't we? OK, he'd never actually said it apart from in the throes of passion but still, it was obvious. He spent time with me. He risked his marriage for me. Of course he loved me. The alternative was a thought I simply blocked from my mind.

I spent the next hour pacing my flat, rationalising that perhaps I had caught him at work, during the middle of a very important project – he had a lot of those – or that he was so overcome with emotion that he couldn't quite articulate his feelings. Men did that sometimes, I knew that, didn't I? It didn't have to mean there was a problem.

But of course, there was a problem. I squeeze my eyes together as I remember, the memory hitting me as viscerally as it did on that dreadful day in the spring. I leave Eve in the cot, the window slightly open and the blankets across her, feeling her nappy just before I do so – see! I'm learning! – and go back into the sitting room, find my hidden wine glass from earlier. Opening a new bottle of red, I pour myself a measure, bigger than before. I'm taking deep breaths. I shouldn't have started to go down this road, shouldn't have opened this particular Pandora's box. It's too painful. It always will be too painful.

When Callum arrived that night, he was wearing the suit he wears for important days at work and the first thing I felt was a swell of relief – I'd been right! I'd simply got the timings wrong, interrupted him partway through a presentation or client meeting, and he'd had to be terse on the phone because he was in earshot of his colleagues. *But why did he call you at all then*, the voice in my head persisted, *why not wait until later? Why would he have looked at his phone during a pitch meeting?*

'Can I get you something to drink?' I'd said, smiling at him. I don't like remembering this part because it makes me sound pathetic, but in the hour since our phone call I'd been putting on make-up, carefully painting on foundation and lacquering my lips, trying to make myself look as pretty as possible. Then I worried that I'd taken it too far, that I wouldn't look *maternal* enough when I answered the door, so I wiped half of it off and started again, going for a toned-down look. The result was probably somewhere in between.

'I'm OK,' he said, striding into the flat, looking around as though I was hiding something there. I thought maybe he wanted to see the tests so I got one from the bathroom and showed it to him, but he recoiled as though I'd done something disgusting rather than given him news of his future child.

'Let's sit down, Caroline,' he said, 'and on second thoughts, I will have that drink. Do you have any beer? Whiskey? Something strong.'

I poured him a whiskey on the rocks, the way I knew he liked it. He didn't speak the whole time, just sat down on the sofa, his hands clasped together awkwardly, his back not even touching the sofa cushions.

'Aren't you going to take your coat off?' I said to him, trying not to think about the last time he was here, when we'd showered together then made pasta in our underwear, listening to James Taylor and drinking red wine. The mood couldn't have been more different. I was starting to feel nervous, sweat beginning to prickle my armpits, my stomach starting to knot with anxiety. Quickly, I poured myself a tumbler of whiskey too, even though I've never been able to stand the taste. I drank it fast, with my back to him, before remembering about the baby growing inside me and clapping a hand to my mouth. Panic gripped me – I shouldn't be drinking at all, but in the strangeness and stress of Callum's behaviour I'd wanted something for the courage. I took a deep breath, trying to think. Surely one wouldn't hurt. It would all be fine.

He kept his coat on, even though it was only spring and the sun had warmed up the flat all day.

'What's the matter?' I asked him, placing the glass of whiskey down on the table in front of him, watching his face closely for clues. I couldn't understand why he was acting like this; it was as if there was a stranger in front of me, drinking my whiskey, sitting on my sofa.

He took a couple of sips, and the alcohol seemed to calm

him a bit, because he reached out for my hand, pulled me down so I was sitting next to him on the couch.

'Caroline,' he said again, 'listen. We need to talk about – about the baby.' He'd paused, taken another sip. 'Are you really pregnant?'

'Of course,' I said, 'it's not the kind of thing I'm likely to make up, is it?'

By this point, my heart was thudding in my chest because I knew that whatever direction this conversation was going to go in, it wasn't going to be good.

'Look,' he said, running a hand through his hair, his thick, brown hair that I loved, 'surely you can understand, Caro, this is complicated. We can't just – I can't just have a baby with you.' He looked up at me. 'I already *have* a daughter, Caroline.'

That was the beginning of the end.

Chapter Twenty-Four

Ipswich
17th August
DS Wildy

Rick and Jenny Grant live in quite a nice house near the Ipswich docks; rows of flowers are planted outside in window boxes, withering in the August heat. It's doubtful that anyone is remembering to water them. Inside, it is newly decorated, the walls fresh with relatively recent paint, a shiny Smeg fridge, a classy-looking island in the middle of the kitchen on which stand endless mugs of half-drunk tea. There are photos of Eve everywhere, with one notably missing from its frame – the one that is currently plastered all over the newspapers, given to DS Bolton at the start of the investigation.

It's too warm inside the house, but nobody opens a window. The family liaison officer pours them all a glass of water. Her face is tight and tired-looking. On the sofa in the living room sits a little pink teddy bear belonging to Eve, and as DS Wildy makes his way into the room, Jenny picks it up and clutches it to her chest.

'Sorry to intrude yet again,' Alex says to her. They have already apologised for upsetting her the other day, but Rick's wall-punching incident has rather evened out the playing field, and all Jenny does now is nod.

'Rick's out,' she says, 'he's joined one of the search parties. It's better for him, I think. He needs to feel like he's doing something.' She gives a weird, nervous laugh. 'Think he's realised that sitting on the sofa all day wasn't doing him any good, after all.'

'Good,' Alex says, 'that's great, Mrs Grant.' He takes a sip of his water, attempts a smile. He wants to talk to her about the things Rick said at the station, his utter conviction that Caroline Harvey is somehow to blame for all this despite the fact that she's lying in the morgue.

'Mrs Grant,' he begins, deciding to jump straight in, 'when you left your daughter with Ms Harvey, were you aware that she had previously had an abortion for a child of her own?'

Jenny stares at him, her eyes widening a little. He can see genuine surprise on her face. The fact came up in Caroline's medical records, but they hadn't thought it relevant until now. It still might not be, but it opens up a conversation.

'What? No. That's not true.'

'It is true, Mrs Grant, the information is clearly stated on Ms Harvey's medical records.'

'When did she have an abortion?'

'A few months before the night of her death. April. It hasn't seemed relevant before, but your husband indicated some – concerns about Caroline to me, about her state of mind. About her desire for a child.'

'God, I had no idea… she didn't tell me,' Jenny says. She clutches the pink teddy tightly, her fingers curling into its lurid fur.

'Do you know who the father might have been, Mrs Grant?'

'Well, Callum, I presume. But I'm surprised she – I didn't think she'd do that. I thought she was desperate for kids of her own.' Jenny pauses. 'Maybe it just wasn't the right time.'

'Do you think there is any chance that your baby was not safe in the care of Ms Harvey, Jenny? That her desire for a child of her own meant she might have wanted to take or harm yours?'

'Not safe? What do you mean? Obviously she wasn't safe, she's *missing*!' She is glaring at him now, and he feels sweat forming on the back of his neck, takes a sip of water. The room is stiflingly hot.

'What I mean, Mrs Grant, is do you think there is any possibility, however remote, that Caroline Harvey could have harmed Eve herself?'

For a second, she stares at him. 'Caroline harm Eve?'

'Yes.'

'Well, I don't think so… I don't know. I don't know. I don't know quite what Rick said to you.' She is worrying at the teddy, pulling a thread from its stomach, winding it tightly around one finger. Tears are beginning to fill her eyes, catching the light in the stream of sunshine that is filtering through the half-closed blinds. 'I never thought this would happen, did I?' Jenny mutters, almost to herself, then looks back up at DS Wildy, raises her voice a bit. 'I can't imagine what's happened to Eve, Detective, but Caroline doesn't have her, does she, because she's *dead*.'

Alex clears his throat. He wishes she'd put down the pink bear, it's distracting.

'Mrs Grant, do you think there is any chance that your friend Caroline was jealous of the fact that you had a child? That there was any part of her that wanted your child for her own?'

*

FEARS GROW IN SEARCH FOR MISSING BABY EVE

Suffolk Police are continuing to search for the whereabouts of missing one-year-old Eve Grant, who was last seen in Ipswich on the evening of 10th August, in the care of a family friend, Ms Caroline Harvey. Ms Harvey was killed on the night of the disappearance.

'We are continuing to appeal to any and all members of the public who may have seen something on the night of the tenth,' a spokesperson from Suffolk Police said. 'Eve Grant was not yet walking by herself, therefore we need to rule out the possibility that she made her own way out of the flat. We are particularly interested in the hours of 6 to 9 p.m., in anyone who may have been seen in the vicinity of Woodmill Road, perhaps carrying something in their arms, an object or bundle, or putting such an object into a car. It is crucial that everyone casts their memories back to that night and if you did see anything unusual or suspicious, please call 0845 54 54 54 as soon as possible.'

On Monday night, baby Eve's parents, Jenny and Rick Grant, made an emotional appeal on BBC One, calling for whoever had taken their daughter to 'please, bring her home'.

Earlier this week a search of the Ipswich marina turned up nothing, and police continue to search the outskirts of Ipswich for a sighting of little Eve. Around two hundred people helped in a search of streets, farmland and woodland through the night and into this morning. Ports and airport staff have also been informed.

The investigation into the death of Ms Harvey continues, with one man in his forties being held in custody.

Chapter Twenty-Five

Ipswich
17th August
DS Wildy

'We're going to have to let Callum Dillon go.'

DCI McVey looks disappointed, an emotion that Alex hasn't often seen cross her face in the years they have worked together. Triumphant, yes; angry, most definitely; scathing, one hundred per cent. But disappointed? No.

The sight of it makes him feel worse.

'We've held him long enough,' he carries on, 'without a confession or hard evidence, we can't keep Callum Dillon in custody any longer than we already have. Unless something vital comes in within the next half hour, we're stuck. His lawyer's practically got a timer set.'

'Fuck!' The DCI gets to her feet, the more familiar expression of deep-seated annoyance replacing her disappointed look. 'Fuck, fuck, fuck. I hate the thought of him out there, roaming around. Jesus, it'd be like the Norfolk thing all over again if something happened. I don't like him going back to Siobhan.' She sighs. 'Did the CCTV from Christchurch Road turn up anything yet?'

Alex shakes his head.

'Nope. Tom's been going through it but it doesn't cover the front of the Dillon house, it only goes up to the crossroads, because of the museum. We've been checking for sightings of the Dillon vehicle – a dark blue Audi, reg plate XE69 JBL, but again, we'd only see it if Callum was turning left out of his driveway. Caroline Harvey's flat is a right turn, it's the opposite direction. Odds are he walked.'

He pauses. 'Look, ma'am, do you think we're barking up the wrong tree here? Rick Grant is convinced this is something to do with Caroline herself, with her wanting Eve – wanting a child of her own.' He stops, trying to collect his thoughts. 'And what if we're wrong about Siobhan Dillon, Callum's wife? She knew about the affair. She would've been angry, upset. She might've gone round there, to confront Caroline, and it got out of hand.'

The DCI is frowning at him. 'That's all very well and good, if you say so, DS Wildy. But if that's your new theory, explain to me where little Eve is now? Why Siobhan Dillon would want to harm a baby she doesn't know?'

Alex groans. 'I don't know.'

The DCI sighs. 'Speak to the French police again, will you? Make sure they searched Siobhan Dillon's belongings along with everyone else's.'

'And Callum?'

'Well, we've no choice, have we? We have to let him out.' She pauses. 'But I want a car watching that house for the rest of the week. If Callum Dillon goes somewhere, we go too. I'm not letting him get away with anything else.'

POLICE RELEASE MAN IN BABY EVE CASE

Suffolk Police issued a short statement today to confirm that the man in his forties who has been questioned on suspicion of the murder of Caroline Harvey has been released without charge. Police are continuing to appeal to the public for any sightings of Eve Grant, who is one year old, and ask that members of the public remain vigilant at all times until the killer is caught. Anyone with further information pertaining to Caroline Harvey or her associates is also asked to call Suffolk Police at the earliest available opportunity.

@JusticeWarrior2003: Jesus, they don't know what they're doing. Why let some lunatic back out onto the streets?

@AndrewWhite: Probably a paedophile. Oh great, he's out.

@SuffolkBoy01: There's too much focus on who killed Caroline. They need to be out looking for the baby #FindEve

@Tasha16: @SuffolkBoy01, come on, mate, you know as well as I do that that baby is dead. And the police know too. That's why they're not even bothering to look for her. There's no point.

@SabahBeautyBlogs: Does anyone else think the TV exec guy is pretty hot? If I was his wife, I don't think I'd kick him out of bed, even after all this! #IWould

Chapter Twenty-Six

Ipswich
17th August
Siobhan

They've sent over a family liaison officer following the search, which was actually about as intrusive as you could get, despite what DCI McVey said. She's a woman called Yvonne with short black hair. She hovers around us all the time, keeps making endless cups of sugary sweet tea and offering Emma biscuits which my daughter doesn't take.

It's as if we've been bereaved, which is ridiculous. The people they should be looking after are the Grant family. No one is grieving in this house – well, not yet, anyway. I am terrified of seeing Eve's parents out on the street when I go to the shops – I don't go anywhere else for fear that I will see her, the mother, her wide tearful eyes and her broken heart. I dreamed about her last night for the first time. The *other* other woman. What does she think of us? Does she believe Callum did it? I'm frightened too of the search party combing the area – part of me wants to join in but I know I wouldn't be allowed. On the news they said they're searching the beaches, and I know that means they're looking for a body.

They've said Callum can come home today, but I've told

him point-blank that I don't want to see him. The lawyers told us that it was the wrong move, that we needed to put a brave face on it, show the public a 'united front'. Patrick O'Connell keeps phoning me, attempting to change my mind for Callum's sake. My own solicitor, a smart, diminutive woman called Olivia Brady, seems to be in agreement. I hired her myself, on Maria's advice, called her after my interview at the station. She specialises in family law too, has been telling me the ins and outs of what could happen if my husband goes to jail.

'But I don't want a united front,' I said to them both, in a flash of honesty where I forgot my promise to Emma, my goal of keeping our family unit together. 'My husband's been sleeping around behind my back for however many months. I'm not feeling very united at all, to be honest.'

Olivia smirked a bit at that, but I was deadly serious. Everyone knows now – the police have spoken to the women in my book group, verified that I was there. They all said exactly what I'd wanted them to. Some of them texted me afterwards, told me the police questions were intense, as if I too am a suspect, as if I too could be on trial. I didn't reply to any of them – I've been trying to ignore my phone since we got back from France, not wanting to see the faux concern in the messages from the uber-mothers; they'll be desperate for gossip, the lot of them. I've told work that I need more leave, just for a few more days. Said I needed to be at home with my daughter, that I'd check in where I could.

I can't manage anything at the moment, not whilst this is going on. I wonder when it will stop, when my total and utter humiliation will finally be complete. Rosa, Callum's cousin, phoned me last night, asking me if it was all true. I could hear her newborn baby crying in the background.

'I don't know,' I kept saying to her, 'I don't know what's happening. I don't know any more than you do.'

Mum's been kept in the dark; Maria says the nurses are being very understanding. 'We pay them enough,' she said. 'Though you ought to think about going to visit soon, S.'

Emma's furious with me. 'Why won't you let Dad come home?' she screamed at me about an hour ago, her body convulsing with rage. Maria tried to calm her down, put her arms around her.

'Dad is coming home, you'll see,' she said, but Emma carried on crying, screaming at me as though I were the devil incarnate. It began to scare me, the expression on her face; there was a wildness to it, a madness I hadn't seen before in my little girl. In the end I left her alone for a while; she went up to her room and put music on, like she always does when she doesn't want to talk to us any more.

Maria and I stayed downstairs; I put the kettle on but Maria poured herself a vodka instead. We sat at the kitchen table, the table full of our family life – the odds and sods drawer stuffed with old phone chargers, pictures that Emma did when she was at primary school that somehow I can't bear to throw away, discarded chapsticks that belong to me.

I keep glancing at the door, as though I'm expecting Callum to walk in at any moment. It's too hot in the house but I can't open the windows; every time I do we can hear the press, who have somehow got wind of the fact that he might be home today and seem to have doubled in capacity in the last few hours.

'It's like being trapped,' says Maria, 'trapped in your own home.' She pauses, takes a long sip of her drink. I don't point out that we're actually in my home, not hers. 'Are you going to let him come back, S?'

She's watching me carefully and I shift a little in my chair, feeling my back sticky with sweat against the chair. The doorbell goes outside, the sound echoing through the house, and all of a sudden I feel defeated, as though there is no point in fighting it all. This is my life now.

'Where else would he go?' I say dully, and Maria nods thoughtfully.

'Not as if he can stay at his mistress's house, is it?' she says, and despite everything I see the ghost of a smile on her face, a naughty smile, like the one she used to do when we were young. She'd do it when our mother's back was turned, if we'd done something we shouldn't have; her face would crack open into a little grin, showing her bright white teeth. I'd always been a little bit mesmerised by it, truth be told. I felt like she was letting me in on a secret every time she smiled. My mother didn't like it – 'Wipe that smile off your face' she used to say, and we'd force ourselves to do straight faces, biting our lips to keep from bursting out laughing. I wasn't very good at holding it for long; I usually cracked and my mother would shout at me, but Maria, she was better. It takes a lot to crack my sister.

'Do you think he did do it, S?' she asks suddenly, and I'm so wrong-footed by the question that my mind goes blank; the words won't come.

The doorbell rings again, more insistently this time, and Yvonne appears in the doorway to the kitchen, clutching a mug of tea and looking worried.

'Sorry to interrupt you, Mrs Dillon, but I've had word that

it's your husband outside. He's at the front door. I think we'd better let him in.'

Maria looks horrified and a spike of panic rips through me; I hadn't really expected him to turn up like this, not without due warning. I am not prepared to see him. Neither is Emma.

'I'll go,' Maria says, 'they're not interested in me,' and I watch as her tall, slim figure follows Yvonne out of the room, towards the hallway and the front door.

'Emma,' I say aloud, alone in the kitchen, and I hurry to the foot of the stairs, trying to make sense of the jumble that is my thoughts.

She's got the door to her bedroom shut and the music is playing; she probably hasn't even heard the bell ring, or the sound of the vultures on the street. Carefully, I push it open, trying to rearrange my features into something resembling calm.

'Emma?'

She's lying on the bed, staring straight up at the ceiling. The expression on her face is oddly blank and I feel a jolt of unease; her body looks odd, laid out like that, with nothing to distract her except the music.

'Are you – are you OK?' I say, and she doesn't seem to register me at first, her eyes continue to look up at the pale cream ceiling, as though lost in a world that I cannot see.

'Em?'

On my second try, she snaps out of it, her vision sliding over to meet my eyes. She sits up slightly, propping herself on her elbows. Taylor Swift's voice fills up the room, too loud and at odds with the strange, stilted atmosphere between us.

'Your dad's here, he's at the door,' I say, and it's as though a light switch goes off inside her brain – in an instant she is up, off the bed and past me, rushing out of the room and down the stairs, leaving the music blaring in her wake. She slips past my side like a ghost; I barely feel her presence.

For a second after she's vanished I stand there, feeling completely invisible. Then I ready myself to go downstairs and face my husband.

*

He looks better than he did the last time I saw him, but still, the man in front of me now is not the same as the man I knew for fifteen years. It's only been a few days but his expression is hardened, closed. Emma is clinging to him as though he is a life raft, her arms wrapped around his middle, the way she used to greet him when he came home from work, back when she was six years old. But she is sixteen now, and their bond remains the same. Unbreakable. I feel a splash of frustration – what more does he have to do to fall from grace in her eyes?

Maria is standing by the door, talking to Yvonne. The front door is closed but through the window I catch sight of the reporters, a few of them smoking, no doubt stubbing out the butts on my doorstep. The sun is blazing through the windows, but inside the house it is dark; most of the curtains are closed.

Callum and I stare at each other.

'Come in then,' I say eventually, my voice sounding wooden. 'You'd better get away from the door.' He steps towards me, and I can't help it – a spasm of fear unfurls itself slowly in my chest.

Chapter Twenty-Seven

Eve has fallen asleep. I reach for her hair, very softly, my fingers stroking the blonde curls like lamb's wool under my touch. Jenny gets to do this every night, I think to myself; she gets to hold Eve close and watch her grow, watch her change just a tiny bit every single day. I thought I'd do that when I was pregnant, get one of those apps that monitors the baby's development. *Your baby is the size of a walnut. Your baby is the size of a grapefruit.* Little pictures on the screen.

For a few weeks after our conversation in April, I thought Callum was going to change his mind. I was overly affectionate towards him, playing the role of girlfriend at every given opportunity, not making a fuss when he was late to meet me, cooking for him in my flat on nights when he told Siobhan he was working late. He hadn't mentioned the baby since that first evening, and yet still, my deluded mind told me that things would change, that he would come to his senses, that once he began to see clearly, he would surely realise how brilliant this baby could be. It could bring us closer, I thought, it could *legitimise* what we had. I let myself imagine it – just for a minute – a world where I wouldn't have to hide Callum's existence from my friends, where I wouldn't have to think about his other life, and where I wouldn't have to compete with his daughter for attention. We could get a place together, kit out a room for the baby – I've always thought yellow would be nice for a baby's room – and cement our life together. He could see Emma whenever he wanted, and Siobhan – well, Siobhan would just fade into the background. Our roles would be reversed.

One Monday, I went for a blood test at Ipswich Hospital. I was alone – of course – but my plan was to show Callum the result when I got back. I knew – I *knew* – that once he saw the official reality of what had happened, once he saw the reality of what we had made together, he would realise how much there was to be gained by us having this child. I wasn't going to find out in advance whether it was a girl or a boy, I thought to myself on the way to the hospital; I wasn't going to find out because I wanted it to be a surprise. Secretly, though, I had always longed for a girl – a little girl that would have my hair and his eyes. I've always liked the name Tabitha.

'First time?' the nurse said, drawing the blood, and I'd nodded, trying not to wince at the sharp sting of the needle.

'Where's Dad today?' she said. She had a nice accent – Northern, comforting, and I warmed to her immediately.

'Oh, he couldn't make it,' I said, and I thought I caught a flicker of pity cross her features so I quickly followed this up with a lie: 'He's picking me up afterwards, though. We're going out for a nice dinner to celebrate!'

'Oh!' she said, looking relieved and immediately perking up. 'Lucky you, pet. That sounds great.'

I lay back, feeling much more comfortable as she bustled about with the paperwork.

'All done!' she said cheerily after a few minutes, 'we'll see you soon, Ms Harvey.' On my way out, she handed me a pack of notes, all the information I'd need for my first twelve-week scan, and gave me a little pat on the shoulder. For some reason, her kindness had made me want to cry. *I have fooled you*, I thought to myself, *I've fooled you into thinking I really am the person I want to be.*

*

The ultimatum came that night, in my apartment. Callum wasn't one for beating about the bush; he was a direct, to-the-point person, and when we first met it was one of the quantities I most admired about him. I've never been particularly decisive.

'Caroline,' he said, 'I can't stay with you if you keep this baby.' He delivered the words with an earnest look in his eye, as though it was a fact rather than a decision over which he did of course have full control. His words stopped me in my tracks, made my heart sink like a stone.

He came closer to me, to where I was sitting on the sofa, a blanket over my knees, playing at being a normal mother-to-be, taking care of myself even though the pregnancy was in such fledgling, early stages.

'You do understand,' he said softly, 'I can't do it to Emma.' He'd paused. 'I know what I'm asking of you is hard,' he told me, as if we were talking about a tricky crossword puzzle rather than a life-altering decision. For some reason, Jenny's words floated into my head. *Misogynist, noun: a person who dislikes, despises or is strongly prejudiced against women.*

I'd stared at him, almost uncomprehending, and he'd sat down beside me, put a hand on my legs. I felt icy cold even though I had the blanket on, as though I'd been submerged in water.

'I've got something to suggest to you,' he carried on, 'an offer, of sorts. To show you how much I care. How much this means to me.'

I could see his lips moving but I was already struggling to focus on what he was saying. Already my mind was spinning into a world of horrible imaginings – a world in which Callum left me alone in the flat, pregnant and unloved. A world in which I faced the humiliation that would bring, and the hardship of bringing up a child whose father refused to acknowledge its existence.

Suddenly, his face was right beside mine, his lips next to my ear. I could feel his breath, warm and sweet.

'If you'll do this for me, Caro, I'll leave Siobhan. I mean it. We can be together, a proper couple. No more lying, no more sneaking around.' He'd paused. 'But I can't give you a baby. I can't do that to Emma. Another child – it would break her heart. She'd feel as though she was being replaced.'

I stared at him, not saying anything. Gently, he kissed the side of my face, trailed little kisses towards my lips.

'Think about it,' he whispered. 'I know I'm asking a lot of you. But I'll do it, I'll leave Siobhan. If you're prepared to be reasonable about the baby.'

He pulled back a little and smiled at me, his head tipped slightly to one side as if everything he was saying *was* reasonable, as though it would be the rational thing to do. My heart was thudding. For over a year, all I had wanted was for him to leave Siobhan – I had asked him to, I had even, one particularly sad night, begged him to. And now here he was, offering it to me on a plate.

'I'd still want to see Emma,' he carried on, 'of course. But Siobhan and I could work something out.' He shook his head. 'They'd never forgive me for having another child, but this way… well, this way we could be happy. Really happy. Just the two of us.' He kissed me again, this time on the lips. 'Isn't that what you've always wanted, Caro? We could go on a mini-break, have some time together, figure out how it's all going to work.'

I felt vulnerable, unmasked by my own wanting. Of course I wanted us to be together. Us being together would catapult me into the world of coupledom, of legitimacy – I wouldn't have to spend weekends alone in the flat whilst my friends and their husbands cosied up with boxsets, I wouldn't always have to be the odd one out at parties. But could I sacrifice a child? Give up the thought of ever being a parent?

As if he could read my mind, Callum started speaking again. 'After a while,' he said, 'after a while, who knows? Emma might come to see you as a mother figure too. She and Siobhan aren't that close. It's me she's closest to. And as long as she knew nothing was changing between she and I, as long as she knew my attention wasn't going to go to a newborn, well…' He tailed off. 'She'd be OK with it.' He nodded, as though reassuring himself. 'She might even be happy for me.'

*

On the day I had the abortion, I was wearing loose, pyjama-like clothes and I had never wanted a mother so badly. My

210

own mother died when I was sixteen, so you'd think by now I would be used to this strange, untethered state of existence, and usually I am, but on the day of the abortion I wanted nothing more than to have her back. I closed my eyes after it was over, and let my head fall back against the seat of Callum's car. Neither of us spoke at first – I didn't feel up to it – but after about ten minutes he began to talk. His words tumbled out of his mouth, faster than I'd seen him speak before; reams and reams of justification. As we pulled up outside my flat, he looked at me, and just for a minute I thought I saw a flash of guilt. But I was so pathetic, so hopeful, that when he said he'd come inside, and tenderly helped me out of the car, I was lost once again.

At least I'll have Callum, I remember thinking to myself as I leaned on him, as we walked to my flat, but I couldn't help feeling like I'd somehow made a bargain with the devil. A silly phrase, really. But that's what it felt like.

Chapter Twenty-Eight

Ipswich
17th August
Siobhan

Inside the house, once the front door is shut behind us, blocking out the press, the atmosphere is charged. For the last few days, I haven't really been paying much attention to the general upkeep of it all, and I see Callum's eyes glance over the pile of dirty dishes from our meal last night, the remnants of slowly congealing food. The fact that we're trying not to open the windows because of the press makes everything worse – the bin in the corner is beginning to overflow, and there is a small row of glass bottles lined up next to it. A fly buzzes dully around the rim of a Merlot.

'Christ,' he says, not one to beat about the bush, 'this place is a tip.' He goes straight to the fridge and pulls out a beer – luckily neither Maria nor myself have touched those – before turning back to look at us. Emma looks like she's going to cry, and I know she doesn't like seeing her father in this sort of state. I watch their eyes connect and I see his face suddenly soften.

'Come here, Ems,' he says, and she walks towards him, her face small and white. Somehow, she looks younger than ever. He folds her into his arms, and I want so badly to join in too, but I can't – it's as though my legs are rooted to the spot. Maria looks at me, and I see a flicker of compassion in her eyes. Not for the first time, I feel truly grateful that my sister is here.

It is she who breaks the silence.

'What have the police said?' she asks him, going over to the kitchen table and pulling out a couple of chairs for us to sit on. Gingerly, I move to sit down, realising as I do so that my whole body aches, a horrible dull ache that makes me want to crawl under the duvet and never wake up. Well, that's not quite true – I would like to wake up, I'd like to wake up in a different life, a life where my daughter loves me rather than shuts me out, a life where my husband hasn't been having an affair, a life where the media aren't camped outside my house because they think the man opposite me might be a murderer. Oh, and a child abductor too.

Reluctantly, Callum lets go of Emma. 'Go upstairs for a bit, Em,' he says, 'or, you know what, why don't you go outside? You look like you've not seen daylight in days. It's lovely and warm out there.' I flash him a warning look – the last thing I want is my daughter getting doorstepped by the press – but he ignores me. 'It's not healthy for you to be cooped up like this,' he continues, 'why don't you give one of your school mates a call? Go do something normal? God knows, we'll all go mad if we force ourselves to stay under house arrest just because of a few bloody hacks.'

He gives her a little grin, and against my better judgement I start to wonder if he might be right, if Emma would be better off getting back to normality a little bit. Whatever that means, anyway.

'I could call Molly?' she says hopefully, already picking

her mobile up off the table. Its rose gold case glints at me, like a little gateway to the outside world. I shudder inside, thinking of the things people will be saying about us on social media. What the uber-mothers will be thinking about me.

'Sure, call Molly,' Callum says, his expression brightening.

'Molly? I don't think I've met Molly,' Maria says, looking questioningly at Emma.

'They're at school together, aren't you Ems?' I say, then worry immediately that I'm talking down to her, as if she is a child. *But she is a child,* part of me screams inside, *she's my child and she shouldn't be having to go through all this.* God knows what the psychology books would say about our family now.

She presses a button on her phone and disappears into the next room, her step obviously lighter.

'Why haven't you been letting her out of the house?' Callum says, glaring at me, 'she must have been going mad cooped up like this.'

'Callum, in case you haven't noticed,' I say, exasperated, 'the bloody world's press is currently sitting outside our door. I don't want Emma getting caught up in all that, I don't want her to see the things people are saying about – about that woman, about the baby, about you.'

He rolls his eyes. 'Siobhan, don't you think she's already seen it all? She's sixteen, for God's sake! She's got it all on her phone. There's nothing a couple of newspaper journos could say that'll shock her when she's got Twitter in her pocket.'

He takes a long sip of his beer. Maria leans forward, trying to take control.

'What have the police said, Callum?' she asks in a low voice, not wanting Emma to hear.

He sighs. 'They don't really have anything against me,' he says heavily, 'the whole thing is ridiculous. I've told them I was in the studio that night, that you and Emma saw the light on, and you'd have heard me come in later. All true, of course. And I appreciate you sticking to it.' He looks at me, and now he does at least look a little admonished, a little less hostile. I feel the guilt again – he doesn't know what I said to McVey, he doesn't know I ruined his alibi. 'Look, there's no point in me denying the affair altogether, Siobhan, but—' He breaks off, suddenly, and glances at Maria.

There's a beat of silence.

'Look, Maria,' he says, 'I know you've been very helpful to my wife, and to Emma, these last few days when everything's been so up in the air, but really, you don't have to stay. I'm out now, at least for the time being, and I can look after things. We don't want to keep you away from your own life any longer than we already have – I'm sure you've got things that you've had to put on hold while this circus unfolded!' He attempts a sort of laugh, to lighten the atmosphere, but my sister is staring at him, stony-faced.

I don't know what to do.

'We do appreciate how much you've helped,' Callum says, continuing because Maria hasn't said a word, 'but there's no need for you to be here if you don't want to be – you could head back to France, or to Woodbridge. I can call you a taxi, seeing as the car's still in France. Or you could go back out there! Hell, if you go to France we might even be able to join you in a day or so when all this has blown over, finish off that bloody holiday!'

The joke, if that's what it is, falls flat around the table.

Maria, on the chair next to me, is stiff, her back straight as a rod and her hands clasped neatly together on the table, as if she doesn't trust herself to let them loose.

'Of course,' I jump in, worried he's offended her, 'Callum's not saying you're not welcome, Maria, you're welcome for as long as you like, it's more that we don't want to impose...' I trail off, realising as I do how much I want her to stay. Callum is acting as though everything is normal, as though we are husband and wife not wanting a guest to outstay their welcome, a team against an outsider, a third wheel. Only it's not like that at all, is it? The bond Callum and I had, the vows we made to each other fifteen years ago in a church, all that is broken now.

It's broken because of Caroline Harvey.

'In fact,' I say, my voice coming out overly loud, 'I want you to stay, Maria. I could use the support.'

I don't look at Callum.

'Of course I'll stay,' my sister says, as if she has simply been waiting for me to come to my senses and confirm what she wants to hear.

Although we are not looking at each other, I can almost sense the connection between Maria and I. Because I've admitted it now, haven't I. I've admitted I need her. And perhaps she needs me too.

'Right, right, fine,' Callum says suddenly, as if knowing he's fighting a losing battle. 'In that case though, do you think you could give me and my wife a moment alone together, please Maria? Or would that be too much to ask?'

He's being rude, but my sister merely inclines her head, her hair dipping down towards the table, then pushes back her chair and gets to her feet.

'I'll go sort Emma out,' she says, before leaving the room. There is something so graceful about her, despite all of this madness. I wish I could see inside her head, see what she's thinking.

And then she is gone, and I am left alone with my husband.

Chapter Twenty-Nine

Ipswich
17th August
DS Wildy

The whole lot of them are gathered in the incident room, DCI Gillian McVey at the front. She looks ruffled, which is unusual for her, and which usually means that Superintendent Khan has been in touch. Alex stands with Dave Bolton and Tom Smith; his colleagues look as exhausted as he feels. Callum Dillon's release this afternoon has put a damper on the entire investigation – Alex watched him and his smarmy lawyer shaking hands outside on the street, the smug grin on Callum's face as he shrugged on his jacket to leave. Perhaps feeling Alex's eyes on him, Callum had turned around to face him through the double glass doors, raised a hand in a sarcastic wave. Alex hadn't returned the gesture, had instead clenched his fists and moved away. Even if the man isn't a killer, there's no doubt that he's a slimeball, an adulterer, and a nasty piece of work despite the outward charm he puts on for his colleagues and his women. If only they could lock people up for that, he thinks.

He's booked in a couple of PCs to keep an undercover car on the road outside the Dillon house for the night, primarily to satisfy the DCI.

On the wall behind DCI McVey there's their timeline, drawn in marker pen on the huge whiteboard that dominates that side of the room. He stares past Gillian to where the photos of Caroline Harvey are pinned to the board, her face staring out at them, unseeing. He hates looking at pictures of the dead – not something he'd really admit to the team here, but the truth nonetheless. Next to her, there's an image of baby Eve, dressed in a blue parka, it must have been taken in winter. You can just about see her hair poking out of the hood. People always say this about their own babies and most of the time it's not true, but in this case, objectively speaking, Eve Grant really does look like an angel.

'Right,' Gillian says, clapping her hands to address the room as though they're a bunch of disruptive schoolkids, which, on a bad day, isn't far from the truth.

'The Super has spoken.' DS Bolton nudges Alex in the ribs. The superintendent is possibly the only one Gillian McVey is afraid of, or at least cowed by.

'Given the fact that we've been forced to release Callum Dillon without charge, and the lack of evidence against him, despite his wife admitting she didn't hear him come in that night, the Super wants us to reassess everything, right from the beginning – and we need to delve deeper into Caroline's own history. Her mental health, her upbringing. We need to know if she was capable of causing harm to Eve, which in turn could've led the Grant parents to kill her – either accidentally or on purpose. This isn't what I would necessarily suggest we focus on, but...' She looks around the room, before coming back to settle on Alex.

'Wildy, you take the lead on that one, seeing as it's your

theory, and Bolton, help him out. I want the rest of you to field the hotline for news of Eve, continuing the search of the area, liaising with the guys in Rouen. No stone unturned, people. We have to find this child.' She clicks her fingers at a couple of the officers. 'Follow up the sighting in Brighton. Find out how far along the beaches they've got. Keep going, people. We're not stopping until we find Eve.'

*

The house where Caroline Harvey grew up is, not to put too fine a point on it, a bit grim. DS Wildy and DS Bolton make the drive from Ipswich to Stowmarket in just under forty minutes.

'Bloody sat nav says twenty minutes,' Bolton grumbles. 'I thought these things were supposed to account for traffic these days?'

'At least we're here now,' Alex says, 'though finding somewhere to park might be a different matter.'

Fifteen minutes later, they're finally knocking on the door of 25 Bircham Road, where Caroline's father, Christopher Harvey, is now the sole occupant.

'Apparently he took the news of his daughter's death somewhat on the chin, which raises questions in itself,' Alex says quickly, keeping his voice low. 'Gillian said he looked as though it hadn't quite hit him yet by the time they had to leave.'

There's no time to say more because the front door is opening, and Bolton and Alex are met with an elderly man, dressed curiously smartly in a grey jacket and trousers, accompanied by a pale blue shirt.

'Mr Harvey,' Alex says, 'DS Wildy, Suffolk Police. And this is my colleague, DS Bolton.'

He doesn't look particularly surprised to see them, but his features do change – a wave of sadness seems to pass over them, a downturning of the mouth and a drooping of the eyes. Alex feels a stab of pity.

'May we come in?'

'Of course, of course,' he says, moving to one side, wincing a little as if the movement is painful. They move through the door and into a dim corridor, brushing past a pile of junk mail on the floor.

'Shall I get this for you?' Alex asks, stooping down to pick up the mail, and the old man nods.

'Thank you – my back isn't what it used to be, I'm afraid, and I just haven't been able to face bending down to scoop all that rubbish up. Looks a mess, I know, but I don't want to risk another fall. I had one last year, you see, and it's not an experience to repeat.'

He takes the pile of mail from Alex's outstretched hand, but not before the policeman has caught sight of a couple of NHS-branded envelopes, the one on top with the word 'URGENT' in red capitals emblazoned across the top.

'Probably all nonsense anyway,' Mr Harvey mumbles, his liver-spotted hand clutching it by his side.

They follow him down the corridor and to the right, into a sitting room that again is strangely dark. The curtains are closed, and the room has an odd, unlived in feel, despite the fact that they know Christopher Harvey has lived here for over thirty-five years.

They sit themselves down on the sofa, which is positioned

only half a metre away from the small television – clearly Mr Harvey is struggling with his eyesight as well as his back.

'Shall I make us all a quick tea?' Bolton asks, and Mr Harvey gives the ghost of a smile for the first time, then raises a slightly trembling hand and points him in the direction of the kitchen.

'Mr Harvey,' Alex begins as they hear the sound of the kettle beginning to whistle in the next room, 'we're here today because we have a few follow-up questions about your daughter, Caroline.' He pauses, inclines his head. 'I'd also like to say how very sorry I am for your loss.'

To his horror, the old man's eyes begin to shine with tears, and Alex wonders if it's true – whether Gillian had in fact left him in a state of shock, whether his non-reaction to the news of her death was symptomatic of it not hitting him yet. Now that it's had time to sink in, perhaps they are encountering a different man altogether.

'Here we are!' DS Bolton comes back into the room, clutching three cups of steaming hot tea, rather precariously balanced against his chest. 'Sorry,' he says, 'there was no milk in, so it's black for today.'

Alex takes another glance around the room, wondering if Christopher Harvey is more infirm that any of them have realised – is he able to get out and about any more, he wonders? It's so at odds with the way he is dressed, the strangely smart suit.

'Are you going out later on, Mr Harvey?' he asks politely as the three of them take their first sips of scalding hot tea, but the old man shakes his head, runs a hand down the breastplate of his jacket.

'No, no,' he says, giving that ghost of a smile again, 'this, well, it's just habit, I suppose. So many years of going into an office, you know, I don't know what else to put on. When Elsie died, I just sort of carried on putting on the same thing, going to work, trying to make ends meet, you know, and then when Caroline left…' he tails off, takes another sip of his tea even though it's far too hot.

'Nothing wrong with a good suit,' Alex says, setting his tea down on the table in front of them and smiling at Mr Harvey, 'and if you're not going out, we'd appreciate an hour or so of your time, to have a chat about Caroline, as I said. Would that be OK?'

'Have you – is there news?' Mr Harvey looks at them both, his eyes slightly milky in the dim light of the sitting room. Alex is itching to turn on the lamp that he can see in the corner, to open the curtains and give this place a bit of air. It is stiflingly warm – does the old man actually have the heating on? In August?

'I'm afraid there's no firm news as yet, Mr Harvey,' Bolton says, 'but we are piecing together a picture of what happened on the night of August 10th and we'd be very grateful for any assistance you might be able to give us.'

'Of course,' the old man says. 'I still can't quite believe it – it was a terrible shock, you see. Even though we hadn't spoken for a while, Caroline is – was – she was my only daughter. My only child.' He passes a hand across his face, looking suddenly ten years older than he is already. 'After Elsie – my wife – died, I suppose I sort of let things drift with Caroline. I was – I was grieving, you see, I didn't really know how to cope without my Elsie. We'd been sweethearts since we were sixteen.'

'What can you tell us about your daughter, Mr Harvey?' Alex asks him. 'What can you tell us about Caroline?'

'She loved drawing,' Mr Harvey says, slowly, 'she would always have a pencil in her hand, you know, Elsie used to tell her not to bite on the end of them but it didn't stop her.' That ghost of a smile again. 'She would do pictures, pictures of us, pictures of animals, she'd take her little pad of paper and some coloured pencils and disappear for hours. She'd show us everything when she got back, and we knew she was good at it. Well, Elsie did. She was good at spotting things like that.' He takes a sip of his tea; the shaking of his hand has become more pronounced, and Alex wonders if he's been officially diagnosed. Perhaps that's what the unopened NHS letters are for.

'And she became an illustrator,' Bolton says. 'You must have been very proud.'

He blinks a bit, then nods his head. 'Yes,' he says, 'yes, of course I was. It was a bit – difficult by that point, her mother wasn't around any more, I suppose I didn't... I suppose I didn't take as much notice of the little one as I should have. But I knew she was doing well, you know, the school would tell me how talented she was at her drawings.' He brightens for a second. 'I think I've still got some of them up in the loft, you know. Some of her drawings, the ones she used to do as a kiddie. Did you want to see them, officers?'

The policemen exchange glances.

'We'd love to,' Alex says at last, 'but perhaps we could all go up there, after we've finished our tea, had a bit more of a chat.' The disappointment on the old man's face is obvious. 'Would that be OK?'

'Oh yes, yes... they're very good. You'll see.'

DS Bolton clears his throat. 'Mr Harvey,' he says, 'you told our colleagues that the last time you saw Caroline was six or seven months ago.' He spreads his palms, hands open. 'To me, that seems an awfully long time considering she was only down the road in Ipswich. Had the two of you had a falling out, anything like that?'

'Falling out? No, no.' Christopher Harvey's face darkens, or it could just be the shadow from the one beam of light that is beginning to stream in through a crack in the curtains.

'Would you normally go months without her visiting you, even?' Alex asks, trying to be gentle. 'Did the pair of you speak often, on the phone?'

He frowns, as though trying to remember. 'I did call her,' he says at last, 'I called her a few times – my eyesight's not what it used to be, mind, but I wrote down her number on a card, in felt pen so I could see it, nice and big, you know. These new phones – I struggle to see the numbers. Everything's so small.'

Alex glances around the room, his eyes alighting on a dusty-looking cream telephone, standing on a small wooden table by the window. Next to it is propped a row of A5 cards, with numbers written on them in black marker pen. DOCTOR STOWMARKET, says the one closest to them, and then, beside it, CAROLINE. He imagines Christopher Harvey painstakingly writing out the digits, pressing the phone to his ear to connect with his child. The sight of the cards is, somehow, unbearably sad.

'How did Caroline seem to you, Mr Harvey?' DS Bolton asks, leaning forward slightly on the sofa, towards where their interviewee is sitting, his body curved into an ageing armchair that perhaps used to be pink.

'She was a good girl,' he murmured, 'she was a good drawer.'

'Yes,' Bolton says, trying and failing to disguise the flicker of impatience in his voice now, 'yes, you told us about her drawings. But other than that, how did she seem?' He pauses. 'Did she ever talk to you about a partner at all, a man she might have been seeing?'

At this, his head jerks up. 'Is that what you think happened? Some bastard hurt my Caroline?'

The outburst is unexpected, and at odds with his thus-far quiet demeanour.

'We are investigating several lines of inquiry to find out what happened to your daughter that night, Mr Harvey,' DS Wildy says, 'but it's crucial for us to understand more about your daughter as part of that process. What kind of person she was, who she spent her time with, what she wanted out of life.'

'She was a kind person,' Mr Harvey says, 'she was always kind. She gave people too many chances.' He stops, hesitating.

'Go on,' Bolton says.

'She wasn't good at – at setting boundaries,' Christopher says at last, 'her mother used to say that, she used to worry a lot about little Caroline.'

He pauses for a second, puts a hand to his head. 'It was hard for her without her mother,' he says at last, 'I should have paid more attention to her. If I had – maybe we wouldn't be here.' His voice chokes a little, and Alex can't help it; he is somewhat relieved to know the old man is capable of showing emotion around his only daughter's death. Even if it is too little, too late.

'She wanted a family,' Mr Harvey says, regaining control of his emotions, looking the officers straight in the face. 'She was a kind person, like I say, but she was also – she was also a jealous one. She wanted things that other people had.' He sighs. 'I think it all stemmed from losing her mother, to be honest. It was hard for her, being the only child; she didn't have anyone to rub her edges off, I suppose.'

The officers exchange glances. 'What makes you say she wanted a family?' Bolton says gently.

'Oh,' he says, 'just little things, you know. She was lonely, it was obvious – she wanted nothing more than to find someone, get married, have children of her own. I think she wanted to make up for her own childhood, perhaps. Start again.'

Bolton raises his eyebrows. 'Nothing wrong with that,' he says, and Christopher shakes his head.

'No, nothing wrong with that,' he muses, almost to himself, 'but she never quite got it. There was a gap in her life, you see. A gap I couldn't fill. We were such a small family, a shattered one, really. Just her and I, rattling around. And nothing ever really changed, no matter how much she wanted it to.'

'Did you ever get to speak to her properly about it?' Bolton asks, and Christopher shakes his head.

'She did see a psychiatrist, once or twice,' he says, slowly, 'I remember being glad she was talking to someone, at least. They seemed to think it was all to do with losing her mother, you know, trying to replace something, fill that void. I don't think anything really ever worked.'

On the table in front of them, the men's teas have gone cold.

Chapter Thirty

Ipswich
10th August: The night of the murder
Caroline

Callum didn't stick to his promise. Even now, the base fact of that makes me feel sick – the abject cruelty of it. He simply went back on his word, once the baby – my baby – had been dealt with. We went on a mini-break and had a lovely time in Norfolk, and I believed everything he said, but then a few days after we got back he changed his mind. Emma was too volatile, he told me, too fragile, and on top of that it would hurt his career prospects. People like a family man, Caro, he told me, as though I was supposed to understand, and the next day he bought me a necklace, silver and delicate, as if a piece of jewellery would make up for the unbearable betrayal. And that was when I knew. It was over, because it had to be. I had been foolish, naïve. I had made a terrible error in judgement. I know that now.

It was after that that I became even more obsessive about babies, about what I had given up.

I'm still watching baby Eve sleep, enjoying the little rise and fall of her chest, when I hear the ping of my phone from the coffee table in the next room. Carefully so as not to wake her,

I close the door and go to pick it up. It is almost eight-thirty; it must be Jenny texting to say she's on her way home from the hospital. I wonder vaguely how Rick's mother is.

But it isn't Jenny. It's the same unknown number from before. *I know what you've been doing.* That's all it says. Only six words, but it's enough to make my blood run cold. Feeling a horrible splash of panic, I go over to the heater and turn it up full blast, before pouring myself another small glass of red wine. My heart is thudding and before I can think too much about it, I hit reply.

Who are you?

Immediately, the three little dots flash up; the unknown number is typing. But then they stop, and the screen is blank again. Maybe it's the wine, but I'm starting to feel angry. Who is it threatening me like this? They can only be talking about Callum. An image of Siobhan flashes into my mind, Siobhan with her long legs and her teenage daughter and her flowing brown hair. Oh, it's not that I've actually met Siobhan. But I've seen her, I've watched them together. That time at Christmas, and another time, too, when they were coming home from Emma's posh private school. The perfect little family, except that he's been sleeping with me the whole time because his wife clearly bores him.

Don't be unkind, Caroline. It's my mother's voice that jumps into my head, like it sometimes does if I'm feeling particularly unsettled. Or tipsy. I shouldn't have had that last glass of wine.

Going to the tap, I run myself a glass of cold water. If Jenny thinks I've been drinking she won't let me watch Eve again, and at the thought of that, my heart gives a funny little squeeze. Eve likes me now, I know she does. She trusts me. Soon, I might even be able to say that she *needs* me.

As if on cue, I hear a little mewling noise from the next room. I abandon my water, the glass only half drunk, and leaving my phone with the horrible message on it behind, I rush into the bedroom, where the cot is. It's still so funny seeing it there, so out of place amongst my belongings. It makes a lovely change, I think to myself, to see this room inhabited by another person, to see a bit of life amongst the mess of my things. My double bed that's only used by me now, my bookshelves full of novels only I will ever read, the photographs in frames that are sparse – there's one of me and Callum that I took last year, but I've turned it to face downwards, I did it the day he told me about the holiday in France. There's a small one of my mother right by my bed – I look at it sometimes before I go to sleep at night. In it, she's gazing straight at the camera, probably at Dad, but she's not really smiling, it's only a twitch of the lips. I've often wondered what she was thinking at that moment, the moment the shutter snapped. Was she happy? It was before I was born, Dad said. All I've ever wanted is someone to share a space with. A family.

When I touch her, Eve is very hot. Despite the window being open, there isn't much of a breeze; the night is too still. It's still light outside, but the day is beginning to fade; a glance at my watch tells me it's almost quarter to nine. I feel her little fore-head, the droplets of sweat forming underneath my palm. She's wearing a pink romper suit that Jenny brought her in – not what I'd choose but never mind – and I tut under my breath, wondering why she hasn't dressed her more appropriately for the weather.

'Come on princess,' I say, gently easing the covers back off her, giving her little body room to breathe. Feeling her skin against mine, I feel a spurt of worry – perhaps this is more than it being hot, perhaps she's ill? I try to think back over what Jenny said when she left, did she say anything about if Eve starts to burn up? Again, I wish I hadn't drank the three glasses of red wine; my brain feels slow-moving and sluggish.

'What's the matter, baby?' I ask her, but Eve's little face is scrunching up, and tears are beginning to fill her big brown eyes.

'Mummy will be home soon,' I say, then regret the words because I want her to want *me*, not Jenny. 'I've got you, I've got you,' I whisper, putting my lips close to the little whorl of her ear. It is tiny, perfect, like a shell.

That's what my baby's ear would have looked like.

Chapter Thirty-One

Ipswich
10th August: The night of the murder
Caroline

It's been ten minutes and she won't stop crying. I am pacing around the flat, cursing its size. She's kicked off her little pink socks in frustration, so her bare feet are flailing unhappily in the air, despite me trying to hold her tightly to my chest, calm her down with my proximity. It's not working.

I've tried giving her the pink dummy Jenny brought with her (why is everything you buy your daughter pink, Jenny?) but she keeps spitting it out, and now I'm worried it's dirty because it's landed on the floor so many times, and my floors aren't exactly that clean. It's been a while since I had the hoover out, put it that way. I pick it up and stick it in the cot, so that at least it's on the clean sheets.

'Don't cry, Eve, please don't cry,' I say to her, but still she wails, and all the time she's becoming hotter and hotter. I can feel the pressure beginning to build up inside my head, forming a tight band of tension across my forehead and the back of my skull. What's the matter with me? Why can't I do this? I bet she doesn't normally cry like this; I think of Rick and Jenny in their lovely house and somehow cannot picture them in this situation. It's me, I think to myself, it's always me, I always get it wrong.

In desperation, I pick up my phone, but I don't know who to call, and all I see is that nasty message again. It's upset me, unsettled me; that's why I had the wine and that's why I can't sort this out and stop Eve crying. It's all her fault, it's Siobhan Dillon's fault. Because it must be her sending me the messages. It must be. I think about calling the number, hover my finger over the button, but something stops me. I don't know what I'd say, I don't know how to deal with a confrontation. I don't want them to know they've got to me.

Going over to the balcony, I open the door and feel a moment of relief as the cooler air hits me. The sky looks beautiful, streaked with pink and gold, and I try to distract Eve with the colours, holding her up to the window and pointing, twisting her little body around so that she can see. The glass obscures part of her view and despite what Jenny said, I step outside with her in my arms, onto the balcony so that she can see the sky properly, the wide expanse of it stretching above our heads. She won't come to any harm – it's not as if I'm going to hurl her over the edge.

A bird flits past, soaring above us towards the waterfront, and I feel a pang of ridiculous jealousy at its freedom. Eve continues to scream and below me I hear the sound of a door slamming, the hiss of a 'for God's sake!' It's the neighbours downstairs; I don't know them, nobody ever talks to each other in this block of flats, but I've seen them around – they're a young couple, younger than me, probably in their mid-twenties. Childless, by the looks of it. People who can't handle the sound of a baby crying.

I stand outside for a few more minutes, jogging Eve up and down a bit on my hip. I feel out of my depth, hopelessly inexperienced. Don't they say you should jiggle babies to get them to stop crying? Something about the movement that helps? I wish I could take her for a walk but I don't want Jenny to come back and find us gone; she must be almost on the way back now.

Going back inside, I try putting Eve back down in the cot, but it only makes the crying worse. Her face is bright red and her mouth, previously a pretty pink pout, is now a gaping scarlet hole, and the sight of it frightens me. I don't know what to do. I don't know what to do.

Chapter Thirty-Two

Ipswich
17th August
DS Wildy

He puzzles over the interaction with Christopher Harvey all the way back to the police station. It is a strange one, all right, and he can't marry up the image of a young Caroline Harvey grieving for her mother, with the sight of her broken body bent over the cot of Eve Grant.

'What are you thinking?' Bolton asks him, as they pull up into the station car park. 'What did you make of Harvey?'

Alex sighs. 'Tell the truth, I felt sorry for him,' he says, and Bolton snorts, turns off the car ignition.

'You're always feeling sorry for someone, Wildy. I thought he was a bit weird, didn't warm to him much. All that stuff about Elsie making the dinner, and the minute she dies the daughter steps in to do the cooking.'

'It was the Eighties,' Alex reminds him. 'Not everyone has quite the modern marriage you have.' The officers grin at each other.

'But still,' Bolton says, 'what kind of father doesn't speak to his daughter for seven months at a time when she lives in the same county? Something about that strikes me as unusual.'

He sighs, scratches his chin. 'Caroline was clearly lonely, a bit troubled, but what does that tell us? There's something not right about this case. Something that isn't adding up. I just wish we knew what it was.'

Alex frowns, one hand on his seatbelt buckle, ready to unclip. 'D'you think we're now—'

He pauses, shakes his head.

'No, go on,' Bolton encourages, and Alex sighs, runs a hand through his hair.

'D'you think we're facing the possibility that Caroline took the child? Did something with Eve because she was so desperate for a baby, went back to the flat, and then it all goes wrong?'

Bolton doesn't reply for a minute or two. 'And who'd want to hurt Caroline, if they knew she'd hurt the baby?'

The question hangs in the air. 'Rick or Jenny Grant.'

'Fuck.' Alex bangs a hand against the glove box, and it pops open, revealing a half-eaten Twix and a torch inside. 'So where does Callum Dillon fit into all this? Or doesn't he?'

'We're missing something,' Bolton says, 'the question is: what?'

*

DCI McVey listens intently as DS Wildy relays Christopher Harvey's story.

'Hmm,' she says thoughtfully, 'it's certainly plausible that she wanted the baby for herself, if she really did have deep-seated issues.'

'Harvey was pretty hazy on a lot of the details, to be honest. Kept going in and out of focus. He said she saw a psychiatrist for a while, but there was nothing concrete he could say. He is nearly eighty, I suppose,' Alex says.

'Hmm,' she says, 'or there is something more, and he's protecting his daughter.'

'Well, he didn't have to tell us anything in the first place,' Alex points out. 'He was the one who came forth with the info, when I started probing a bit into Caroline's background.'

'So you're wondering if Caroline really did hurt Eve, after all?' DCI McVey fixes her gaze on Alex. Her eyes are bright and direct.

He hesitates. 'I don't think we can rule it out, ma'am. Not yet, anyway.'

Chapter Thirty-Three

Ipswich
17th August
Siobhan

To be honest, I'm exhausted with listening to Callum. His hands are gripping mine across the kitchen table; Maria has finally gone up to bed, and I haven't seen Emma for hours. The music blaring from her room has stopped, leaving my husband and I in relative silence. It's almost ten o'clock, and my stomach growls in hunger. I haven't eaten since breakfast.

'Siobhan,' he is saying, 'we have to face this together. Don't you see? A united front. If this thing breaks us, we're putting not only ourselves in danger but Emma too. She's still a minor, she's not old enough to live by herself! If they manage to bang one or the other of us up for something we didn't bloody do, then what will happen to her?'

'She could live with Maria, obviously,' I say, but I'm only playing devil's advocate. Deep down, I know what he's saying is true, it's what my solicitor Olivia has said, but I don't want to give him the satisfaction of being right. I can't stand the thought of our daughter fending for herself any more than he can, especially considering her state at the best of times.

'Plus, the lawyer fees are already through the fucking roof,' Callum says, letting go of my still-unresponsive hands and grasping at his hair as though he wants to pull it out. 'If this carries on, if they question me again or find some ridiculous piece of trumped-up evidence, how are we going to cope? How is our daughter going to survive the gossip – you know what people can be like.'

'We have some savings,' I say, my voice still cold, but Callum snorts in exasperation.

'Don't be absurd, Siobhan. It's not as if the money you've made from your work covers even half of the mortgage.' He leans towards me, taking my hands again, as though he hasn't just dismissed my career in a single sentence.

'Look, I know you're furious with me, Siobhan. I know that. I know I don't deserve to have you as my wife—' at this, to my surprise, his voice breaks a little, but I promised myself that I wouldn't feel sorry for him, and so I don't.

'I know what I did with Caroline, starting to see her, it was wrong. It was a disaster. It's the worst thing I've ever done.' His eyes are beginning to shine now, a glaze of emotion which could be real and could be fake.

'But Siobhan, the stuff the police are saying.'

'They've let you out.'

He sighs. 'You and I both know it's not over yet, Siobhan. They let me out because they had to. Not because I'm off the hook. The first person the bloody police force ever suspect in a case like this is the – the boyfriend. Or whatever.' He looks down at the table and I know he's wishing there was another way to phrase it, that he didn't have to sit here, telling his wife about his moonlit life as another woman's boyfriend.

'Look, if you and I can stick together, just until this is over, I'd really, really appreciate it.'

I can see the muscle in my husband's jaw tightening as he speaks; he's forcing himself to keep calm, not to get annoyed with me. I've known him for almost twenty years – I know how his body works, even when he thinks I don't. He is easy to read, sometimes.

'What do you mean by "stick together"?' I say, keeping my own tone calm and quiet, not wanting to wake my sister or Emma.

'Well,' he says, 'we show the world – the media, the police – that we're a team. Husband and wife. You standing by me would make everything so much easier; I mean look at you, Siobhan. If you put your trust in me, everyone will. If you can find a way to forgive me for messing everything up, for behaving like a moron, then other people might too.' He raises his eyes to meet mine. 'If you don't think I'm a child-stealing murderer, there's a chance that the police might come to their senses and realise that I'm not.'

I wait, letting the moment stretch out. In and out, in and out, the muscle in his jaw pulses. It's making me feel anxious just looking at it.

'It wouldn't be for that long, not if you didn't want it to be,' Callum says, his words coming more quickly now; my silence has unnerved him, he's less sure of his footing. 'But I hope, Siobhan, that in time you might forgive me.' He's trying hard to connect with me, I can feel it, but I have to stay strong, to keep my heart hard and closed against him. If I give in, I will be lost.

'We've been married for fifteen years,' Callum says softly, 'surely that counts for something?'

This I can't let go.

'Yes, you would think so, wouldn't you, Callum?' I say. 'Fifteen years of marriage is quite a long time. But you were happy to throw it away the moment Caroline Harvey walked in, weren't you?'

He looks taken aback; the unease flashes across his features like a cloud passing across the sun.

'I've already told you – it was a mistake, Siobhan,' he says, and all the time my eyes are focused on his jaw, popping in and out, in and out. It's almost rhythmic. Mesmerising.

'A mistake is one night, Callum,' I say to him. 'A mistake is a drunken encounter, a one-off, a lapse in judgement. Not an extended affair. That's something else altogether – it requires planning, consistency, deception spanning weeks and months.' I stare at him. 'And it's not the first time you've done it.'

He's beginning to panic; he knows I'm right. After all, he's known me for as long as I've known him – he knows when I have the upper hand. But I don't think I'm quite as easy to read as my husband – I never have been.

'Right,' he says, getting to his feet, pushing back his chair with such force that it startles me, just for a second. 'Right. If that's the way you want to play it, Siobhan, if the safety and togetherness of our family means so little to you that you can't see the bigger picture here, then fine. Fine. Let's let the police come up with some cock-and-bull story because they've no other leads and pin the whole thing on me, shall we? Let's let them accuse me of not only murder but child abduction too. Let's let them haul me through the courts and throw me in prison, let's lose the house because we can't afford the mortgage, let's give all the money you and I have both worked for to some poncy, overpaid lawyers who will forget about me the moment the cash hits their account.' He's breathing hard, panting.

'Let's let our daughter fall by the wayside, let's say goodbye to fifteen years of marriage and parenting, let's offer ourselves up to the media circus out there and let the likes of the *Daily Mail* rip us into shreds. Does that all sound like a good idea to you, Siobhan?' A speck of spittle flies out of his mouth and lands on the table in front of us, glistening in the semi-darkness of the kitchen. Neither of us have bothered to turn on the little lamps, the expensive fittings that usually make it feel like home.

I wait a moment, leave him panting there in the kitchen, and although my heart is racing, I force myself to look him in the eye. I hate the things he is saying, but when it comes to Emma, I know he's right. She *does* have to be our priority – as a mother, I need to keep her both emotionally and financially stable. God knows I haven't done a very good job so far.

'That isn't what I'm suggesting, Callum,' I say slowly, 'as you well know.'

'Then what are you suggesting, Siobhan?' he asks me angrily. Upstairs, I hear the creak of a floorboard and have a sudden mental image of Emma sitting at the top of the stairs, like she used to when she was little, listening to us argue.

'Keep your voice down, Callum,' I tell him, crossing to the kitchen door and poking my head out to check the stairs.

There is no one there, of course; at sixteen Emma is past that stage. Thank God.

'What's your master plan here?' he asks me, his tone sarcastic, and when I look to his fists, I see they are clenched at his side. I stare at them, wondering if I can trust him, whether I believe his protestations of innocence.

'Listen,' I say to him, 'this is what we're going to do.'

Chapter Thirty-Four

Ipswich
10th August: The night of the murder
Caroline

The screaming hasn't stopped. I want to call Jenny, ask her to help me, but every time I think about dialling her number, I stop myself. I can't bear the thought of her rolling her eyes at Rick and his mother, having to come home because *Caroline can't cope* with the simple and normal fact that a baby is crying too much. I can't stand the thought of never being allowed to look after little Eve again.

'Please, Eve be quiet!' I say, and I try putting her back down in her cot in the bedroom, going into the next room and leaving her alone, even though it's a wrench and my gut twists as I listen to her cries. I close the door of the kitchen, shutting myself in, but it's pointless; the flat is tiny and her screams reverberate around it. Frantically, I reach for my phone, ignoring the fact that I've got an unopened message, and google 'what to do when your baby won't stop crying'.

Remember that your baby loves you but is having a tough time, the first article reads, and I feel a stab of anxiety. My baby doesn't love me because Eve isn't my baby. She loves Jenny, not me. Just like Callum loves Siobhan, not me.

I don't know how much more of this I can take.

I run my eyes back down the list. *Leave your baby in its cot, let it cry itself to sleep. Sometimes that's what your baby needs!* Well, that's not an option. If Jenny comes back and finds her bawling, it will be the last time I get to look after her.

Wrap your baby up snugly. Not in this kind of heat, that's surely the last thing she needs, but maybe I am wrong. I put a hand to my head, trying to stop the panicky thoughts getting in. Maybe I've been wrong all along – after all, I'm not a mother, how do I really know what a child needs?

But she's so hot already, she's sweating.

Give your baby a cooling bath. I pause, thinking of my tiny bathroom. No one else ever uses it now; I tried to get Callum to begin leaving things here – a razor, deodorant, signs of life – but he never did. It is as though our relationship never existed, as though I have been erased. But Eve could use it, I could give her a bath. She'd be nice and clean when Jenny got home.

Brightened by the idea, I head into the bathroom. It's small, a showerhead over the tub, my collection of shampoos and conditioners lining one side. Carefully, I move everything onto the side. I hardly ever use the bath for myself, I don't really like the opportunity to wallow. I can still hear Eve crying; quickly, I put the plug in and turn on the taps, testing the water with my fingers to check it's not too hot or cold. I don't know how much water to put in, I realise, I don't know how much a baby needs. Surely not as much as an adult. But perhaps to cool her down I need to fill it enough so that she could be fully immersed?

Standing, I wonder whether to put any kind of soap in, then reason that the main purpose is just to cool her down, so I don't need to. In the bedroom, I touch her forehead again – she is boiling. Carefully, I strip off her little pink romper, slowly releasing each of her limbs into the air, feeling the Baby-gro damp with her sweat. Poor thing, I think to myself, you poor little thing.

Chapter Thirty-Five

Ipswich
17th August
Siobhan

The feel of Callum's fingers in my own makes me feel slightly nauseous, coming over me in waves the same way it used to when I was pregnant with Emma, all those years ago. I suffered from sickness terribly – hypertension, causing the vomit to rise up in my throat almost every day without fail. The third trimester was the worst; at times, I remember wishing I'd never got pregnant in the first place, never subjected myself to this horribleness. But then when Emma was born, she was so perfect, so totally mine, that the months leading up to her birth and the horror of the caesarean were forgotten, wiped clean like a slate. For the first few years of her life it felt as though we only had eyes for each other – my daughter and I against the world. Even Callum was left out. But then, as the years went on and she grew older, things shifted – it was me who was the one on the outside, the interloper. Whatever closeness we'd had between us ebbed slowly away. And I want to get it back.

'All right?' Callum's fingers squeeze mine and I force myself to squeeze back, do what we've decided. The look of relief on his face gives me a tiny rush of power – he needs me now, more than he ever has before. The front door opens, and there they all are, the cameras flashing in our faces, the microphones being thrust into the August air. Callum's lawyer puts a hand on his arm, his teeth glinting white in the sunshine. Gradually, they quieten down, hyenas ready for their prey.

I clear my throat.

'My husband and I wish to thank the media and Suffolk Police for all they are doing to help bring Caroline Harvey's killer to justice and to find baby Eve. However, whilst it is true my husband had a—' my voice falters, but I push on, 'relationship with Caroline Harvey, there is no doubt in my mind that he is not the one behind this terrible murder.' At this, I pause, turn to look at him, feel our eyes burning into each other. 'Callum and I have been married for fifteen years,' I say, 'and whilst I am saddened that our trust has been broken, both of us are confident that it is something we can rebuild. I stand by my husband and we ask that we are left to pick up the pieces along with our young daughter, Emma. We wish the very best of luck to all those giving up their time in the search for Eve, and of course, our deepest condolences go out to the family of Caroline Harvey at this dreadful time.' Another pause, a nod from his lawyer. 'Callum is a good man, a good husband, and an excellent father to Emma. He is an innocent person, who made one mistake, and I love him very much.'

That last sentence was a bit too much; the words make me feel sick and strange. There is a beat of silence, and then, when they all realise that that's all they're going to get, the crowd start shouting once more.

'Are you going to divorce your husband, Mrs Dillon?' one screams at me, 'aren't you embarrassed by what he did to you?'

I ignore both questions.

'If Callum didn't kill Caroline, who do you think did?' shouts another, and at this I shake my head, lifting my shoulders to indicate that I have absolutely no idea. It's difficult to strike a balance between looking ignorant and uncaring. And yet it is hard for me to summon sadness at the fact that my husband's lover is dead.

I'm not saying I can't. I'm just saying that it's hard.

*

Back inside, Maria is waiting for me. As Callum goes upstairs, she takes me by the wrist, holding me too tightly, like she used to when we were small.

'Are you sure about this?' she hisses at me, her voice urgent. 'Are you sure you know what you're doing, Siobhan?'

I wince. 'You're hurting me, Maria,' I say, trying to twist out of her grip.

She relents a bit, easing off the pressure with which she's grasping me but keeping her fingers looped around my wrist, my body held close to hers.

'I just want you to think about it,' she tells me, 'think about what he did to you. And think about what's best for Emma.'

I stare at her, confused. 'I'm *doing* what's best for Emma,' I say, 'Emma is the reason I'm standing by him. I thought that was obvious, Maria. I'm trying to prioritise my daughter.'

I shake myself free of her and continue up the stairs. I can feel her staring after me all the way up to the top, her eyes on my back until I disappear from her sight. She doesn't like me not doing what she wants. She never has.

Chapter Thirty-Six

Ipswich
10th August: The night of the murder
Caroline

She loves the bath! Finally, finally she has stopped crying, and the silence is so new and fresh and such a *relief* that I almost want to laugh. Her little hands splash at the water, her fingernails tiny and perfect, and as I gently wet a flannel and sponge it against her back she gives a squirm of delight.

'There you go, baby,' I say to her, running the flannel across her forehead, hoping that it helps to cool her down, 'there you go, little water baby. You are a little water baby, aren't you? Yes you are, yes you are!'

The noise of her giggle is the best thing in the world.

I wish I had some toys for her to play with, a little yellow duck, or one of those books made of inflatable plastic. Maybe I'll get some, for next time I babysit – now that I know she likes the bath I can do it whenever she wants, it could be our thing. Fun time with Auntie Caroline. *Yes*.

I squirt a bit of my shampoo into the bath because I haven't got any proper bubble stuff, swoosh my hand around in the water to create white foam that Eve immediately reaches for with one of her chubby little hands. I scoop a blob of it onto my finger then place it onto her nose; it makes her look even cuter and I wish I had my phone to take a quick snap. It would be nice to have a picture of her, to remember what a happy time we're having, to prove to myself that I *can* do this, that I made the right decision leaving Callum, that some day I too will have a little girl of my own.

'You stay there for a minute, Eve, there's a good girl,' I say and I stand, smiling down at her as her little legs make splashes in the water. She's sitting up, perfectly content, and I quickly look around for my phone, check in case it's somehow fallen into the bag of her things that I've placed on the side. But no, all that's there are her nappies and a few wooden toys that Jenny packed – not suitable for the bath, I don't think.

I must have left it in the kitchen.

'One sec!' I say to Eve, even though she's totally oblivious to me, is enjoying the water too much to notice if I'm there or not, and I hurry into the next room and spot my phone on the surface, lying next to the kettle. When I grab it, there's another message. And this one makes my blood run cold. It's from the unknown number again.

I'm here, Caroline.

I stare at it, shocked, my heart beginning to race. It is only a minute, maybe two, before I stuff the phone into my pocket with shaking hands and go back towards the bathroom, wanting to immerse myself once more in the happy world of Eve at bath-time. What do they mean, *I'm here*? Downstairs? In the *flat*? What if the downstairs security has broken again? My heart begins to thud. I haven't heard anyone come in, but they'd be being quiet, wouldn't they? I need to lock the door, get Eve into bed. If this person really is downstairs, I don't want them coming anywhere near my baby. Sorry, Jenny's baby, I mean. I know she isn't mine.

The phone in my pocket, I walk into the bathroom. For a second or two, I stare.

And then I scream.

Chapter Thirty-Seven

Ipswich
18th August
DS Wildy

DS Wildy is out in the corridor by the vending machine, debating between a Twix and a Mars bar, and about to call Joanne to tell her he won't be home in time for dinner tonight for the third night in a row, when Dave Bolton appears by his side, slightly breathless and with brighter eyes than Alex has seen any of the force have in days.

'The French police have found something in the grounds of the Dillon family villa,' he says. 'They've just emailed it over – thought you should come and have a look.' He glances at the pound coin in Alex's hand. 'The Mars bar can wait,' he says. 'This is big.'

Back inside the main room, the team are gathered around DCI McVey's computer. She's the only one with her own office – the Ipswich constabulary is a relatively small force – and as far as Alex has experienced, her office is usually pretty out of bounds. In other words, she's precious about her personal space, so this really must be something good.

'Sorry,' he says by way of apology as he enters the room, 'I was just trying to get through to Joanne.'

Gillian McVey nods, barely looking up at him. She has a reputation for being hard as nails; Alex knew it when he joined the team. He's always wanted to be one of those people whose reputation goes before them, too, but unfortunately the main impression he's given people in his time here is that he's too *nice*. But he can't help it – he feels sorry for people. And in this case, there are so many victims – not least poor Siobhan Dillon whose husband was having an affair right under her nose, and Jenny and Rick Grant, whose faces grow more and more haggard every day, despite the fact they're in their early thirties.

If only he could find the baby, at least it would put some of it right. But even Alex knows that outside of the first forty-eight hours, the chances of finding Eve Grant alive are pretty bloody slim. The best they can hope for is a body, some sort of closure for the parents. Perhaps that's what this is.

'What did the French find?' he says, and McVey beckons to him to come look over her shoulder.

On the screen is a little pink object, laying on a police evidence table. Alex leans closer, squints at it. It's a child's dummy. He feels the hairs on the back of his neck stand up.

'It matches the one that belonged to Eve Grant,' McVey says, clicking through to more photos. 'And it was found in the villa, during a search of the grounds carried out by the guys in Rouen for us. Took them a few days to unearth it.' She taps the mouse, showing them photographs of the outside of the villa, the land that rolls down towards the bottom of the huge hill. Alex stares at it, the luxury of the place. Orange markers denote the spot where the dummy was found, a patch of earth not too far from the swimming pool.

'Christ.' Alex frowns, his mind beginning to race. This could change the whole investigation yet again. 'So we're saying Callum Dillon took Eve's dummy all the way to France with him? Why?'

Gillian shrugs. 'Some sort of twisted keepsake? Happens more than you think. But he'd obviously tried to get rid of it – though what I don't get is why you'd throw something like that in the grounds. I mean, it wasn't even properly buried. Surely there are better places to hide it.' She gives a grim smile. 'Do we think this means *Eve* is in France?'

McVey shakes her head. 'I mean, it's possible, we can't rule it out, but it's highly unlikely that the Dillons would've been able to get a one-year-old that didn't belong to them across the border. Not on a plane.' She pauses. 'But we've spoken to border control anyway, they're going through the CCTV at Southend and Caen again now. Just in case we missed something the first time.' She gives a little snort. 'But come on, a one-year-old? That's a pretty significant thing to miss.'

She glances across the office to DS Tom Smith, who is one of the newer recruits, and the one who went through the airport CCTV in the first place to check the Dillons' travel times.

'I don't think he'd have missed it, boss,' Alex says quietly, but Gillian just rolls her eyes.

'Always the nice guy, Wildy. I've been in this game long enough to know that sometimes we miss even the unmissable.'

She sighs. 'Callum's lawyer isn't going to like this very much though, is he? If it's hers, it's a direct link between him and that night.' She pauses. 'His wife didn't do an awful lot to clear his name when I spoke to her, either. She can't verify that he was in the studio. She went to bed alone after her book group, didn't even hear him come in, despite what she said originally. She's not convinced of his innocence, no matter what she's saying to the press.'

'Well,' Alex says, knowing that the DCI likes a devil's advocate, someone to challenge her, 'the dummy could be a link between the *villa* and that night. Don't forget, Callum wasn't the only one staying there.'

McVey nods, frowning. 'True. But either way, this could be a bit of a game-changer for us. It's been sent to the lab; I've asked them to fast-track the DNA. If it belongs to Eve Grant, we might be able to bring him back in, charge him this time.' She runs a hand through her short blonde hair and exhales loudly. 'I'd love something to wipe the smug smirk off Callum's face. Did you know I actually think he tried to *flirt* with me the other day before we let him go? Even his arse of a lawyer looked embarrassed.'

Alex winces dutifully. 'Are you going to let the parents know about the dummy?'

The DCI shakes her head. 'Not yet. Not until we've talked to Callum again.' She sighs, and Alex knows she is thinking of Eve, of the tiny, innocent girl who will likely never be reunited with Jenny and Rick Grant. 'Poor little mite.' There is a pause, and then she says, 'I'm going to request a digger for the ground around the villa. If the dummy's there, we can't rule out that there might be more to find.'

Chapter Thirty-Eight

D S Wildy watches as McVey lays into Callum, whose lawyer is starting to look distinctly uncomfortable, despite the greased forehead and power suit. Patrick O'Connell has slicked-back hair and clean, clipped nails, and most of the time his smile is as smug as Callum's is; Alex can certainly see why the Dillon family hired him. He's obviously done his absolute best to rid himself of his native Irish accent, but, pleasingly, it slips in here and there. He is tapping a finger against the table, his eyes darting around the room whilst Callum sits wide-legged across from the DCI. There is something offensive, insulting even, about the spread of his legs, and Alex can feel dislike for the man radiating off him.

'Right then,' he says to himself, 'let's see what you've got to say for yourself, Callum smug-arse Dillon.'

Interview Room 3
Present: DCI McVey, Callum Dillon, Patrick O'Connell,
acting solicitor for Callum Dillon

DCI McVey: *I think we've all had enough of messing around and wasting time, don't you?*

CD: *No comment.*

POC: *My client has thus far complied with all of your questioning. No attempts have been made to waste police time. You have already held my client for the maximum amount of time this week, and to bring him back in so soon after his release is nothing short of ridiculous. Mr Dillon has a family to get back to, responsibilities in his work. It is unacceptable to continue this ludicrous line of back and forth questioning, hauling my client in and out of custody, if you've no idea where you're going with it.*

DCI McVey: *I've got every idea where I'm going with it, thank you. Mr Dillon, by your own admission, you flew to France with your family on 11th August, last week, the day after your long-term girlfriend Caroline Harvey was found dead in her apartment. You stayed in Saint Juillet for a total of two days before you were apprehended by our colleagues in Rouen. Prior to that, you say you had no contact with Jenny and Rick Grant, nor with their baby, Eve Grant. [pause] So please, Mr Dillon, explain to me how a dummy belonging to Eve Grant was found at the holiday villa where you had been staying?*

CD: *A what?*

DCI McVey: *[pushes a photograph across the table to him] A dummy, Mr Dillon. As you can see here. This dummy is identical to an item that belonged to Eve Grant. It was bought for her by her mother Jenny. Purchased from Mothercare last year. And now it turns up, hundreds of miles away, at the very villa you'd decided to holiday at. So, Mr Dillon, I'm going to ask you again – how can you explain this, please?*

CD: *I can't explain it. It doesn't make any sense.*

DCI McVey: *I put it to you that it does make sense, Mr Dillon. I put it to you that the reason the dummy was there was because you had it on your person on the night of 10th August, after you killed Caroline Harvey and disposed of the body of Eve Grant.*

POC: *Objection to that statement – there is no evidence that my client disposed of anyone's body. Or that the dummy you have found is the same one belonging to Eve Grant. So using the term 'belonging to Eve Grant' is in fact completely inaccurate.*

CD: *I don't know how the dummy got there. Maybe it was left over from another family.*

DCI McVey: *Isn't the villa owned by your sister-in-law, Maria Wilcox?*

CD: *Yes, it is, but she rents it out. Have you even asked her? There could've been another family staying there before us.*

DCI McVey: *We have checked the records, Mr Dillon. The house hadn't been rented out in a few months. And Maria Wilcox doesn't have any children. She also has no connection to Caroline Harvey. You are the connection, Mr Dillon. You are the one with the motive.*

CD: *[silence]*

DCI McVey: *The dummy is identical to the one that Jenny Grant describes leaving with Caroline Harvey on the night of the murder. It is currently being tested to see if it contains traces of her DNA. If it does, Callum, then I have to say, things aren't looking up for you. It would be a lot easier for everyone – including yourself – if you confessed to what you'd done.*

CD: *I've never seen that dummy before in my life.*

DCI McVey: *[pushes a photo of Caroline Harvey across the table to him] She was a beautiful woman, Caroline, wasn't she?*

POC: *I don't see how that is relevant.*

DCI McVey: *Would you say she was prettier than your wife, Mr Dillon?*

POC: *Again, irrelevant and unnecessary questioning, designed solely to upset my client.*

CD: *I don't know. It doesn't matter.*

DCI McVey: *Did you ever have plans to leave your wife for Ms Harvey, Mr Dillon?*

CD: *[pause] I don't – I hadn't really thought.*

DCI McVey: *You'd never thought about it? I have to say I find that hard to believe.*

CD: *It was a difficult situation – look, I'm not proud of it. But having an affair doesn't make me a murderer, does it? As I keep saying.*

POC: *Of course it doesn't.*

DCI McVey: *It suggests a lack of morality, though. Wouldn't you say?*

CD: *No comment.*

DCI McVey: *Mr Dillon, from accessing your phone records, we can see several recent correspondences between you and Ms Harvey, the last of which is from you, telling her to leave you alone.*

CD: *I don't think I used those words.*

DCI McVey: *[reads from paper in front of her] When I get back, I think it's best we don't speak any more. Please, stop calling me.*

CD: *You see! When I get back. Why would I have used those words if I was planning to top her the night before I went?*

DCI McVey: *Mr Dillon, you had been to Ms Harvey's flat many times before, had you not?*

CD: *You know I had, yes.*

DCI McVey: *So it's fair to say you knew the layout well.*

CD: *It's a small flat. There wasn't much to know.*

DCI McVey: *But you did know about the exit route at the ground-floor level, which led to a communal garden, didn't you? You did know that the CCTV cameras had been smashed a few weeks back?*

CD: *Yes.*

DCI McVey: *You knew that there would be very few people around at that time of night and that if you wanted to leave through the garden, you could.*

CD: *What are you getting at?*

DCI McVey: *Mr Dillon, did you know that Ms Harvey was babysitting Eve Grant that night?*

CD: *Of course not. I hadn't spoken to her. You just read me the last message I ever sent to her. [pause] Shit. [wipes eyes] Look, you've got to remember that I've lost someone too, Detective. I've lost Caroline.*

DCI McVey: *Spare us, Mr Dillon. Had Caroline ever mentioned Eve Grant to you before?*

CD: *[pause]*

POC: *You don't have to answer that.*

CD: Yes, she – she did once or twice. A while ago. She liked Eve. She liked babies, children, you know. Lots of women do.

DCI McVey: Lots of people do. Not just women. [pause] Do you like children, Mr Dillon?

CD: Jesus Christ, what are you implying?

POC: I object to the implications of your question, Detective.

DCI McVey: Why did you take Eve Grant from Caroline's apartment, Mr Dillon? Why did you clean the flat with bleach after killing Caroline Harvey?

CD: I didn't. I DIDN'T!

DCI McVey: Where is Eve Grant now?

CD: I. Don't. Know.

Chapter Thirty-Nine

Callum's lawyer, Patrick O'Connell, has come back to the house with him. The pair of them disappear off into my husband's studio, taking with them a bottle of whiskey (oh, stop being such a cliché, Callum), and Maria and I sit at the kitchen table, trying listlessly to eat a lasagne that she's made. Yvonne, our family liaison officer, has gone for the day, and I'm rather hoping that she doesn't come back. I'm sick of her snooping around; I feel like she's been watching us, listening in on our conversations. That's the absolute last thing I need.

Emma appears at the doorway.

'Why did they call Dad back today?' she asks, her voice small. She's wearing jeans with a rip in the knee, a white T-shirt that could do with a wash.

I swallow the bite of lasagne that I've been pushing around inside my mouth for the last thirty seconds.

'Sweetheart, I don't know.'

But she's not looking at me, she's looking at Maria, and as I look up, a spark of something seems to pass between them, like a jolt of electricity that zips straight by me.

'Have they found something?' she asks, and Maria gestures to her to come sit with us, patting the chair next to her at the kitchen table.

I take a sip of my glass of red wine; it tastes vinegary and strange, has been sitting out on the side for far too long in the heat.

'Emma,' I say, 'nobody's told us anything. Dad's with his solicitor in the studio, and Patrick is one of the best lawyers around. He'll know what went on today, and he'll know what to do.' I reach out a hand across the table to stroke hers, but her skin is cold, unresponsive to my touch.

'Are you feeling all right?' I ask her, because all of a sudden, I'm noticing how pale she is, the tiny beads of sweat that are sitting along her hairline, just visible against her skin and the blonde of her hair.

'You must be tired,' Maria says suddenly, and getting to her feet, she stands and puts a hand on my daughter's shoulder. 'Why don't you go back upstairs, have a little lie down? I'll bring you up some painkillers.'

Wordlessly, Emma does as my sister says, standing up and moving away from the table, almost as though she is in a trance.

'Emma?' I say, astonished, but Maria turns back to wince at me and puts her hand on her abdomen.

'Period pains!' she whispers, mouthing the words, 'she told me earlier. It'll pass!'

The pair of them disappear from the kitchen, leaving me sat in front of the plate of congealing lasagne, wondering what on earth that was about.

I'm shut out, I realise, *I'm shut out of even the things going on in my own home.*

Slowly, I get to my feet and begin cleaning the table, scraping the messy lasagne off our plates and into the waiting bin. I slug the rest of my red wine, wanting something to take the edge off. I can't stop the jealousy swirling around inside me – first my husband, then my sister – it seems Emma is prepared to be close to anybody apart from me. What do I have to do to be her mother again? What do I have to do for her to let me in?

Chapter Forty

France
19th August
Adele

The female police officer is tired. It's been a long day, and the heat is getting to her – she's too hot in her uniform and she resents the fact that whoever owns this house is clearly making more money than she will ever hope to – for as long as she is in the police force anyway.

The villa is huge, lavish almost, yet it has an eerie stillness about it. The place has already been scoured for DNA, the belongings of Callum, Siobhan, Emma and Maria have been carefully searched and are now in messy, careless piles near the door, ready for someone like her to clear up. She can't wait until the day she doesn't have to do menial jobs any more, can move onto the exciting stuff. No more transcripts and emails, no more making cups of coffee. But most of the people who rise up in this particular force seem to be men. She sighs, grits her teeth. *Just get on with it, Adele.*

Bending down, she reaches for the nearest suitcase, powder blue and padded, the name Siobhan Dillon written neatly on the attached luggage tag. The woman's clothes are nice, high quality – she touches a silk dress almost reverently. The design is British.

She hasn't been told all the ins and outs of the case, but knows her colleagues are liaising with the English police to get to the bottom of a murder case. She wasn't able to pick up much from the interview transcripts she's painstakingly typed up – pages of *no comment* that give nothing away. She gives a little shiver when she thinks of the English police, all those miles away, desperately searching for answers. These clothes belong to the wife – Adele feels sorry for her. Deciding to be kind, she begins to fold them, taking care of the frills and creases. She stacks them neatly into the suitcase and zips it up, ready to be sent back to England.

Beside the pile of female clothing is another pile, mainly consisting of shorts and T-shirts, obviously belonging to the husband. Adele knows he is the one in trouble, the unfaithful one, the one arrested on suspicion of murder. She decides not to bother folding those – sounds like he doesn't deserve it. She looks around for his suitcase, but sees only two other bags – one clearly belonging to the teenage daughter, and another, a holdall, with the name Maria Wilcox on the side. Nowhere is there a suitcase that looks as if it could belong to the man.

Frowning, Adele gets up and begins to search the rooms, going into each bedroom, checking the cupboards in case the suitcase has been left behind by the officers here before her. She checks underneath the beds, on top of the wardrobes, all the places one might normally put a suitcase. But there is nothing. She even checks the bathrooms, but sees only her own reflection – confused and tired-looking, staring back at her in the huge walled mirrors.

Returning to the hallway, she looks again at the piles of clothing. Did Callum and his wife pack together, share a suitcase? It doesn't look as though it would all fit – Siobhan Dillon has a lot of clothes. Adele pulls her telephone out of her pocket, presses it to her ear and waits.

Chapter Forty-One

I am still holding Eve, standing in the bathroom as the steam from the water glistens in the air. My hands are shaking, my whole body is shaking. Around me, everything looks the same – the gleaming white bathroom, the cold water in the bath, the brightly coloured shampoo bottles and toilet roll and toothbrush, mocking me with their normality. The bag of nappies, unused and redundant. Her skin feels funny, as if it is stretched too tightly across her tiny little bones, and the silence, the awful silence, is all around me. Around us.

A speck of water drips from the tap into the bathwater, the splash making me jump. Carefully, gently, slowly, I place Eve down onto the fluffy white towel I'd laid out for her on the floor. It is way too big for her, it would have swaddled her several times over. I stare down at my hands as though they are not my own. Her eyes are shut, the dark lashes sweeping the thin skin of her small cheeks. The hands that are not my own lift her again, and I feel the wetness of her against my chest, my chest that is warm and beating and alive. *This is a joke*, I think, *or a hallucination*. At any moment I will wake up, snap out of it, Eve will open her mouth and cry and cry and the flat will fill with noise again, glorious, delicious baby noise that I will never wish away again. Her eyes will meet mine, those gorgeous eyes, and I'll cuddle her to me, dry her off, put her back in her little pink playsuit and tuck her up for another try at going to sleep. Jenny will come home and she will be so pleased that I've bathed her, so very very pleased, and she'll smile at me and say that Eve can stay over, if she wants, she can sleep here all night because she's so happy here, look at her, she's so content.

But of course, none of that is happening.

Desperately, I put my mouth close to hers, wanting to feel her soft breath against my face. Please, I think to myself, please, I'll do anything. Nothing happens. I place my mouth against hers and breathe in, as steadily as I can, keeping her little chin lifted, trying frantically to remember the first aid we were taught back in school. I pull back, stare at her chest to see if it's moving, then do the same thing again, breathing into her mouth for the count of a second then pulling back.

The moment feels as if it has lasted forever but suddenly, there is a movement, and her bare chest rises with a tiny, soft sound. Immediately, I am crying, and for a horrible second I think I have imagined it, but no, she's breathing, and I pick her up, oh-so-gently, and her eyelids flutter open to reveal the beautiful brown eyes beneath.

'Eve,' I say, 'Eve.' My heart is beating so fast and I feel as though I am going to be sick but none of that matters because she's alive, she is, she's alive and she's safe and I've got her, I've got her now. She coughs, a strange little sound, and water spills from her mouth. I pat her back, over and over, murmuring to her, tears slipping down my face. I thought she'd drowned, I thought she was dead. Oh Eve. Oh Eve. I don't deserve to be looking after her.

*

My legs are beginning to go numb; I realise that I've been sitting on them, staring at Eve, terrified to take my eyes off her in case she stops breathing again. But her little face looks OK now, her skin has returned to a normal colour, and her eyes move around the room, with no sign of anything untoward. I don't know how long we have sat here for – time has become elasticated, stretchy, something I cannot and do not want to grasp hold of. I hear my phone begin to ring, the tinny, electronic sound seeping into my consciousness, but I ignore it. It doesn't matter – all that matters is Eve.

It might be a minute later, it might be an hour, but gradually I become aware of another noise, a different sound to my ragged breathing and Eve's gentle stirs. It is a knocking, persistent, and for one mad moment I am convinced it is the police, they are here, they know what almost happened, they know I'm not a fit babysitter, they know a child almost drowned on my watch. But then I realise – and this realisation is even worse – that it will be Jenny, Jenny is back, she will come in here, and I will have to tell her what might have happened, listen to her berate me, clutch her daughter to her chest and tell me I'm never allowed near her again. And then I remember the message, the reason this happened, the reason I was so stupid and selfish and lost concentration. *I'm here.* It hardly seems to matter any more. All that matters is the baby in my arms, the fact that she is alive.

I pick Eve up, holding her body close to mine, and I go back into the bedroom, place her carefully in the cot. I move as if in a dream, my limbs heavy, disconnected with relief, and I am almost fascinated when I catch a glimpse of myself in the mirror that hangs on the back of my bedroom door. I look the same – my eyes are red, and my skin is blotchy with tears – but other than that the same brown eyes stare back at me, the same hair tied back to keep the heat off, the same silver necklace bumps around my collar bone. How can I look the same, after what has just happened? How close I came?

The knocking continues, and I shout out 'Just a minute!', trying to buy a little more time. It will be Jenny, I know it will. My breathing is still strange and I force myself to take deep breaths, in and out for the count of five. Eve is fine, isn't she? She didn't drown. She is fine. She will be fine. My voice echoes around my head, bouncing off the walls of the room as though I am in an echo chamber.

'Caroline!' the voice calls from outside, but it's not Jenny's voice. I take a deep breath, my mind racing. There is a little peep-hole in my door, and I put my eye to it, press my cheek against the wood. But the person on the other side of it isn't the one I'm expecting. The image is blurry, but I think I recognise it – the dark hair, the hazel eyes. It looks like her. It looks like Callum's wife.

Chapter Forty-Two

'The suitcase.'

DCI McVey strides into the middle of the open-plan office, her hands spread out as though it is obvious.

For a moment, Alex is nonplussed. 'What suitcase?'

'Callum Dillon's suitcase. The French police have just been in touch – a young constable, that Adele, has just been over to the villa to pack up the family's clothing but it turns out there's nothing to put Callum's in.' She spins round, facing them. Dave Bolton frowns.

'Did he share with his wife, with his daughter?'

'They think not, it wouldn't all fit. Besides—' DCI McVey leans over Alex's shoulder, taps a few keys at his computer. 'Don't you think Callum Dillon is the kind of guy who'd have his own luggage?' The screen fills with photographs of him, mainly taken locally, at various charity events and benefits. There is one of him walking not far from a minor celebrity; they look as though they are leaving an airport. Callum's hand trails behind him, pulling along the silver handle of an expensive-looking black case.

The DCI nods. 'He had it in the airport CCTV, too. It was on the tapes, clear as day.'

'So where is it?' Bolton asks, and DCI McVey laughs, though the sound is harsh and cold.

'That, Dave, is the million-dollar question. *Where is Callum Dillon's suitcase?*'

'Want us to ask him about it, boss?' Alex says, but the DCI shakes her head quickly.

'No, no I don't. I don't want him knowing anything at this stage – it gives him time to prepare a cover story back at home with his lawyer. Gives him time to have a nice little think. No, if that suitcase is in France, our colleagues over there will find it. And if it's been used to keep Eve in, they'll find that too.'

And find it they do. It's just under two hours later when the phone call comes. DCI McVey's voice changes as she answers it. The suitcase is black, the name tag ripped off it, found on the verge half a mile away from Maria Wilcox's villa, almost as though someone might have thrown it out of a moving vehicle. It's empty, the lining slightly ripped. Alex looks at the photos.

'Maria Wilcox told us that Callum and his daughter took a road trip one day alone,' he says slowly, 'he could've thrown it from the car then, couldn't he?'

'Going for testing now,' the DCI says, 'and I've reminded the lab what the word urgent actually means, seeing as they haven't even got the dummy swab back to me yet.' She rolls her eyes, but Alex can see that the mood in the office is brightening, now that the investigation is beginning to get somewhere.

'France have brought in Superintendent Pascal,' the DCI says, 'and the entire area is being swept again. This time – and God knows how they'd have got it there – this time, they're looking for a body. I think we've been focusing on the wrong place.'

All of them stare at the small black suitcase on the screen, and Alex knows they're all thinking the same thing. Just big enough to hold a baby.

Chapter Forty-Three

France
19th August
Adele

Adele watches as the dust churns up around the villa, settling onto everything it touches. It is a shame, really, she thinks, the place is so beautiful. She thinks of the wife's fancy dresses, the glistening blue of the swimming pool. A place of luxury, ripped apart in the search for the child.

It is only her fourth month in the Rouen police force, the process is new to her. Her superior told her she could stay, help with the search that will continue this evening. They are pleased with her for spotting the lack of suitcase, for her sharpness, her speed. The English police are excited, they think this will be what they need.

Despite the lingering heat of the day, she feels a shiver go through her at the thought of the wife, finding out what her husband has done. Adele doesn't have a partner, *non,* and this case hasn't made her any more inclined to find one, much to the chagrin of her parents back in Paris.

Around her, the machine digs up more and more earth, the green, flowered gardens surrounding the villa transforming into mounds of sandy dirt. Pink roses fall to the floor, beheaded by the excavations. Further down the hill, more police are searching manually; the surrounding houses are all holiday lets but their bins have been emptied, the nooks and crannies of the hill have been splayed open in case they are hiding the baby. The sun is beginning to set now, they will not be able to dig for much longer.

Part of her wants them to find her, part of her does not.

'*Il y a aucun espoir pour le bébé,*' her superior had said to her gently, this morning, 'there is no hope for the baby.'

Above them, the huge rock towers, blocking out what is left of the dwindling sunlight. It gives away nothing, and still the search for Eve Grant carries on.

Chapter Forty-Four

Her hair is longer than I thought it was, that's the first thing I notice about her. I've always known she was beautiful, of course, but in the flesh it is even more obvious, she is even more striking. It doesn't surprise me, exactly, but it distracts me, and for a second or two I just gaze at her, in the way that Callum probably does, staring at the fineness of her features, much finer than mine, much finer than Jenny's.

'Can I come in?' she says, and without waiting for an answer she seems to slip past me, through the open doorway and into the flat. She must have noticed my stained face, but she doesn't say anything, and not knowing what else to do, I close the door behind us and follow her. She's gone into the kitchen, her long limbs making the journey from the front door in just a few strides. Behind us, the bedroom hums, baby Eve sealed off from her.

'Were you in the bath?' she asks me, and I realise that the bathroom door is ajar; she can partially see the half-full tub, the light is on and there is a towel strewn on the floor. The bag of Eve's things is hidden from view, on the ottoman to the right of the door.

'Now isn't a good time,' I say eventually, finding my voice at last – my priority has to be Eve, making sure she is all right after what so nearly happened.

'Why not?' she asks me, and her tone is light, as if we are playing a game or discussing the options for dinner tonight. There is something similar to him in her gestures, the way she turns her head.

'Why are you here?' I say, and at that she laughs, a strange, high-pitched sound. She's wearing loose clothing, a T-shirt and a pink skirt that floats around her knees. My own shirt is wet from where I held Eve's body against me; I see her eyes flicker over the large damp patch.

'I'm here because you don't seem to be getting my messages,' she says, smiling at me again, 'so I thought I'd deliver one in person.'

Despite everything, I feel a further stab of horror when she says this.

'You're the one who's been texting me those things?' I say, and she nods, still smiling.

The bedroom is just metres away; the room feels like it is pulsing.

'I have to do something,' I say to her, 'I can't talk about this right now. I'm sorry – I'm sorry about Callum, about everything, but I can't do this now.'

The smile drops off her face as quickly as it came.

Somewhere in the room, my phone beeps with a message.

'You don't get to choose when we talk about it,' she hisses at me. 'You didn't care about me when you were with him, did you? You did exactly what you wanted; I've seen you.' Abruptly, she stands up. We're almost the same height, but

I am larger than her, I feel every ounce of weight on my body as she looks at me.

'No,' I say, 'that's not what I – that's not how it was. I never meant to hurt you.'

She laughs, head thrown back a little, teeth flashing in the light of the kitchen.

'Come on then,' she says, 'let's have a look at your little love nest. I'm curious, I have to say.'

Before I can stop her, she is darting past me, pushing open the door to the kitchen. Too late, I see one of Eve's little pink socks on the sofa, discarded beside one of the cushions. She must know I don't have children, but she doesn't seem to notice it. She turns around and her gaze is fixed solely on me. I am what she wants.

Chapter Forty-Five

She can barely look at me. I stare at her, up close, drinking her in, this woman I have obsessed over for months now, ever since I saw her with Dad one evening after school. I was with my friend Molly – we were supposed to be doing homework but her parents were away and so we'd gone into town. I saw Dad kissing Caroline, in the doorway of a pub, on the wrong side of Ipswich where we never really go. My heart had skipped a beat and I'd pushed Molly in the other direction, not wanting her to see. I kept waiting for Mum to confront him, to tell me, but she never did. She's pathetic. She doesn't stand up for herself, and none of this is Dad's fault – it can't be. It's this woman, bewitching him. *Caroline.* I have seen her from afar, of course, but in person she is different, somehow. Less shiny. Less vibrant. She is pale, her skin slicked with a shine of sweat – I feel a flicker of pleasure that I might actually be scaring her.

The kitchen is emptier than I thought it would be – there are no signs of my dad. None of the paraphernalia we have at ours, the trinkets Mum keeps, the photos on the walls of us playing happy families. I don't like those anyway – they're all a lie.

'Do you know who I am, Caroline?' I ask her, keeping my voice low and soft like I have practised. I'm having to improvise everything now, just a bit, because she's not how I was expecting – I expected her to be tough and snappy and combative. Perhaps I'm more intimidating than I thought.

She nods, wiping at her face; it looks tear-stained already. Then to my horror, she puts out a hand towards me, as if to touch me.

'You're Emma,' she whispers, 'you're Callum's daughter.'

I nod, never breaking eye contact with her. Her eyes are slits in her face, red and puffy from crying.

Around us, the room is very silent, silent and still. There is an emptiness; I can sense it. Devoid of life.

I take a step towards her, feeling a flicker of enjoyment as the look of panic flashes across her face.

'Why do you think I'm here?' I ask her, tilting my head to one side.

'I don't know,' she says. 'I don't know what you want from me.' Her gaze darts around my face and I smile at her, feel myself struggling to suppress the beginnings of a giggle.

'So why my dad, Caroline?' I ask her, taking a step towards her, watching with a sense of fascination as her hair falls partly across her face. She needs to pluck her eyebrows. I'm trying to work out what my dad saw in her, what he wanted from this weird empty flat and this tear-stained woman that he couldn't get at home from me and Mum. I want her to stand still, like a waxwork in a museum, I want to be able to examine her from all sides as though she's an exhibit.

We're standing by the kitchen counters. There's a lone wine glass next to the sink, a small fridge on the other side of the draining rack. No fridge magnets, no lists of things to do like there is on ours. A small life, I think, too small for her, so she had to start in on someone else's. A splash of anger curdles in my stomach. She's not even looking at me.

'What's your plan, Caroline?' I ask her, tilting my head to one side, forcing her eyes to meet mine. She looks glazed almost, as if my words aren't quite filtering into her consciousness.

'Emma,' she says finally, her voice quiet, too quiet, 'I can't do this right now. Now is not a good time for this conversation. I have to – I have to…' Her eyes dart away from me, towards the door that leads out into the hallway and presumably to a bedroom. A bedroom where she's happily been fucking my dad without any care for me at all.

'You don't get to decide on that,' I say, and then she actually glances down at the watch on her wrist, an annoyingly elegant-looking brown strap with a gold face. Did he buy her that?

'You don't understand,' she says, and her voice is even softer now, almost a whisper. I hate the way she's looking at her watch, dismissing me, dismissing my family. Taking only what she wants. She doesn't care about me, she doesn't know how much I need my dad, how much I need him to stay with us, stay with me.

'Don't tell me that I don't understand!' I say to her, and my voice rises, almost to a shout. Her eyes flick to the door again and I can see a vein pulsating in her forehead, horrible and blue. She looks ugly now, I think, she looks ugly and scared.

'Why didn't you reply to my messages?' I ask her, and she stares at me, confusion in her eyes. I feel a slap of satisfaction – she obviously doesn't think I'm capable of any of this, she thinks I'm a silly little girl, everyone does. I've heard them talking about me – *hormones, her age, a stage*. But they've got it all wrong. I'm angry – with Mum for not doing anything about it, with Maria for not even noticing, with Dad for letting this woman trick him. I know about her, about what kind of woman she is, and I'm here to show her that I meant what I said – she shouldn't take what isn't hers. I don't. Yet here she is, standing here, refusing to apologise, refusing to engage, yet happy to take my father like picking a cherry from a tree.

I don't think so, Caroline.

Chapter Forty-Six

Ipswich
10th August: The night of the murder
Caroline

I have to get her out of here. It's almost eight thirty and all I can think about is Eve, little Eve in the cot in the next room, alone. I worry about the water still being in her lungs, about secondary drowning – she needs me to watch over her.

But still the girl needles at me, standing in front of me as though squaring up to somebody in a fight. What does she want from me? Why won't she leave me alone? I feel as though I am inside a nightmare, like the ones I used to have after Mum died, when the walls are closing in and the ceiling is getting nearer and nearer until it traps me, coffin-like, underneath its terrible weight. I need to be with Eve.

'Emma, please,' I say, trying to sound normal, to sound calm, when inside my head there is a roaring, rushing noise, like water speeding down a mountainside, an avalanche of panic that I can barely control.

'Please leave,' I say quietly, 'I promise to talk to you about this but now is not the time.'

'I won't leave until you tell me it's over,' Emma says, smiling at me weirdly, her mouth twisting up at the sides.

'It's over,' I say, 'it's over.' I nod my head madly, thinking desperately that this will be it, this will be all she wants, for me never to see Callum again and for her to leave before Jenny comes back.

'How do I know you mean that?' Emma says, fixing me with those blue eyes, the bright, bright eyes that remind me now of her father's, and I feel, in spite of the chaos in my head, a spurt of fury and frustration. This hardly matters to me, now, how can it when I came so close to losing Eve? How can it when I almost let the worst thing imaginable happen, the worst thing a person could do? Why can't she understand that?

'Just go will you, Emma!' I say, lifting my head, thinking that perhaps she will respond to strength rather than weakness, but at my sign of annoyance, my *insolence*, her eyes widen and I see the muscles in her neck begin to strain.

'Go?' she says, 'I'm not going anywhere, Caroline, and certainly not because you tell me to. You've no right to talk to me like that.' She comes closer to me, so close that I can smell her perfume; something sweet and heady. I feel sick, bile rising in my mouth. I have to get to Eve.

As quickly as she came close to me, she moves away, the strange little smile still playing on her lips. Unease stirs within me – she is unpredictable, angry.

And then, 'Why don't we have a cup of tea?' she says.

Chapter Forty-Seven

I don't know how to get her to leave. I don't want a cup of tea, to get involved in whatever strange power play Emma is carrying out. All I want is to be able to think, to control my thoughts and work out what to do.

The sound of the kettle boiling begins to fill the room, the hot bubbling noise surrounding us, trapping me in. Ignoring Emma's gaze, I put both hands to my face and take deep breaths, in and out like my mother used to show me before she died. What would she think of me now? If she knew what I had almost done, what my inexperience, my stupidity, my careless-ness nearly led to? She'd be ashamed. Horrified. Disgusted.

Pressing my palms into my eyes, not caring what I look like, I try to think. Suddenly, I know what I have to do. I know there is only one way out.

'Emma,' I say, and as the flick of the kettle switch goes off and she looks down, I reach my right hand out, grab a long, silver kitchen knife from the rack next to the sink. In my hand, the black handle is firm, solid, and my grip is steady. Calm.

She turns to face me, and I take a step forward.

Chapter Forty-Eight

Ipswich
10th August: The night of the murder
Emma

The sight of the knife startles me; I didn't think she had it in her. The kettle, boiling hot, sits beside me, ready for our tea. I was going to chat things over with her, force her to see my side of the story. Force her to see how much she'd hurt us. Make her feel bad for what she has done. Make her feel guilty. We're going to France tomorrow, so that even if she tried to talk to him then, she wouldn't be able to. We'd be miles away. I worked up the nerve to come round, knowing that in less than 24 hours' time, I'd be on a plane. I'd be safe.

But I don't think that's what she has in mind.

'Put the knife down,' I say to her, not smiling any more, because even though I came here, I did this, I didn't think she'd react in this way. Not really. I thought I had the measure of Caroline Harvey, but it turns out that perhaps I was wrong.

'I want you to leave,' she says, and she moves towards me, the knife outstretched. It's a kitchen knife with a sharp, clean edge; the silver blade sparkles under her horrible kitchen lights.

I hate myself for being scared. I hate her for using this against me.

'What are you going to do?' I ask her, willing my voice to

come out strong and taunting rather than shaky and frightened. 'D'you think my father is going to come near you ever again if you hurt me, Caroline?' I force out a laugh, my eyes never leaving the knife. 'I bet he wishes he'd never come near you in the first place. You're messed up.'

She shrugs, the knife moving up and down, cutting through the air. The vein on her forehead is still there, snaking its way unattractively across her skin.

'Put the knife down,' I say again, and I make a leap forward, intending to grab it off her, but before I can do so she drops it, the weapon clattering onto the cheap plywood floor. I dive for it, grab the handle and stand up, breathing heavily, my long fingers curving around the plastic. It feels strange underneath my palm. I feel as though I'm watching myself from above, looking down on my body as I face Caroline across her kitchen.

I want to put it down, or throw it out of the window, anywhere that it's not in her grasp, but she's only a metre away from me and I can't risk letting go of it in case she grabs it again. I dart my eyes to the left, checking to see if there are any more but I can't see any. She'll know, though. She might have a whole drawer full of them. My heart is thudding and my hands feel slippery. Somewhere in the room, a phone beeps with a message – hers or mine, I can't be sure.

I'm pointing the knife towards her, my eyes still on her face. I want to get out of here, now, the ideas I had about confronting her feel stupid, dislocated from reality, and suddenly all I can think about is being back at home with Dad, putting my feet on his knees as we watch TV, waiting for Mum to come home from book group. I don't want to be here in this weird little flat with a knife in my hand. But I don't want her to hurt me, either. I don't know what to do. I drop the knife.

Chapter Forty-Nine

Ipswich
10th August: The night of the murder
Caroline

The moment she drops it, I reach down for it, intending to grab it and put it away, make her leave and get back to the baby, but she mistakes my actions for a threat and lunges down too, obviously fearful that I'm going to hurt her.

For a moment, our hands collide, skin against skin, and I feel a flash of anger as her hair whips across my face, her blue eyes flashing just like her father's. Her legs kick out into mine and my legs buckle underneath me, pulling me over so that my body slams against hers, pinning her beneath me. The knife is in my hand and I twist my torso upwards, trying to get away from her, and at that second there is a cry, the cry of baby Eve, piercing and loud through the small flat.

The shock on Emma's face is obvious and immediate. The crying continues, unmistakeably a baby, and Emma's face changes, screws up as though pain is ricocheting through her.

'Is that your baby – is that my father's child?'

'No— '

I begin to say, but it's too late, my hand around the knife has gone slack as I listened to Eve and Emma grabs it from me, and pushes it into my stomach with a horrible howl of rage.

Chapter Fifty

The blood is immediate and shocking. I let go of the knife at once, horrified by what I have done, but it doesn't stop me from feeling the soft push of the blade as it slides into her abdomen, sickly and wet. The noise of the baby crying has stopped, but someone is screaming, and I realise it's me – an earthly, unnatural sound. Caroline is making a noise, too, but it's quiet, a low, guttural groan. I ease myself out from underneath her, knowing I have to call the ambulance, do something quickly, stop this from happening.

'Caroline!' I say, 'Caroline!' She doesn't answer, keeps her eyes shut and clenches her hands to her stomach, her fingers around the knife. Her body is folding in on itself like one of the paper dolls I used to make with Mum when I was little. The blood is pooling onto her white blouse, and her face, already pale, is paler still, as white as the walls of this silent, empty flat.

I kneel beside her, put my hands to her face, not knowing what to do, how to stop what is already happening. I want to remove the knife, to pull it out of her body but I'm scared that if I do so the wound will deepen and I will cause even more damage. It looks so brutal, embedded in her stomach like that, and I feel the panicked tears come to my eyes. *What have I done?*

'I'm sorry, I'm sorry,' I say desperately, but her eyes are squeezed shut with pain and when I put my face close to her mouth, I can hear that her breathing is ragged. I look around for my phone but I don't know where it is, it's not in my pocket, and I don't know what to do, I don't know what to do, I don't know what to do.

She opens her eyes, just for a second, and I stare into them, dark brown pools of pain.

'Phone,' she says, gasping, and on cue, there is a buzzing noise and I see it, on the side next to the kettle, the rose gold case winking at me as though nothing has happened. The notification is from Mum, telling me that she's leaving book group soon, will stop at the shop on the way back. She thinks I am at home; so does Dad, unless he has been in my room. He won't have, they never do any more. 'Popping to shop en route. Do you want anything?' the message says and I feel a twinge inside because Mum is always trying so hard, so hard to be close to me, and I won't let her because I'm so angry with her for letting this happen, for letting Dad stray.

Caroline groans again, and I steel myself to dial 999, because I have to, don't I? I have to save her life. But I'm scared. I'm so scared. I don't know what to do when they come – to run, to stay. If they'll arrest me, if they'll believe my story. I swallow. I'll call 999 in a minute, but first I need someone to help me, to tell me what to do. I need to call the one person who I know I can count on, the one person who will help me. My fingers slippery, I press the numbers and hold the phone to my ear.

'Please come,' I say, 'something's happened.' My voice breaks, and I begin to cry.

Chapter Fifty

The station phone rings as he's about to finally leave for the night, and Gillian McVey dives for it. The office seems to freeze, his colleagues pausing to hear, although the DCI's face is unreadable. It always has been, Wildy thinks.

She replaces the receiver after a few minutes, then turns to face the room.

'That was the lab. They found traces of Eve's DNA inside the suitcase, remnants of saliva inside the lining. No blood, but skin cells, too. Same for the pink dummy – it was definitely hers,' the DCI says. She pauses. 'They also found a smear of blood – small, easy to miss in the lining, but there. It's a match for Caroline Harvey; we think it must have been transferred by Eve herself. Additionally, they found fibres of a blanket, which we can assume is the one Jenny Grant said was missing from her cot. He must have wrapped her up in it and stuffed her inside, used it to transport the body out of the flat.'

'No more on the body itself?' Bolton asks, and for a moment the room seems to hold its breath, but Gillian shakes her head.

'Not yet,' she says, 'but I'm afraid we have to work on the assumption that Eve was dead when she was put in the case. If she wasn't when he took her, she would be soon – she'd suffocate inside there.'

Her words are heavy, and Alex feels his gut clenching, the twist of disappointment. He knows that a week into an investigation is unlikely to have a positive outcome, but still, this kind of confirmation is always unspeakably horrible, and relaying it to Rick and Jenny Grant will be even worse.

'I think there are two reasons why Callum would've taken Eve from the flat,' the DCI continues. 'First, she died in the struggle with Caroline, she was collateral damage and he had to remove the body. Second,' she holds up two fingers, 'he wanted to make Eve look like the target, throw us off so that we didn't connect him with the murder. Safe to say either way, his plan hasn't worked. With his lack of concrete alibi and Jenny's own suspicions about him, the link to the suitcase is enough to charge. Put it this way – Callum Dillon won't be taking another holiday for a very long time.'

*

Bolton claps him on the back; Alex hasn't even noticed him approach. He is sitting at his desk, his bag packed to leave for the night, staring at the photographs of Siobhan, Callum, Jenny and Rick, turning everything over and over in his mind. *Why* does he still feel as though something isn't right?

'All right?' Bolton says to him. 'The DCI wants one of us to go with her to the Dillon house, be there to enjoy the final reckoning. Thought you'd be the man for the job.' He stares at Alex expectantly. There is a pause.

'No,' Alex says, 'you're all right, actually. You go, mate. I'm going home.'

His colleague shrugs, claps him on the back again and practically skips over to where Gillian is waiting by the station doors. Alex turns away from them, back to the board where Eve's face is staring out at them, her bright little eyes and her curly blonde hair. *Someone's baby*, he thinks, *someone's baby is gone*. No matter how glad the force is to charge Callum, nothing will ever change that. He thinks of the search parties that have been working tirelessly all week, the sniffer dogs roaming through the countryside, the fruitless Facebook appeals, kind strangers wanting to help. Has it all been for nothing?

The thud of it hits him, slowly and depressingly. After all that, it is what it seemed: another nasty man and a dead baby on the books. A statistic, soon to be forgotten. All at once, he wishes he were back at home with Joanne, eating pasta together and talking about nothing, the sun shining through the window and all of this darkness far, far away.

'DS Wildy?' The DCI is calling him, and he turns around, crosses the room to where she's standing, her jacket on ready to leave.

'Didn't want to come?' she says questioningly, frowning at him. 'You've done a lot of great work on this case, Alex, don't underestimate yourself.'

'Right,' he says at last. 'Yes. I'll come.'

The DCI frowns at him, but her gaze isn't unkind. 'You don't have to,' she says, 'if Joanne's waiting up.'

'No,' he says, taking a deep breath, his resolve stiffening.

He thinks of Jenny Grant's face, of Siobhan Dillon's anxious eyes. 'I want to see him get what's coming. I'll come.'

She looks pleased. 'Uniforms are out front, they're going to accompany us to the property,' she says. 'Get your game face on, Wildy.'

Chapter Fifty-Two

Ipswich
19th August
Siobhan

I have come to dread the sound of the doorbell ringing; every night for the last week it has haunted my dreams. When it happens tonight, I am upstairs, folding bedsheets, trying to keep up some semblance of normality for Emma, for us all. Maria is downstairs in the kitchen, loading the dishwasher accompanied by a glass of cool white wine. Callum is in Emma's room, the pair of them cosied up together, thick as thieves. What they're talking about, I don't know – I only know that I'm in here, like the mug I am, busying myself with laundry because I'm too frightened to look at what might be going on beneath the surface of our lives. The façade we have built. But then, I think as I run my hand flat over a flowery pillowcase, aren't I as guilty as anyone in that respect? I have kept up the pretence of our marriage for all of this time, and look where it's got us. Look where it's got *me*. Folding laundry on my own.

At the sound of the doorbell, accompanied by a loud, insistent knocking, my stomach drops like a plane cut out of the air. I drop the pillowcase, redundant now, and go to the window of our room, pull aside one of the thick, heavy curtains that

I've never really liked anyway. Callum often wanted to keep them open, let the world see us. It excited him; it doesn't now. Now, we hide away. There is a police car outside the house, and another one, a follow-up rounding the corner of our road, past the park, the tall dark trees overhanging the pavements, and past the row of neighbouring houses, the inhabitants of which have all taken to looking at us lately as though we are vermin. Perhaps we are.

In the next room, I hear Emma's voice, raised, panicked. All of us know that someone at the door at this time in the evening is hardly going to be good news. Despite myself, as I descend the stairs, I find myself hoping against hope that this *will* be good news, a get out of jail free, a last-minute redemption for the Dillon family. Of course, it isn't.

'Police!' comes the shout outside; we have taken too long to respond and I can't help myself, I cringe at the idea of our neighbours drawing back curtains, opening windows, wanting to see what drama this stifling hot summer has brought to our unhappy household now. *It doesn't matter,* I tell myself, *it doesn't matter what anyone thinks.*

Maria appears, her hands slightly wet from the dishwasher, skin glowing pink in the light of the hallway. Time seems to slow down as my husband emerges, Emma trailing behind him, tears already filling her eyes.

'Go back upstairs, Emma,' I say, but the words are futile, she ignores me as though I haven't spoken at all. Is this what it has cost me, my turning a blind eye? I am not just a doormat to my husband, but to my daughter too?

I open the door with my left hand, watching my wedding ring glimmer gold. It is a burden I don't want any more

– I imagine myself ripping it from my finger, casting it off into the sea, watching it flow away like the women in films do. Maria's words in France come back to me, *I don't know why you wanted to get married at all*, and in this instance, I can't remember either. She was right, I think; she was right about Callum all along.

It's DCI McVey, and the man, DS Wildy, the one I thought had kind eyes. They look harder tonight, little chips of steel in his face. His gaze moves past me to my husband.

'Callum Dillon,' he says, 'we are arresting you for the murder of Caroline Harvey and the abduction and suspected murder of Eve Grant. You do not have to say anything, but it may harm your defence if you do not mention, when questioned, something you later rely on in court.'

I stand to one side, invisible, as they barge their way into the house, to where Callum is standing, in a crumpled shirt and jeans, a mess of a man, a shell of himself.

'You can't do this,' he is saying, 'you can't do this. You've no evidence!'

'New evidence has come to light,' DS Wildy is saying, and I feel nausea worm its way up my throat, viscous and embarrassing. 'If I were you, I'd get in the car.'

'Siobhan,' he says, then desperately, to the officers, 'my wife will tell you, I was home that night. I didn't have time to kill anyone, I don't know what evidence you've found but it's not true, it's planted, it's a set-up!'

I don't say anything; my mouth feels as though it is filled with ash. Behind us, Emma is crying, noisy, unchecked sobs, and I go to her, put my arms around her, feeling her shaky body collapse against mine. For once, she doesn't resist, and despite everything it is so lovely to hold her again, to feel close to her, even if only physically.

'Siobhan,' he says, 'please. Please. Get Maria. Get her to come to the station, to talk to them.'

'Maria?' I say, confused, 'why do you want Maria?'

She is behind me already, her hand on my shoulder. She is an inch or so taller than me; her hair brushes mine. I can smell her perfume, musky and sweet.

'Tell them!' he says to her, as the police snap handcuffs around his wrists and he instinctively strains against them, 'tell them, Maria.'

I turn my head to look at her, but her face is impassive. She is still holding the tea towel, the picture of domesticity, of innocence.

'Tell them what?' she says, her head on one side. 'Callum, there isn't anything to tell.'

He lets out an anguished sound, and his body bucks against the officers, a movement that frightens me.

DCI McVey looks at me, and I see a flicker of empathy in her eyes, the same look that made me tell her the real timings of that night, tell her that I didn't see Callum come home after all.

'I'm sorry we've had to do this so publicly, Mrs Dillon,' she says softly. 'If the press bother you too much, please do give me a call. You have my number. We can sort something out for you.'

I nod numbly, my arm still around my daughter's waist.

'Please,' I say, 'call me Siobhan. I don't want to be known as Mrs Dillon any more.'

She nods, a quiet acceptance, and the three of us watch as my husband is dragged outside, into the waiting police vehicle, the light falling around him, enveloping him in its darkness.

The front door shuts behind him, and my sister, my daughter and I stand motionless in our hallway, the only sound Emma's quiet sobs, and the ticking of the clock that hangs on the wall. Watching us all, keeping our secrets.

'What evidence do they have now?' I say aloud, and my knees feel weak at the thought of it – blood, a body, a murder weapon? What ties my husband to that night? What kind of man have I spent my life with?

'Mum—' Emma begins to say, but Maria steps forward, ushers us both out of the hallway, back into the brightly lit kitchen. The dishwasher is humming, and the surfaces are sparkling; my sister has cleaned the whole room for us.

I sink down onto a kitchen chair, feel the muscles in my shoulders knot and unknot as I lean forward, run a hand through my hair.

'I just want to know,' I say, feeling desperation bubble inside me, 'I just want to know what happened that night. The truth of it. The whole truth.'

Maria sighs. 'S,' she says, 'I don't think we ever truly will.'

'Emma,' I say, 'come here and let's—'

There's a sudden movement behind me, and when I turn around, I see that my daughter has already vanished upstairs.

Maria and I stare at each other. 'Let her be,' my sister says, 'she's dealing with a lot. Give her a bit of time.'

Chapter Fifty-Three

Ipswich
21st August: Two days later
Maria

It's a few days after he's charged when I go to visit him. The summer heat is about to break, all of us can feel it in the air. He doesn't look well, I have to say. He looks as though he's lost weight already, the skin practically hangs off him. It's not a good look.

'What are you doing here?' he says to me, and I tut at him, shake my head.

'That's no way to greet your sister-in-law, is it, Cal?'

'Ex sister-in-law soon, thanks to you,' he growls at me, and I can't help but smile.

'Yes,' I say, 'it's funny how things work out.'

As he turns his head, I catch sight of a bruise, near his temple, purple in the harsh prison lighting. He's being held in custody until the trial. They haven't got a guilty plea from him yet. I expect they will soon.

'Ouch,' I say to him, 'that must have hurt.'

He doesn't respond.

'Are you going to tell her?' he says eventually, dragging his eyes to meet mine, and I can't help but enjoy the look of defeat on his face. 'You know I was at home that night, you know I was in the studio. You could've told them that, told them about us. I was begging you to.'

I think of him, straining as the police held him, asking me to tell them. I'd enjoyed that moment, if I'm honest.

'No,' I say, 'no, Callum, I'm not. Why would I tell her? She's my sister. I don't want to hurt her. Neither do you, any more than you have already. If you tell her, you'll lose more than you already have – do you think your daughter will forgive you for me, as well? Do you think either of them will even come visit you if they know that Caroline wasn't the only one?'

'You're pathetic,' he spits at me, a little bubble of spit collecting at the corner of his mouth. 'You're a witch, Maria.'

I narrow my eyes at him. 'Well, that's your side of the story,' I say, 'but I warned you.' I lean closer to him, relishing the way his eyes change. That's fear. I did that to him.

'Where did you put her?' he whispers. 'What did you do with that little girl?'

I stare at him, adopt an innocent expression. 'I kept her safe,' I say. 'Eve is perfectly fine, Callum. No thanks to you. You ought to be thanking me for getting you off a double murder charge. At least now you might only face the one. They're not going to find a body.'

It takes a second and then he groans, the sound escaping from his lips. It's the sound of defeat.

'You're sick,' he says, 'you're sick in the head, Maria. You know that, don't you?'

'I'm just not my sister, Callum,' I say softly, 'And I won't be second-best.'

He flinches, and in that moment I wonder at how I could

have done it, how I could possibly have found him attractive. How I could have let him touch me, kiss me, whisper in my ear. How, in that moment all those months ago, on a walk last spring, down by the stream, I could have let him inside me for the very first time. If I'd never found out about Caroline, perhaps it would still be going on. But I did, I found out because of Emma's little temper. I have to admit, I wasn't expecting it. But that's what men like Callum are like, I suppose – never content with one. Not happy with two. Callum Dillon had to have all three of us.

It's just a shame he didn't know about my taste for revenge.

Chapter Fifty-Four

Ipswich
10th August: The night of the murder
Maria

When Emma called me that night, I had just left Callum's studio, the taste of him still on my lips. The air in Christchurch Park was hot and still, the August heat creeping under my hastily buttoned blouse, permeating my still-sweaty skin. I was hurrying back to my car, parked across the grass so that no one would see it near their drive, but I'd stopped moving, listened to Emma's hysterical words down the phone. My sister was at her book club, she'd be back relatively soon – we'd been risky that night. Too risky. I'd never been to the studio before, didn't want to be anywhere near the house, but he'd begged me.

'Please,' he'd said, 'I need you, Maria. Siobhan won't be back for hours. Emma won't notice, not if you come through the side gate. Her bedroom faces the other way.' He'd lowered his voice. 'Don't you want to take the risk?'

I suppose I was flattered. What we had had always been fun, for him at least, and for me it was a way of proving myself, of showing that no matter how hard my perfect little sister tried, she'd never really win. She'd never have the perfect husband, the perfect child. Callum wanted *me*, not my sister. I enjoyed it, that feeling. It was addictive. I've always liked exerting power, particularly over men. I've avoided marriage, steered clear of children, but I've enjoyed getting the best parts of everything my sister worked hard for. Sex with her husband. A bond with her daughter. None of the drudgery that comes with it.

'Where are you?' I'd said to Emma on the phone, confused. Callum had said she was up in her room, in the house. Listening to music, railing at the world like she usually did. Avoiding her family. But she wasn't in her room. She'd snuck out.

When she told me, I was confused; the Woodmill Road address meant nothing to me. I thought perhaps she was with a friend, or a boy, had got herself into some kind of trouble and needed her auntie to help. It was a bit annoying; I'd planned to go home and pack my bags for France, but she was crying so hard that I could barely understand what she was saying and so I began to walk faster, eager to be away from the park before Siobhan returned home. If Siobhan ever found out about my affair with Callum, I'd lose all of it, you see. I don't want to end up like my mother, no, I've always been a key part of this little family and that's the way it had to stay.

I made it to my car, Emma's hysterical sobbing in my ear. Pressing the phone to my cheek, I tried to understand what she was saying. When I finally did, the words made my blood run cold.

*

I arrived at the flat just after nine. I didn't think much of the area – it was the shitty part of Ipswich, nowhere near as nice as where my sister lives. There was graffiti on the outside of the building and the CCTV cameras were smashed in. I took the lift to the fifth floor, holding my breath to avoid the stench of urine. Emma was waiting at the front door of number 43, blood all over her hands and her top. I winced at the sight of it. My own blouse was done up wrong, I realised, but there wasn't time to sort that now. I hoped I didn't smell of her father.

Without saying anything, I followed Emma into the flat, into the kitchen where the woman named Caroline Harvey was lying on the floor, her stomach soaked with blood and her face very pale. Emma was whimpering, which wasn't particularly helpful, and as I stepped toward Caroline she made a little sound, and her eyelids flickered. She was still alive.

'Shall we call the ambulance now?' Emma asked urgently, but I held up a hand, my eyes on Caroline, stopping my niece in my tracks.

'Tell me again,' I said. 'Tell me again who she is, Emma.'

'She was sleeping with Dad,' Emma whispered, 'she was his lover.'

I'll admit it was a shock. I felt my face blanch, the colour draining out of it, as I realised just how much of a fool I had been. I'd been no better than my sister, after all. His lover? Siobhan was his wife; *I* was his lover. That was the way it was.

'For how long?' I kept my voice casual, not wanting to show my hand. Nobody knew about my affair with Callum, and it was going to stay that way.

Emma was shaking. 'I don't know exactly. Months.'

'And the baby? You said on the phone there was a child.'

Emma flinched at the words but pointed at the bedroom, her hand shaking as she did so. I followed her finger through the sets of open doors, saw the cot and the small bundle inside.

'Is it his?'

'I don't know,' Emma said desperately, 'I don't know.' She was starting to hyperventilate, cause a scene. I needed to get her out of there, I needed to be able to think.

'OK,' I said, 'listen to me carefully, Emma. This is what I want you to do.'

'I will deal with this,' I said, 'I will deal with it all. But I need you to leave, to leave now and never come back. Go straight to your room, put music on. If your parents ask, you were in all night.' I took her shoulders, my fingers digging into my skin. I felt sorry for her, but more than that, I saw an opportunity.

'Do you understand, Emma? If you become involved in this it will ruin your life. Your mother's too.' I bent her face close to mine.

'I care about my sister more than anything in the world,' I said, 'and I won't have this break her heart. You must promise me never to tell, do you swear?'

Her eyes were so bright, staring urgently into mine. Quickly, I hugged her, pulling her body to me, her arms around the back of my neck. I'd have to wash this blouse.

'You didn't do anything wrong,' I whispered, 'you didn't do anything wrong. Now go.' Emma took one last look at Caroline, prone on the floor. I couldn't tell if she was still breathing. Then she walked to the door, turned to face me one more time.

'Speak to nobody,' I said, 'go straight home.'

'What will you do?' Emma cried, 'Will you save her? Will you get the ambulance here in time?'

'Of course. I'm going to sort it,' I said. 'I'm going to sort it all out for you. Just don't break your promise, Emma. No matter what happens.'

I reached for her one more time, grabbed her chin in my hands and tilted it towards my face. 'I'm trusting you, Emma,' I said, 'and I love you very much.'

'Thank you,' she whispered, and then she was gone. Well, if we weren't bonded enough before, we certainly were now.

I took a deep breath, trying to think, trying to make sense of it all and not get distracted by Caroline's moaning. The flat was weird – a sad, empty little place. None of my interior design eye, though it could've done with it. I couldn't stop thinking about what Emma said; I'd tried not to react, but inside I was seething. Callum had been sleeping with *this* woman, at the same time as he was sleeping with me, at the same time as he was married to my saint of a sister. *I* was supposed to be the fun one, the bit on the side. The one who made his life exciting, made the humdrum of his marriage worth living. Me. Not her. Who even was she? Had he been prepared to leave my sister for her? He'd never been prepared to do that for me, never even entertained the thought. No, I was fun Maria, no-strings Maria, exciting Maria. But clearly even that wasn't enough.

I went over to her as she lay bleeding on the floor. I'd told Emma I was going to call the ambulance, and I thought about it, really I did – I even picked up the phone ready to dial. Caroline saw me do that, and mumbled something, though it was hard to hear as she wasn't in a good way.

The flat wasn't too far from the hospital – someone would've been there fairly quickly, I reasoned. I felt her neck carefully, using my sleeve to cover my fingers. A pulse – weak, but there. But she'd seen me now. And she'd seen Emma. And she was a bit of a threat, if I'm honest.

So I put my hand on the handle of the knife in her stomach

and I twisted it, hard, once, then twice. I didn't look at her whilst I did it, I'm not a complete monster, but anyway it seemed to do the trick, because she went quiet after that, and when I felt her neck a few minutes later, that little weak pulse had gone. Not his lover any more, then. There's nothing sexy about a corpse.

I paced around the flat for a minute or two afterwards, staring at her things, the wine glass on the side, the tiny collection of paperbacks, the row of children's picture books in the bedroom. There were no other signs of a child in the flat, other than a bag of things by the side of the bath, which was still half-full of greying, scummy water. I didn't touch any of it, but I let the water out of the tub, using my sleeve to cover my hand again, and watched it swirl away. On the side in the bathroom was her mobile phone. I couldn't resist a quick look, and there it all was. Callum. Callum. Callum. Reams and reams of messages and calls.

I felt angry all over again, and worse than that, I felt betrayed. I stuffed the phone in my pocket, dismantled it when I got home and threw it out with the weekly rubbish. Keeping Emma's secrets, right until the end.

Her body was horrible – there was blood spooling all over the kitchen floor, and the knife was sticking out of her at an odd angle now after my twisting. Glancing around the living room, my eyes fell on it, and my stomach clenched with anger.

It was Callum's suitcase. A little black one, stowed in the corner under the TV cabinet. I'd seen it before, at the house, and once when the four of us – me, Siobhan, Emma and him – went away together, two years ago, before any of this started. Before Callum decided one affair wasn't quite enough for him.

I went over to it, and yep – there was his nametag, bold as brass. Anger curdled inside me. They'd been away together, they must have. Me, I was relegated to quick shags in the studio; he couldn't even be bothered to leave the house. But she got mini-breaks. In that second, I was glad I'd killed her.

My phone pinged with a message, Emma panicking, wanting to know what I was doing. *Think*, I forced myself, *think*. There was the baby, possibly his baby. People took babies all the time, didn't they? You heard about it on the news. I could make it look like a kidnapping. No one would look anywhere near Emma. Someone wanted to take the baby; Caroline was trying to stop them. Yes.

I pulled the knife from her stomach, getting blood on my sleeve as I did so, and wrapped it in a plastic bag I found in her drawers. *Not very environmentally friendly, Caroline, keeping so many of them stashed away.* I dragged her into the bedroom, used bleach from her cupboard to clean the floor, wipe down the surfaces that Emma said she'd touched, working quickly, quietly. It was almost quarter to ten, growing dark outside. I stared at Caroline's face as I moved her, at her boring brown hair, her pale, mousey skin. What was so special about her? What did she have that I didn't? I couldn't for the life of me work it out. She was light, I'll give her that, and I decided to position her just so, make it look as though she was protecting the baby until the end.

I picked up the suitcase, which was empty, and then I wrapped Eve up, really carefully, I didn't want to hurt her. I used the pink blanket in her cot, twisting the material round and around so that she'd be warm enough, talking to her quietly all the while, keeping her calm. She stared at me a lot, those big brown eyes. At one point, she reached out for me, but I avoided her grabby little hands.

I put another bag around her torso, just to be safe, stop any trace of her getting onto me or my car although I'd already laid a sheet of plastic ready for the trip to France tomorrow – the auction furniture was horribly dusty. For one moment I thought she was going to cry, but thank God she kept quiet. I put her inside Callum's suitcase, just for a few minutes, upright, her head at the top, with the zip unlocked so she could breathe. I popped a dummy in her mouth just in case she cried, a little pink one I'd found lying in the cot, and then I wheeled the suitcase quickly out to my car, wearing one of Caroline's coats, the hood pulled up. I don't think anybody saw me. There are loads of vehicles round by that block of flats; it's not exactly the nicest area. Not like Siobhan's road, where an unusual car would've stuck out like a sore thumb.

In the car, I opened the case and lifted her out, placed her carefully on the backseat. The car was already loaded for the journey to France the next day – I'd been planning to take over some pieces I'd picked up in the auction house: a bookcase and a lamp, and a nice rug that was perfect for little Eve to snuggle against. She fitted quite neatly inside the roll. It was risky, I knew it was, but it was do-able.

That night at mine, I dyed her blonde hair dark with the L'Oreal I use for myself – no time to do a skin test, but I had to hope for the best! I didn't know whether there'd be people out looking for her; I thought not if she belonged to Caroline, not until someone discovered the body, but I may as well be on the safe side. I did my own roots at the same time – covered up those pesky greys. The colour change suited the baby, actually.

I washed the blood off the knife using bleach, then popped it in my drawer along with the rest of the cutlery. It's nice and sharp, it'll be useful for cooking. Waste not want not, after all. It had done its job.

That evening the baby slept at mine, next to me in my bed. She was a good girl, she didn't cry much, and I fed her milk from the fridge and a bit of porridge that I found in the back of the cupboard. In the morning we were back in the car, ready for the drive to France. It was only as I was backing out of my drive that the idea came to me: the perfect way to get revenge on Callum. It wasn't *my* fault, after all. None of this was my fault. I was saving my niece, saving my sister. If you thought about it, I was doing a good deed. And maybe, just maybe, I'd be able to save them both from Callum as well.

I brought the suitcase back with me to my sister's house in the morning, empty and ready for our holiday. I left Eve in the car for five minutes, dummy in, sleeping happily in the roll of the heavy red rug curled up on the backseat. Nobody noticed as I shoved the suitcase in their hallway cupboard, then beamed excitedly as Siobhan came down the stairs.

'I can't wait for you to see the villa!' I said, giving her a hug, and she rolled her eyes in exasperation.

'Callum still hasn't packed; says he can't find his case.'

'Have you checked the cupboard under the stairs?' I asked, wide-eyed, and then he came down, grinning at me in that way he always does, the way he thinks I can't resist. But I can resist, Callum. I'm not as much of a pushover as my little sis.

'Good idea,' he'd said, and he found it in seconds, in the cupboard where they always keep their luggage. For a fleeting second, I saw a beat of confusion flicker over his face and knew he must be remembering the mini-break, wondering if he'd left it at Caroline's, and I held my breath for a moment. But the moment passed as quickly as it came and he shrugged to himself. I knew he'd just think he'd forgotten, that he had brought it home after all.

I waved at them all, then hopped back into the car, set off for Dover. Eve was good as gold the whole way – I stopped for some baby bits at a petrol station, even made a joke with the woman on the till. The car was locked the whole time of course; Eve was perfectly safe. I felt invincible, to be honest. You'd be surprised how often people get away with things in broad daylight.

If I'm honest, I was going to kill her. I couldn't see any other way out. I'd make it quick and neat, I thought, dump the body somewhere between Suffolk and Dover. They'd all think it was Callum, that he'd taken her off in his suitcase and got rid of the evidence. But when it came to it, I couldn't. She looked so small in the backseat, so innocent. I'm not a monster, after all. And to tell the truth, that's when I began to panic.

We were approaching the Channel Tunnel. I needed to buy myself a bit more time, time to think, but I was starting to sweat and my thoughts were colliding into each other like those magnetic balls on children's games. I had to get her out of the car. But we were on the motorway by this point, in heavy traffic, there was nowhere I could stop and the Channel was approaching. I had no choice but to keep driving.

The drive through the tunnel was the worst bit; my heart was hammering and I felt sure they'd see the guilt on my face. But I flashed my frequent traveller pass at them, and when they shone the torch into the car all they saw was the furniture, and my coat in the backseat, covering the end of the rug where Eve was sleeping. It was dark; nobody saw a thing and they waved me through, bored and eager to get off their shift. Once I was in France, I could think more clearly. I could make a back-up plan.

I decided to drop her at the remotest hospital Google could find me, not far from a domestic violence shelter. It was risky, of course it was, but at that point I didn't know what else to do. She was getting hungry; I hadn't fed her for hours and guilt squeezed my throat. I didn't have it in me to kill her, especially when she reached out to me, grabbed a handful of my hair. She was a sweet baby – she didn't deserve to die. So I had to think on my feet.

I found a piece of paper in the glove compartment, scribbled a note in French and tucked it into her blanket, careful not to touch any of it with my bare fingers. *Please take care of Delphine.* I've always liked that name. I tried to keep calm, thanked God for the proximity of the domestic violence shelter; I expected they got babies abandoned at the hospital all the time. She certainly looked the part, now, with her dark hair and dark eyes, and I hoped that with the note, nobody would have any reason to look at her and suspect her of being a missing baby from back in Ipswich. I left her round the side of the hospital; the front of the place would've had CCTV, and besides, I figured someone would walk round the side eventually, especially if she cried. The hard part done, I headed over to the villa, just in time to meet them off their flight. Time for the holiday to start.

'So glad you came!' I said, opening the doors of the villa with a flourish. I was proud of how nice it looked, and my new lamp was going to be a lovely addition.

I watched as Callum bounded forward into the house, suitcase in hand. I smiled to myself, just a little smile, nothing too big. If only he knew where it had been.

Emma was pale when she arrived, of course – well, who wouldn't be, after last night! – but I grinned at her, squeezed her hand comfortingly. I suppose she might have taken it as more of a warning because she looked up at me, wide-eyed, but I smiled at her again, nodded my head to confirm it was all sorted. I waited until before dinner to tell her about Caroline – how sorry I was that she'd passed away before I could even call 999. How we'd left it a bit too late. I thought she might be sick when I said that, but I convinced her that the right thing to do was to act normal, come for dinner and play along. I told her it wasn't her fault. I told her nobody would ever find out, to delete all our texts and calls and put the whole sorry business out of her mind. I told her everything would be OK. I think she believed me, but she wasn't herself for the rest of the evening. She's nowhere near as good as I am at playing along.

We had a nice evening, that first night in France. We had some wine, talked out on the balcony. I didn't drink as much as my sister. I rose early the next morning, pretended I'd been at the patisserie in the village. The others were sleeping, hungover. I threw Callum's suitcase into the verge, three miles away from Saint Juillet. The dummy, I dropped on my way back to the house. I kicked the earth around it a bit with my sandals, covered it in dust, but I'm not surprised the police found it. They were supposed to.

Then I sat back and waited for the doorbell to ring, for the police to come for Callum. I knew they would eventually, after all.

Chapter Fifty-Five

Ipswich
3rd September
DS Wildy

Two weeks later, Alex Wildy is at home with Joanne when the phone rings, the DCI's name flashing up on the screen. They're watching a sitcom together, the light, canned laughter washing over them both, Joanne's feet tucked underneath Alex's legs. He is – well, he wouldn't say happy, the stress of the last few weeks have pretty much put paid to that – but he is content. Trying to be content anyway, safe in the knowledge that despite not having a body to bring closure to Eve Grant's parents, they are at least confident that they have got the right man.

'Wildy.' Gillian McVey's voice comes down the line, urgent and fast. 'Can you get to the station, asap? There's been a development in the Grant case.'

On the sofa next to him, Joanne's expression is already changing to one of disappointment; she knows what an evening call from the DCI means, has got used to it over the years, the cut-short times together, the half-finished boxsets. It comes with the job, but that knowledge doesn't make it any easier.

'Will do,' he says, and he's already standing up, pulling on his jacket and grabbing the car keys, glad he hadn't indulged in the beer Joanne had offered him earlier. She kisses him goodbye, and he promises her he'll be home soon, before she knows it, but he can tell from her eyes that she doesn't really believe him – he's not sure he believes himself.

His heart is hammering as he makes the short drive to the station, pulling up haphazardly a few metres beyond his usual parking space, leaving a window rolled down in his haste to get inside.

It's almost nine o'clock but the station is buzzing, a weird energy filling the room, and Alex makes his way over to where the DCI is standing, one hand on the phone pressed to her ear, the other on her hip. He catches her eye – she looks tired, but there's a spark in her face that he hasn't seen for months, not since the case last year where they got a last-minute confession in a particularly nasty domestic violence dispute.

A few seconds later, she puts down the phone after nodding twice with a crisp few words in French.

'That was a hospital,' she says slowly, 'a hospital in rural France, *Foundation Lenval*. They've got a baby they think might be Eve.'

For a moment, time seems to stand still, and then everything moves into action – McVey is shouting instructions, Dave is frantically tapping at his computer, pulling up the location of the hospital, and Alex is questioning McVey, asking what, how, when.

'It's a remote hospital in rural France, nowhere near Rouen,' McVey is saying. 'I spoke to one of the nurses fifteen minutes ago, when I first rang you, and she was very upset. Said her husband had been on a business trip to Rouen and heard the locals talking about the case. Seems a child, a little girl, was brought into the hospital where she works on the 11th – two days after Eve went missing here – and that they'd all assumed it to be French. Dark hair, dark eyes, they think about one year old so not speaking yet, obviously. The child had evidence of water in her lungs, they'd been treating her over the last week or so but hadn't put two and two together that it could be our Eve – her hair was dark, and she was left on the doorstep with a letter in French claiming she was a child named Delphine. Apparently there's a domestic violence centre in the next town, they get a lot of babies left on the doorstep. It's not uncommon, the nurse said, and whilst the search for Eve has been everywhere here, none of it was broadcast in France – not Jenny and Rick's appeal, or our appeals for information – nothing. It all went out on the BBC and local news here. It wasn't until this nurse's husband mentioned it to her and she googled a photo of the baby that she alerted anyone.'

'Jesus,' Alex says, 'do they really think it's her?'

McVey shrugs. 'They're emailing through photos now – Dave, get ready for them will you?'

'Here,' Dave shouts, and the rest of them gather around him, like vultures to a corpse, only this time Alex is hoping against hope that this case is going to be different, that the baby on the screen will be Eve, that he will be able to go to Rick and Jenny Grant with the news they have been praying for, the news they all thought was never going to come.

The images download, three of them. A little girl in a hospital cot, eyes tightly closed but face calm, a pink rosebud mouth formed into a little pout. A picture of her with her eyes open, looking straight at the camera, clad in a blue gown with the hospital logo emblazoned upon it. And a photo of the whiteboard clipped to the end of her cot, the writing in French: *Baby Delphine, parents unknown.* Her hair is dark, not the blonde angelic curls they've been looking for, but at the very crown of her head there is a lightness, a brighter shade coming through that is inconsistent with the rest of her hair.

'It's her,' McVey says, and Alex feels a whoosh inside him, a flood of adrenaline that has him gripping the back of Dave's chair, his knuckles white. The room is a cacophony of noise.

'Thank God for that,' Dave is saying, a smile breaking out on his face. 'Jesus, that poor little girl. But it could've been so much worse.'

The words hang in the air; they all know how much worse it could have been.

'I'm going to go straight out there myself,' DCI McVey is saying, 'I don't want anything going wrong.' She nods at Tom. 'Can you book me onto the next flight to Rouen?'

Her eyes land on Alex, and her voice softens a bit. 'Want to accompany me, Wildy?'

He thinks about it for a moment, then shakes his head. 'No,' he says, 'I'm going to go tell the parents. I want to be there when they find out.' He is caught up in the adrenaline, giddy with the good news. It's not until he is on his feet, phone in hand to call Jenny Grant, that the thought hits him. It hits them all.

'Wait,' he says, 'How did he get her out to France?' He is thinking fast, staring at the images of Eve. The nurse was right; she does look French, the dark eyes, the hair. But not even Callum Dillon could have got a living baby on an aeroplane without anyone noticing.

The DCI is with him, her eyes locked onto his. The realisation hits them both at the same time. There is no way a living, breathing child could have got through airport security without them noticing, not without a passport. And the CCTV doesn't lie – Siobhan, Callum and Emma went through to France alone.

'He didn't,' she says slowly, 'he didn't do this, did he? Callum didn't take Eve from that flat.'

'No,' says Alex at last, 'no, I don't think he did.'

Chapter Fifty-Six

Ipswich
3rd September
Siobhan

It's September, the first day back at school, when they arrest my sister. The first I hear of it is her phone call from the station, and her voice is so different; reedy and small, so far from the confident way she usually speaks. Emma is in class, thank God.

I arrive at the station in my work clothes; I'd made the choice to go back into the office after everything died down, face the music as it were. It wasn't as if I'd done anything wrong, except trust the wrong people.

DCI McVey was the one to greet me; we've developed a bit of a rapport, her and I, and I can't say I dislike her any more. There's something nice about her, sisterly.

She tells me Maria has admitted everything – the affair with my husband that both of them worked so hard to conceal, the abduction of Eve to France, and the murder of Caroline Harvey.

'When we told her there was no other way Eve could've got to France, she broke down,' McVey says. 'I think she'd been struggling with the weight of it, to be honest. Sometimes that happens, you know – people think they can live with themselves, but they can't. Forensics found Eve's DNA in her flat, too – we'd never searched it before. We'd never thought of Maria as a suspect.' She purses her lips. 'She's a smart woman, your sister. She knows the game is up. If she pleads guilty, she'll do less time.'

'What will happen to Callum?' I ask, and she tells me he'll be released this afternoon without charge.

'But it's up to you if you want to have him home, Siobhan,' she says, and I smile at her, shake my head. I've already filed for divorce, and it seems silly to go back now.

'I'm so glad the baby's OK,' I tell her, and she nods, pats me on the arm.

'She's back with her parents now,' she says softly, 'they're very lucky.'

'Do you want to see your sister?' she asks me, and I think about it for a moment.

'No,' I say eventually, 'no, I don't think I do.'

The DCI smiles, and I see something flit across her face – something like pride. I am learning, I think; I'm learning that not everybody in my life is worth my time.

'OK,' she says, 'since she's admitted it, it won't go to trial. So we won't need to see you again, Siobhan, all being well. You and your daughter take care of yourselves. And stay strong.'

'I will, Detective,' I say, 'I will.'

She nods, gestures behind me, and I see Callum being escorted down the corridor, his face haggard, a bruise above one eye, but in his normal clothes, his hands free of cuffs.

'Siobhan,' he says, and I look at him, this man I married, this man I trusted with my happiness for all of these years. The TV exec without a job. The father who has broken his daughter's trust for the very last time – not even Emma can look past the affair with her own aunt, though she seems to blame Callum rather than Maria, about whom she has been silent and sad.

'Looks like you're a free man,' I say, and he stares at me, his eyes hollow. He might be a free man, but he's lost everything now, as a result of his greed.

I smile at him, pityingly, and make my way outside into the sunshine, where my daughter is waiting in the car. We go home together, and that night I hold her to me, safe in the knowledge that she is mine, now, for always. That night, I dream of our future, our life as mother and daughter. We will move away from here, somewhere new, a fresh start. We will tell each other everything, all of our secrets and fears and hopes and dreams. We will be as close as can be, two peas in a pod. Forever and ever. I know we will.

Epilogue

Letter to inmate number 357284: Wilcox, M.

Dear Maria

I hope you're OK and that prison life is bearable. Thank you for what you have done for me. I am grateful for it every single day.

I know now what my father was like, what sort of man he was. I know you didn't mean to get mixed up with him, and I'm sorry that you did. I want you to know I don't blame you for that. For any of it. Not after what you did for me.

I am at uni now, studying to be a lawyer. When I graduate, I am going to take on cases like ours. I want to make up for it, for what I have done. I want to get you out. I think of you every day.

I love you more than anyone in the world. Always.

Emma x

Acknowledgements

There are so many people involved in making a book and I'm grateful to every single person who has got me to this stage – my third book! I never thought I'd achieve my dream of being published so to be on book three feels like quite something. My agent, Camilla Bolton, for her unwavering belief in me and her brilliant ideas, my editor, Charlotte Mursell, who is a true star in every sense of the word – thank you both for supporting me and helping me to be a better writer with each book (one hopes…).

Thank you to Anna Sikorska for designing my favourite jacket yet, and to the wider team at HQ for doing such a wonderful job of getting my books into readers' hands. Thank you to Lisa Milton, Georgina Green, Alexia Thomaidis, Hannah Sawyer, Lucy Richardson, Sarah Goodey – I feel so lucky to have such a great publishing team behind me. You're the best.

Thanks as always to the extraordinary team at Darley Anderson, particularly Mary Derby, Kristina Egan and Georgia Fuller for selling my books into other territories, and to Roya Sarrafi-Gohar and Rosanna Bellingham. Thanks to the HarperCollins US and Canadian teams for getting behind my first two books and helping me build sales over there.

I'm very lucky to have such supportive family and friends around me – thank you to my brothers Owen and Fergus for helping me solve plot problems and only asking for a small cut of the royalties, my wonderful Mum for always believing in me, my Grandma and my Dad for always championing my books and telling other people about them too. Thank you to the Wildy family – Hugh, Linda, Katherine and Rob – for being so supportive of my books. And thank you to Alex, for telling everyone we meet to buy my novels, for not letting me get away with procrastination, and for being my partner in crime.

And last, but absolutely not least, thank you for reading this book. It always makes my day when I get messages from readers telling me they've enjoyed my work, and for everyone who has read my first two and this one too, thank you from the bottom of my heart. Authors would be nowhere without their readers, and I hope you all enjoyed *The Babysitter*. I would love to hear from you if you've read any of my books so please do get in touch if you'd like to using any of the methods below.

Instagram: @phoebeannmorgan
Facebook: @PhoebeMorganAuthor
Twitter: @Phoebe_A_Morgan
Website: www.phoebemorganauthor.com

Don't miss *The Girl Next Door*, the gripping
psychological thriller from Phoebe Morgan…

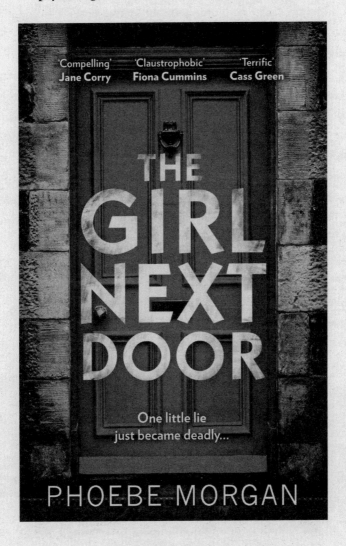

'Compelling'
Jane Corry

'Claustrophobic'
Fiona Cummins

'Terrific'
Cass Green

THE GIRL NEXT DOOR

One little lie
just became deadly…

PHOEBE MORGAN

Available now!

Looking for your next spine-chilling thriller
with a twist you won't see coming?

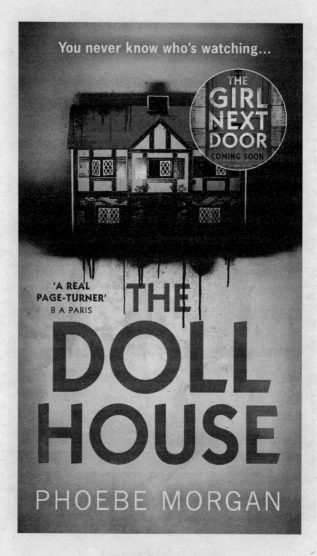

Available now!